ABSOLUTION

A Hunter Novel

J. V. SPEYER

For information contact:

Jessica Voloudakis
Writing as J. V. Speyer
138 Franklin Street, Braintree, MA 02184
857-212-6355
jvspeyer@gmail.com

Book and Cover design by Bad Doggie Designs
Edited by Quiethouse Editing
ISBN: 978-1-7329315-4-1

ACKNOWLEDGMENT

Thank you to my editor, Quiethouse Editing, and my cover artist, Bey Deckard.

For Sophia

The first time my father drove through southeastern Massachusetts with me, we passed a sign for Assonet. After giggling like a twelve-year-old, he asked me to find out what Assonet was.

This book is the answer to that question.

CHAPTER ONE

Luis carefully dressed in his official FBI-issued dark suit and tie. Getting shot had sucked. Recovering from getting shot had sucked more, however much Donovan tried to help. At least Luis managed to find productive uses for his time. He'd gotten some help for his depression, which could only be for everyone's benefit. He wouldn't describe himself as "cured," but he was doing better and that was the important thing. He should know. He was a professional, after all.

He'd sat down and written a book too. It was an account of the Rabbit Tracks Killer case, one he'd solved a few years ago back in Iowa. It had been an ugly, messy case before the Bureau was called in, and untangling it had taken everything they had. Luis had concerns about writing about such a recent case, but at the end of the day, the benefits outweighed the risks. People needed to be more aware of potential dangers closer to home. They had a mental image of bogeymen hiding in bushes waiting to ambush people, and sure, that happened. But most homicide victims were killed by people they knew. Even spree killers tended to go after acquaintances.

The Bureau was willing to let him publish it too. No one could have been more surprised than Luis, but the Bureau had taken a lot of public image hits in recent years. They'd do just about anything to burnish their reputation. Ultimately, writing had given him something to do and kept him productive while on leave.

He'd also spent some time chatting with Captain Lightfoot. Sometimes, he went to see the ghost. Sometimes, Lightfoot stopped in to see him. He tried not to think about it as weird. Eventually, he'd stop trying and just get used to it. Either way, he was adapting to this new skill whether he wanted to or not. If he was going to run around seeing dead people, he might as well learn to control it.

Doctors had finally cleared him to go back to work, and he was more than ready. He'd helped out from home when Kevin, his partner, asked, but that was different. He could answer Kevin's questions while sitting in his underwear on his couch, or out walking in the woods. Now, he was putting his suit and tie back on and getting back into the swing of things.

A horn blared outside, and Luis ran to catch his ride. Kevin had one of the work SUVs today, the dark American-built SUVs with tinted windows that no one ever believed weren't Fed cars.

"I see we're jumping right into something fun," he said with a grin as he slid into the passenger seat.

Kevin gave him a subtle little smirk. "It was actually Holcombe's idea. You mentioned the neighbors had been calling the police."

Luis' cheeks grew hot. "I'm writing my congressman and telling him to ban painkillers," he muttered. "Or at least to require anyone on them to be gagged for the duration." He'd talked a lot in the immediate aftermath of his injury. He still didn't know everything he'd said.

"Hey, don't be ashamed." Kevin pulled out onto the road, framed by a cacophony of honking horns. He returned fire with an upraised middle finger and continued. "Most of what you said was stuff we needed to know, even if you'd rather not have said anything. But, yeah—she figured the neighbors would have less to say about a Brazilian guy 'poking around' the condo if they saw you were in law enforcement."

Luis squirmed and sat up a little straighter. It might be a winning strategy with some neighbors. Others wouldn't care. It was a nice gesture on Kevin's part though and on Holcombe's. They were putting in the effort, so Luis needed to do the same.

"So what's been going on around the office since I've been out?" he asked, to change the subject.

"They finally moved us out to Chelsea with the rest of the Boston field office. I guess they got sick of paying that prime downtown rent." Kevin rolled his eyes. "Fontana got a date. I was shocked, considering how much time he spends bitching about how he can't get laid. It's about time, you know?" Kevin's smile turned into a wicked grin. "And you know what? He found his date on Mixr."

Luis' brain shorted out for a second. "Wait a minute. Fontana likes guys?"

"So it would seem. Said Mixr tried to set him up with you too. Showed me the screen shot. Even though your profile said you didn't want any white guys and was set to 'inactive,' it still tried to match you up with Fontana." Kevin glanced at him for a second but had to look back at the road before he missed his turn.

Luis braced himself for the sharp corner. He could have sworn at least one wheel left pavement, but no one else seemed at all concerned about it. There had to be a special insurance rider just for Boston drivers. It was the only way Luis could see anyone being willing to insure anyone around here.

"They need to fix their algorithms. And they need to add another setting—no bricks."

"Bricks? Is that a new slang term the kids are using these days?" Kevin sped up to keep someone from passing him on the right.

"It is. One I just made up, just for Fontana. He looks like a brick, he thinks like a brick, he talks like a brick. He's a brick." Luis wrinkled his nose. "Or has he somehow found a way to think outside the box now that I've been out of action?"

"No, he's still a brick." Kevin laughed. "Same as he ever was. Maybe he'll loosen up now that he's feeling more open about his sexuality."

"We can only hope." Luis relaxed a little and grinned as they eased onto the crowded highway and oozed their way toward Chelsea.

He'd hoped there wouldn't be much fuss when he got back to the office. He'd never been the kind of guy to enjoy that sort of thing. Chances were pretty good he'd get his wish, since he didn't get along all that well with his coworkers.

Dennis, the guy who ran the coffee kiosk on the ground floor, greeted him in a professional way and didn't acknowledge he'd been out for an entire season. It was a good sign.

When he walked up to his desk to find balloons, cards, flowers, and a brand-new bulletproof vest that said WEAR ME instead of FBI on the chest, he had to bow his head to the inevitable. Somehow, it was worse than the cheering, hooting, and clapping that went along with his entry into the bull pen.

"Welcome back to work, Agent Gomes." SSA Holcombe smiled as she strode in from her own office. She looked sincere at least.

Luis tried to remind himself that she was sincere. It was okay for him to be wary, but he was trying to learn to trust again. He should write this stuff on his hand or something.

"It's good to have you back. We've had requests for your insight from Weymouth PD, from Providence PD, and from Naugatuck PD. If you'd like to take a look at those cases, they should be on your tablet."

"Yes, ma'am. With pleasure." Luis took his seat as the applause died down. He didn't know how to take the response, so he pretended it wasn't happening.

"All right. Borchard, you've got that wire fraud case. Wragge and Fontana, I've got a gem for you. Join me in my office. Rourke, you're finishing up that child porn case, if I remember correctly." Holcombe met each man's eye as she spoke to him.

Kevin shuddered as he took his seat at the desk beside Luis'. No one liked working kiddie porn. It gave veteran agents nightmares for weeks. "Yes, ma'am. I cannot wait to go put some bracelets on these bastards."

"Neither can I." Holcombe rubbed her knuckles with a tiny, grim smile on her face. "It's going to be fun. In the meantime though, let's make a point of getting there first."

"Got it."

Everyone turned to their tasks, and the workday began.

Luis could hardly believe how easy it was to fall into his old routines. He'd been gone for three long months, longer than he'd been in the Boston office to begin with, but he fell right back into the rhythm of his work. The only difference between now and the spring was Donovan.

He got a selfie from Donovan at ten fifteen, just in time for a coffee break. The picture featured Donovan sitting on a bench at a picnic table, at some wooded location where the leaves were just now starting to turn. He looked amazing, with his dark, softly curling hair and his big dark eyes. *Guess where I am?*

Luis didn't have to do a lot of guesswork. He'd read the news over his morning coffee. Someone had found a floater in one of the state parks in the southeastern part of the state that morning. *Freetown State Forest.*

No fair! You cheated!

Luis chuckled. *I'm a well-informed citizen.*

See? Cheating.

Luis sent him a selfie back, including all the flowers and balloons. He didn't include the vest. Donovan still flinched when he saw the scar from the surgery after Luis had been shot. Luis didn't think Donovan would see the humor in WEAR ME.

Then he got back to work. The cases Holcombe had assigned him wouldn't require him to travel beyond a quick if frustrating trip down to the South Shore. They were simply consulting cases. He'd gotten them all the time when he'd been at Quantico. Local offices would get a case that stumped them but didn't justify a change in jurisdiction. They'd ask for a consult or just a fresh set of eyes. Luis liked doing this kind of work. Sometimes, they'd find links to other cases, and sometimes, they'd just manage to help solve a local and isolated case. Either way, Luis got to go away feeling like he'd done something good.

The first case, the Weymouth case, involved a serial attacker who preyed on people in churches. The case involved sexual crimes, but unlike the bulk of sexual attackers Luis had seen, the assailant didn't select victims by gender. They did seem to be drawn to the five Catholic churches in Weymouth but struck each of them an equal number of times—and in order. The next one on the list was St. Jerome's.

He frowned. Only people between twenty and fifty were attacked, and the attacks always took the violence to an extreme. Attacks happened on Fridays, like clockwork, and they happened between 8 and 9:30 p.m. He did some digging and found a man in the area who'd made some violent social media posts about Catholicism after the Pope issued a statement condemning current American immigration policies. He sent the information to the local police department, including a profile of a typical hate crime attacker. He'd almost certainly have to go down to Weymouth and look further into it, but with any luck, this would give Weymouth PD enough to narrow down their suspect pool.

The case in Connecticut was a little more complex. Naugatuck had seen a series of small explosions with little damage and no casualties. Residents were spooked, claiming terrorism, but police weren't sold. "These look like every other bored teenaged pipe bomb maker, but we haven't managed to find him. And we don't want to ruin his life because he's bored and doing something stupid to let out a little teen angst," the detective on the case told Luis over the phone. Det. Lovell sounded nice and sympathetic, although Luis had to wonder if "something stupid" would be so innocent if someone had been hurt.

"Pipe bombs aren't something to play with," he reminded her, "but you're likely right. Where have the bombs been left?"

"Mostly in empty fields or vacant lots. They've been pretty obvious when they've been found, and the only real tell my bomb squad's found with them is that they've been sprayed with a commercially available substance that's supposed to repel dogs."

Luis nodded slowly. "I see. I think your bomber's most likely a girl."

"I thought most bombers were male." He could hear the frown in Lovell's voice.

"They are. But girls are socialized more to show concern for others and punished for 'what-ifs' more than males are. They're also encouraged to show more compassion. She'd be devastated if something happened to a dog, so she takes steps to keep a dog from picking up a bomb that might well look like a stick. She's most likely young, a teenager like you said. Look at kids who stand out in high school chemistry class. My best guess is she's bored, like you said, and doesn't have a lot of friends. And when she's been through whatever kind of prosecution you decide to give her, find some way to occupy her time productively. It sounds like she's got a good heart. She just needs some guidance."

The third case wasn't so easily resolved. A young woman of twenty-two years had disappeared from East Providence after a Tinder date. There were no clues. The only reason police had taken the case was that she'd left behind a cat she adored, and because the occasional Tinder date gone awry had become something of a stereotype. "We can't be positive she didn't leave on her own," said Detective Gutierrez, when Luis called him. "She's twenty-two, and there's no sign of a struggle. She seemed fine the day she disappeared, and there's no indication of foul play beyond the cat."

"Hm." Luis looked the file over. "Angela Kasperson. Her family reported her missing?"

"Yeah. Her phone is gone, and it seems to be turned off. The last place it pinged a tower was Seekonk."

"Interesting. Do we know anything about her Tinder date?"

"Not without a warrant. And the judge isn't keen on giving us a warrant without proof that there's a problem here." Gutierrez let out a long-suffering sigh. "I get that people are entitled to privacy. And I get that twenty-two-year-old people sometimes make irresponsible choices. But, damn it, she's been missing for five days now, and it doesn't look good."

Luis frowned. It didn't look good at all. He knew, in his heart, that Angela Kasperson was dead. He couldn't prove it, but he knew. "Based on this file you sent me, she doesn't seem like the type to just run off. She's a nurse. She's responsible for the cat, and she sends money to her sister too. She's not going to risk her sister and nephew going without. Seekonk is over the state line. Check with other departments anyplace in Massachusetts for anything of hers that would justify bringing in federal resources. I'm not hopeful, but if she is alive, we don't have a lot of time to waste."

"Thanks, Agent. I appreciate it. I'll see if we can find any trace of her and get back to you."

"Thank you, Detective. I hope we can find her soon."

Luis looked at the time. In the old days, he'd have just kept working until he couldn't stay anymore. Now though, he got up when Kevin waved his keys at him. He was going home. He and Donovan had a date tonight. If Gutierrez came up with anything, he'd call. Until then, there was nothing Luis could do.

Donovan had a spring in his step when he got to the office on Thursday morning. Yesterday had been Luis' first day back on the job, and as near as Donovan could tell, everything had gone swimmingly. His colleagues had engaged in some good-natured but minor ribbing, and he'd gone back to work without any significant hiccups.

Donovan had been worried about it. He knew Luis had been worried about it too, even if he didn't want to admit it. Things had been uncomfortable with the Boston field office when Luis had been hurt. While the team had been working on things, and Luis had been working on things, there was no way to tell how things would pan out until Luis put on that sexy fed suit of his and showed up.

But he had, and things had gone well, and now, everyone could sit back and relax.

He waved his cup of Dunkin' at the receptionist and plopped himself down at his desk. His chair even felt more comfortable. How was that even possible? He had to be imagining things. Maybe he was a little uptight about the whole return-to-work thing, but he hadn't thought he'd been anxious.

"Don't get comfortable," Lt. Power barked at him from the door to his office. "Get in here, Carey. I've got a case for you."

Donovan counted to five. It was early yet. He'd be less inclined to get truculent with Power when he'd had some coffee. Right? He had to hope right.

He grabbed his coffee and headed into his superior's office. "You have a case for me? Is it higher or lower priority than the quadruple homicide out in Colrain, the Back Bay stabbing that had every property owner clutching their pearls for weeks, or the John Doe in Barnstable, who showed up without his head, arms, or legs?"

"This one involves a body found in a state park—state forest, actually. And—"

"Wait, another one found in Freetown?" Donovan put his coffee down on Power's desk and sat down. "What the hell is going on down there?"

"What the hell is going on with you?" Power scowled at him. "How did you know it was in Freetown?"

"I was just there yesterday." He narrowed his eyes at his boss. Maybe it had slipped Power's mind. The guy had a lot of people to manage. "For another DB. Do you think this is serial?"

Power looked like he wanted to say something cutting in response, but then he thought better of it. "Freetown has a bit of a history. It used to be a major dumping ground for gangs from Providence, Boston, Fall River, or New Bedford—

hell, sometimes they'd drag bodies up from Connecticut. It's a big place, with a reputation for a bunch of spooky crap, so they felt like they could get away with more. My gut's telling me it's something along those lines." He looked down and away. "Er, there was a serial killer there for a while, back in the day. But the MO here is completely different, and he was a lot closer to New Bedford."

Power wrapped a dark hand around his coffee cup and took a long, pensive sip. Donovan found his eyes drawn to an angry red scar on his superior's hand. It had been there for as long as Donovan had known him, and it had never faded. It was hard to remember sometimes that Power had been out there in the trenches like the rest of them, but then Donovan would glimpse that scar.

"Sometimes though, you'd get some really weird types. Cultists, Satanists, you know. And they'd do their dirty business in the state forest too. I don't know why. There are something like six cemeteries on the property, so they likely put some kind of significance on that. I don't know. We could be looking at some kind of kook like that.

"Whatever it is, the victim was ID'd as a missing person from East Providence in the wee hours of the morning today. So that takes the case federal."

A knot formed deep in Donovan's gut. "And

let me guess. Boston office, profiler . . ."

"You got it. I don't mind saying, I know you don't like working with the feds, but I'm damn glad we had the profiler involved with that Sudbury case. It got a little dicey a few times, but in the end, he was right. And he caught the guy, when it counted." Power gave him a measuring look. "Do you have an issue working with Agent Gomes again, Detective?"

Donovan chuckled. "No, sir. Not at all. We resolved our differences." Considering that Donovan had swallowed Luis' cock so deep last night he'd seen stars, he'd say they'd more than reconciled. He didn't think his commanding officer needed to hear those details.

"Excellent. He and his partner, the guy with the mustache, they're on their way down to Freetown now. My guess is that they'll get lost, since everyone's GPS takes them to the wrong place. I'd head down to Freetown and try to meet up with them if I were you. You know the place better than they will, since you've at least been there once."

"I'm on it." Donovan got up and headed out. The freshly dead took priority over victims whose cases had lingered, as a general rule. Newer cases had a higher likelihood of being solved. It might frustrate the families of the quadruple homicide out west or the Back Bay stabbing victim or the Barnstable John Doe, but facts were facts.

Donovan drove as fast as he could get away with, but he knew he wouldn't beat Luis and Kevin there. He knew they wouldn't get lost, either. Their GPS would tell them one thing, but the ranger in charge of the park had told Donovan all about the ghosts plaguing Freetown State Forest during yesterday's visit. If Freetown had ghosts, they'd have found Luis by now. And Luis wouldn't need a GPS to navigate once he found a friendly or at least cooperative soul.

According to Luis, ghosts were more or less humans who were just dead. At least, they were just like humans when it came to psychology. Luis could turn an awful lot of people cooperative, and they didn't need to be alive for him to do it.

Donovan got to Forest Headquarters in about an hour, and just as he'd expected, he found the big black "Feds Here" SUV sitting in the parking lot. He pulled in beside it. He couldn't help but feel like it was sneering at his little Ford, and he shook his head. He wasn't about to start putting human sentiments onto cars now. He would only find madness in that direction, and in this job, he didn't need the help.

He jogged into the main room at headquarters, where he found Luis and Kevin talking to two rangers. One was the ranger Donovan had spoken to only yesterday, Martin O'Leary. He was a shorter guy, pushing sixty, with merry blue eyes and a grim sense of humor. The other ranger was new to Donovan. He was tall, with light-brown skin and black hair. He stood a little closer to Luis than Donovan would have liked and kept stealing sly little glances at Luis too.

Donovan frowned. He was out, sure, but he didn't make a big deal out of it. He hadn't made any announcements or declarations about his relationship at work. It would be great if he didn't have to. He didn't want to go around marking his territory like some kind of wolf or angry Chihuahua. And wouldn't it be up to Luis to put a little bit of distance between himself and this other guy?

He stepped forward. "Ranger O'Leary. It would be great if we could stop meeting under these kind of circumstances."

Luis, bless him, made a beeline over to Donovan. He didn't put his hands on him or try any kind of PDA. They were both too professional for that, but the gesture set Donovan's racing pulse at ease. "I should have realized you two knew each other, when you mentioned you were out here yesterday." He grinned at Donovan, beautiful and strong.

Donovan's knees almost buckled under the weight of all that beauty and the memory of what they'd done last night. "Yeah, Ranger O'Leary and I go way back. Way back to yesterday afternoon." Donovan and O'Leary laughed. "I'm afraid I haven't had the pleasure of meeting your other friend?"

O'Leary took on the introduction. "This is Ranger Ruben Noguera. He was the ranger on duty when the poor girl's remains were found. He'll take you out to the site. I'm getting too old to be climbing around all over this place, and ever since the news hit the media, people've been lighting these phones up. Would it kill someone to call about fire risk?"

Noguera shook Donovan's hand. He had a firm grip, but something about him rubbed Donovan the wrong way. It was probably just the way he'd been looking at Luis, like a dinner laid out for his consumption.

"You know these agents?" Noguera asked, in a perfectly friendly tone.

"We worked together on a case a few months ago, and we've kept in touch." Donovan forced himself to stay civil. "Is the crime scene team out there yet?"

"They are." Noguera gave him an odd look but pressed on. "That pathologist from the ME's office, Dr. Wong—he's a character, isn't he?"

Luis coughed into his hand, and Kevin looked away, whistling. Donovan shot them both looks he hoped were withering before replying. "He takes his job very seriously. I'm sure you're too professional to take his . . . quirks personally."

"Sure. I guess a few social skills are bound to slide when you spend your days with folks who can't talk back." Noguera shrugged. "It's going to be a bit of a hike. It's better to just take the truck and hike in from the road."

"You're the expert." Kevin gave him a bland smile. "Lead on."

They piled into a dusty pickup truck with the park's logo on it and headed out to the scene. "They found her at the Ledge, in the quarry." Noguera snorted. "I'm not sure why a couple was up at the Ledge in the first place. It's hardly my idea of a romantic place to watch the sun rise, all things considered—"

Kevin jumped in. "Why's that?"

Luis cleared his throat. "It's got a reputation for suicide."

Donovan and Kevin both gaped at him. "How the hell do you know that?" Donovan asked him. "You're not even from here. You're from Florida, by way of the great swamp that is Virginia."

Luis ducked his head and blushed. "It was a long drive, man. In all honesty though, the Ledge has a pretty dark history. For whatever reason, it seems as though even people who weren't showing symptoms of suicidal behavior made impulsive suicide attempts. Survivors claimed an urge just came over them. Some even allege they were pushed, even though they were alone at the time." He shrugged and looked out the window. Whatever he saw made him do a double take, because he turned his gaze inward again.

"There's a reasonable psychopathology behind it, of course," he added, with half a glance at Noguera. "Particularly as some of the other stories about the area got to be more widely known."

"Yeah, I hear what you're saying." Noguera nodded, an easy grin splitting his handsome face. He switched to Spanish for a moment, and whatever he said left Luis laughing.

Luis shook his head and steered the topic back to the case. Donovan brushed his hand over Luis' as a thank-you. Luis tried not to speak languages the rest of them couldn't speak if there wasn't a job-related reason to do so. "Where was she found?"

"She was in the water. The dude jumped in to try to save her, but it was pretty clear she was no longer among the living when he turned her over." Noguera steered them onto an unpaved road, and Donovan grabbed onto the passenger-assist bar.

The forest was pretty, Donovan could admit that much. The trees were barely starting to show their color, and everything seemed vibrant and alive. Well, everything except for the cemeteries. They passed two on their way down, old faded things with tilted headstones and more shadows than anything else. Luis kept his eyes on his phone as they drove past. Donovan would have given anything to know what he saw in those old boneyards, but he couldn't ask.

Wong and his team were at the scene when they arrived. So was the FBI's crime scene team, led by a slender young man Kevin introduced as Maxwell. Maxwell and Wong were already toe to toe when the truck arrived. Their arrival seemed to have quieted voices, but no more than that.

"You're allowed to touch the body. That's it. You have no authority to go messing around with hard evidence. It's not yours. If it's not human remains, you don't get to put your grubby little hands on it. In fact, it's interfering with a federal investigation, punishable by a fine, up to five years in prison, or both."

Donovan inserted himself between the two, aware that he was only making himself more of a friend in Wong's eyes. It couldn't be helped. "What's the story, Dr. Wong?" he asked, leaving the Feds to soothe their own.

"The story is that *Mr.* Maxwell is an officious little twerp who doesn't know how to do his job. And while I can't issue a finding until I've completed my autopsy, I can say your victim met with foul play." He pulled back the tarp covering the remains and pointed to extensive bruising around her throat. "Manual strangulation, with serious defensive wounds. This is definitely murder."

CHAPTER TWO

Wong came back to them with the official ID the next morning. Angela Kasperson's sister confirmed her identity based on a tattoo on her side. Floaters, even after only a day or so, tended to be somewhat gruesome in appearance, and the face wasn't always the best guide. Wong brought out a photo of the tattoo for the sister, so she didn't have to see her sister in such a state. Luis almost gave Wong credit for sensitivity, until he found out his brother had coached him to do it.

The sister, Marissa, cried in the conference room as Luis and Donovan sat down with her.

"We're very sorry to be the bearers of bad news," Luis told her in a soft voice. "And we're very sorry for your loss."

"I'm just—why is the FBI involved?" Marissa sniffed. "Do they always get involved with missing nurses?"

Donovan put a hand on Marissa's shoulder. "They do when the case crosses state lines. The

Providence detective looking into Angela's disappearance had already asked Agent Gomes to take a look at the case, as it happens. He's a profiler. The detective couldn't say anything at the time, but I think he suspected foul play."

"Absolutely." Luis nodded at Donovan. "We've all learned the hard way that saying the wrong thing at the wrong time can lead to family members taking the law into their own hands. We're working on a warrant to get the records and information for her Tinder date for the evening, but he may not be responsible for what happened to her."

Marissa buried her face in Donovan's broad chest and burst into a fresh round of sobs. "Who else could it be?" she wailed.

Donovan patted her back. "Did she have any enemies? Any disgruntled patients or family members of patients?"

"No. She worked in the maternity ward. Everything was going great for her." Marissa sniffed loudly. "She had a lot of friends, and they were all good people. She didn't do the Tinder thing often, it was just hard to meet people with her schedule, you know?"

"We're cops, ma'am," Luis assured her with a small smile. "We understand, and we're the last ones to judge. We're just trying to get a complete picture of who your sister was, so we can find and catch the person who did this. It won't bring her back, but it will stop him from doing this to another family."

She nodded and seemed to get herself under control. "Detective Carey said you're a profiler? Like on that TV show?"

"That's right." Luis sat on the edge of the table. "Exactly like on the TV show, just without all the international intrigue. Our whole job is to analyze a crime for behavioral clues to help solve crimes faster and, hopefully, with a greater degree of accuracy."

Marissa narrowed her red puffy eyes at him. "So there's more to it than just my sister's case."

Donovan sighed and stood up a little straighter. "We don't know that for sure. Freetown State Forest has a pretty grim history as a body dump site, and the spot in the park where your sister was found has a unique history of its own. There's no doubt that Angela met with foul play, but we can't say whether or not the other remains are related at this point." He looked away and winced. "And by that I mean, we can't say because we need a lot more information, not because we're hoarding information from you. It can seem like we're keeping things quiet just to keep things quiet, but we don't want to present you with facts that are just speculation."

Marissa paled and covered her mouth with both hands. Her chest heaved, and Luis wondered if she was going to start screaming again, but she got herself under control. "I . . . My God. How does something like that happen?"

"People go missing all the time, Marissa." Luis tried to keep his voice calm. She wasn't accusing him of moral failure. It just felt like it because he was conditioned to think that way. "Not everyone has family they're close with to sit up and force the authorities to take a closer look. The saying 'The squeaky wheel gets the grease' comes from somewhere, I'm afraid. No one can solve a crime unless they know a crime happened."

"I guess not." She bowed her head. Her shoulders shook, but she didn't break out into sobs again.

"And the fact that you did that means we go over those cases that were ruled suicides again. Some of them weren't ever identified, Marissa. Because you advocated so forcefully for your sister, those victims will get another look. And if it is a serial killer who's been getting away with it, you'll be the one who dragged him into the light." Donovan met her eyes and held them. "If there's any comfort to be taken here—and I know that's a stretch, under the circumstances—it's that a killer will be stopped."

She closed her eyes for a second. "Is it selfish to wish he could have been stopped some other way?"

"No." Luis shook his head. "Not at all. You know, when I was a kid, my mom was killed. And it set me on the path to where I am today, which is great and everything, but I'd still rather be some street rat in the *favela* and have my mom than all that. It's not selfish, it's natural, and it's perfectly okay." He gave her another little smile. He wasn't sure what else to do there. He wished he had Donovan's ease with grieving relatives. Luis understood the process. He'd gone through it himself, and he'd written a few papers about it. He'd just observed it so often he found himself becoming numb.

She returned the smile, a little shakily. "I'll go through her things, once they let me into her apartment. If I find anything or think of anything, I'll let you know."

Luis smiled as gently as he could. Family members rarely found anything the forensic team didn't, but he guessed he shouldn't be so judgmental. They knew their loved ones best, and a technician wouldn't recognize the significance of something like a necklace or a ring unless it was out of place.

"Thanks, Marissa. And we'll keep you posted too, as much as we're able." Donovan shook her hand, Luis followed, and they left to go back to the crime scene.

Donovan didn't say much until they got back out to the car. Once they were on the road, he turned to Luis. "That's new. I've never seen you open up so much to a victim before."

Luis blushed and looked away. "It's a thing," he said. "It's come up with Father Geoffrey, and it's something we're working on. I've tended to be pretty oblique about myself and my background, which contributed to some of the problems I've had since I joined the Bureau. With my coworkers, I mean. It doesn't let folks off the hook for racism, but I have to admit that some of my reactions come from some of the things I've been through, and it can come off as standoffish or rude if people don't know better. It's not like I need to be ashamed of any of it. It just is, and I have no reason to hide it."

Donovan smiled and took Luis' hand. Luis relaxed into the touch. "I'm proud of you," he said in a quiet voice. "I'm glad you're doing better."

"Well, the alternative was pretty awful, so there's that." Luis grimaced. "It's grim work sometimes, and it's sure not easy, but it's worth it. We're getting our happily ever after, so I'll do whatever it takes."

He would, too. He'd always been willing to work for his happiness with Donovan as long as there was hope. He had his concerns about working on a case together again, but they'd get through it. Like the alternative to recovery Donovan had mentioned, the other option was too awful to contemplate.

"So I've got to ask," Donovan said after a few seconds. "Freetown State Forest has a reputation, right?"

"Place is full of ghosts." Luis chuckled. He didn't need to ask what Donovan was getting at. "Most of them were kind of static though. I guess the technical term is residual? They weren't interacting with the modern living world at all. They were just kind of re-creating the past. It was kind of interesting to see that past, but not helpful. Some of them were a little more aware. One chased after the pickup truck the other day, when you first joined in. Or when we first joined in, depending on your point of view. Anyway, he chased after us for a while, yelling at us to 'Get off his lawn.' "

"Wait, what?" Donovan burst out laughing. "You're joking."

"Nope. Angry old white guy sitting in an old lawn chair, drinking a beer. If it weren't for the glow, and the fact that none of you could see him,

I'd have thought he was alive. He chucked the beer at the truck, and another one appeared in his hand. If I have to be a ghost when I die, I aspire to that level of badassery."

Donovan pulled onto the highway. "Luis, you don't even drink."

"I'll throw something else then. Or I'll start drinking ghost beers just so I can throw them at passersby." Luis grinned. "I still feel like I'm lost at sea with all this ghost stuff, but I'm getting there."

"Have you thought about reaching out to a professional?" Donovan sped up and passed a tanker truck. It seemed a little early to have so many home-heating trucks on the road, but Luis supposed he was still new to winter around here. Maybe people liked to stock up. People were already muttering about the Blizzard of '78 like it was a bogeyman hiding in their closets. Was that normal, or did they know something he didn't?

"No. The last thing we need, as an agency, is to have it get out that an agent in the Boston office is seeing a psychic." Luis made a face. "Defense lawyers, the media, and half of Washington would be all over that like flies."

"Valid, I guess. I still think it might help you. If nothing else, you'd get better at shutting them out when you wanted to."

Luis grimaced but left it alone. Sometimes

he'd been tempted, but it wasn't worth it. He still felt like he was on thin ice with the bureau. He wasn't about to jeopardize his standing by wandering around the new age store and investing in crystals and sage sticks or whatever. He was a professional, he believed in science, and he was going to go with what had always worked for him.

They pulled into a parking lot near the crime scene and hiked in. The Ledge and its environs made Luis' insides twist. He knew the water at the bottom of the Ledge—an old quarry that had become a pond—had a bottom. It felt, even from the pond's edge, like he could jump in and dive right through to the center of the earth. The Ledge had been roped off with crime scene tape and had state troopers guarding it, but Luis wouldn't bet money on the scene's integrity.

Movement in the bushes, movement no one else saw, made him look up. When he directed his gaze toward the disturbance, he saw the figure of a short slender woman with long blonde hair. She was dripping wet, but the ground underneath her was dry. She smelled like blood and death.

"Your treasure hunters missed something," she told him.

Her accent might have been the worst mixture of everything Boston and New York had to offer. Rhode Island, then. Luis moved over to where the ghost stood and squatted down to examine the find.

When he was sure no one could see him, he whispered, "Can you tell me who killed you?"

She frowned, blinking in shock and confusion. Luis figured it had been a long time since anyone had responded directly to her, if ever.

"I don't remember. That part's all a blur." She stared at Luis, as if she couldn't quite figure him out.

Luis sighed. It had been a long shot. He'd have had to find a way to prove it, beyond the word of a ghost. "That's common with trauma. I got shot in May, and I don't remember it either. It was worth a try. If I come back, alone, will you talk to me again?"

"You want to?" She tilted her head to the side. "I'm no one. Never was."

"You always were. And we're going to find out what happened to you."

"Heads up," the young woman told him. "And my name's Jennifer."

Jennifer disappeared, and Luis heard a soft, quiet crunching as someone approached him from behind. Someone put a hand on his back, right between his shoulder blades.

"Ranger Noguera." Luis stood up and smiled, turning around. "Thanks for joining us."

"No problem." Noguera stood a little closer, close enough for Luis to pick up his aftershave. It had a pleasant cedar scent, and Luis found himself smiling. He didn't get the sense that Noguera was all that interested in him, which made his flirtations a little repulsive, but the aftershave still made him smile. "And please, call me Ruben."

"Ruben, then." A few months ago, he would have considered going home with Ruben. He fit all Luis' criteria at the time. He was interested, Latin, and well groomed. He was built too—obviously spent some time in the gym. Now, Luis could just appreciate his cooperation. He only wanted Donovan. "I don't suppose anyone gave you any evidence bags?"

"Not me, but I think Agent Rourke has some. Why?"

Luis gestured toward the ground. "Because the evidence techs missed a spot yesterday." He pulled out his phone and took a picture of Jennifer's gift to him—a set of brass knuckles, broken, and stained with blood.

Ruben whistled. "How the hell did they miss that?" He looked up and winked at Luis. "Those are some mighty fine eyes, that you picked up on them so fast."

Luis blushed and ducked his head. "I wouldn't go that far. I didn't see them yesterday.

Hey, Kevin, do you have an evidence bag?"

Kevin rushed over and donned a pair of gloves. Together, they filled out a label for the bag and put the broken brass knuckles inside.

"Think they're the murder weapon?" Donovan asked. He took up a position at Luis' left shoulder, conspicuously right between Luis and Ruben.

It was a weird thing for him to do, but maybe he felt as weird about the way Ruben flirted as Luis did. Or hell, maybe Donovan just liked Ruben's aftershave too.

"We'll have to ask Maxwell. I don't know, but it's worth a look." Kevin frowned. "Let's get this back to the lab."

Luis nodded. He could feel something watching him from the trees, and it wasn't Jennifer's ghostly eyes either. He wanted to get away sooner rather than later. "Let's head out," he said, and stalked back to the car.

Donovan gripped the steering wheel. He was pissed. He didn't know who he was pissed at yet, but he was pissed. "So Ranger Rick was friendly." He tried to keep his voice neutral as he drove back to FBI headquarters.

"It's Ruben," Luis said absently. He'd

jumped into Donovan's car very casually, and Donovan was trying to look at it as a good sign. "He was a little flirty, wasn't he? It's not the most professional behavior I've seen, but I'm sure it gets lonely up in those woods. Looks like the warrant to search those Tinder records came through. SSA Holcombe is dealing with the company right now."

"Good." Donovan couldn't trust himself to go after them. Right now, he didn't know if he could stop at just the case. "You seemed kind of encouraging."

Luis picked his head up and looked out the windshield, blinking for a moment. "I did? I sure didn't do it intentionally. I'm sorry. I didn't want to antagonize the guy working with us at ground level, but I don't think I made any overtures." He looked back down at his tablet. "I mean he's not hard on the eyes, but one partner is enough for me. I don't want anyone else."

Donovan relaxed his death grip on the steering wheel. He shouldn't be so uptight. What did he expect Luis to do, slug the guy for standing too close? "I know. I'm sorry. I just got so jealous. I know I can be a little weird that way, but this was like a wave hitting me."

Luis put a hand on Donovan's thigh. It didn't feel like a prelude to sexy times. It was just warm and reassuring. "I guess I can see that," he said with a hint of laughter in his tone. "To be honest, I was a little confused at first. No one's gotten jealous before. No one's given a crap before. It's kind of nice. I mean, don't take it to an extreme, but it's nice to be wanted." His cheeks darkened. "And before, yeah, I might have gone for it. That was before I remembered what it was like to have more than a quick fuck in my life." He lifted his eyes to the road and paled. "Gah! Prius!"

Donovan laughed and swerved to avoid the Prius doing forty in the center lane. Luis' reactions to Boston driving never failed to get a laugh out of him.

They made it back to the FBI offices in Chelsea and headed upstairs. Luis turned the brass knuckles over to Maxwell, who cursed at having missed them the day before.

"How did we not see them there?" he moaned. "Wong's never going to let me live this down."

Donovan exchanged glances with Luis and Kevin. "You don't actually have to tell him. I mean his interest usually ends with the autopsy."

Maxwell shook his head. "He's been creeping around here trying to horn in on my evidence. I'm getting ready to Mace him, I really am."

Kevin grinned. "I think Wong has

transferred his affections, Donovan. It's your lucky day!"

Donovan laughed and put a hand on Maxwell's shoulder. "Sorry, man. I wish I could feel bad about this, but it gets him off my back."

Maxwell stepped back, topaz eyes wide. "Wait, no. He's hounding me and trying to interfere with evidence. That's not affection."

"Wong's a special kind of guy." Luis gave him half a grin. "His brother's a Boston cop. He's a little easier to deal with, as it turns out."

Donovan turned to stare at Luis. "Wait, how do you know that? I didn't know that." He couldn't be suggesting what Donovan thought he was suggesting. Could he? No, Luis had told him he didn't want anyone else.

"I looked him up while I was recuperating. I had nothing else to do." Luis shrugged. "I'm a profiler, a federal agent, and a detective. I'm a professional nosy little fucker, Donovan. It's not like I can stop just because a doctor wagged his finger at me. If he gets to be a huge hassle, call his brother and his brother will straighten him out."

Donovan wondered if Luis had been behind the sudden drop in irritating phone calls from Wong. He caught Luis' eye, and Luis just winked. Warmth spread through Donovan's chest.

Maxwell lifted his head, impressed.

"Thanks, Agent. I'll get his information from you. And I'll get right on analyzing these."

Luis never gave himself enough credit for his people skills, but he'd just earned himself a friend for life in Maxwell. Donovan wished Luis could see it.

The trio retreated to a conference room to take a look at the evidence so far. The office was quiet at the moment, with most of the agents being out working on their own projects. Donovan didn't miss the other agents. He hadn't quite forgiven them for their attitude toward Luis before his injury.

They took seats around the small table in the conference room. It would be their official "war room" for the duration of the case. Kevin stuck a photo of Angela on the wall. "First confirmed victim."

Donovan frowned. "You're sure it's serial, then." He rubbed at his face.

"You got another body in the same place two days ago, right?" Kevin raised an eyebrow. "A floater?"

"Yeah. She'd been there a few days actually." He grimaced and looked away. "I think Wong is still trying to decide if it was suicide or homicide. The length of time makes it hard to tell if she was pushed or if she jumped. There's no way to tell from her position at impact because she moved around while she floated."

"Okay. Gross, but okay. Do you have a name for the victim?" Luis sat up a little straighter and turned to Donovan.

"No. She's still a Jane Doe."

Kevin made another column for Possible Victims and added Jane Doe. "I think we need to do a search for recent 'suicides' and suspicious deaths at the Ledge. How far back do you want to take it?"

"A year?" Luis tapped his pen against the table. "It's a place to start, at least. If we find a lot of victims, and a strong pattern, we can go back further. Keep an eye peeled for a blonde named Jennifer, by the way."

Kevin jumped, just a little. Donovan grimaced. "That's not a hunch, is it?"

"She pointed me to the brass knuckles." Luis dropped his voice. He always did, when he talked about ghosts in a setting where other people might hear. It had to be hard for him, a guy who'd always lived his life out loud, to be so secretive about anything. "I'd never have seen them on my own. They were in some brush and stomped into the dirt."

"I see." Kevin screwed up his face. "I'd expect the dead to be a little less helpful, you know?"

Luis shrugged. "Remember that time we went to Minute Man National Park looking for Riordan? There was a ghost woman who'd been drowned in a well. She was looking you over like you were on the menu and she was starving. That was pretty unhelpful."

Kevin's eyes bulged, and his face lost about half of its color. "Maybe don't share those things anymore?"

Luis' dark eyes sparkled. "You asked. So we know we've got at least two victims, possibly three. The thing is, the killer had a lot of rage toward Angela. Her body was a mess. The brass knuckles suggest premeditation—he was always going to attack her."

Donovan closed his eyes and bowed his head. He was a cop from a family of cops. He'd seen a lot of violence and a good amount of horror. These guys steeped themselves in it, on purpose, to save the rest of the world. "So you're saying he's done this before."

"Absolutely." Kevin nodded. "He's an angry kind of guy. He wouldn't be able to hold this kind of rage in for long."

Luis was staring at his tablet again. "So," he said after a moment. "We've got the autopsy results on Angela, which is great. And I've got the results on your Jane Doe, Donovan. Jane has extensive premortem facial injuries, but her COD was drowning. We do have bruising on her arms and legs that might be perimortem. It suggests she was thrown into the quarry, maybe while unconscious."

Donovan recoiled. "That's repulsive. Who does that?"

"Someone with a lot of anger and hate in his heart. And a lot of upper body strength." Luis swiped right. "Angela's COD is blunt force trauma consistent with battery, combined with manual strangulation. No water in her lungs. She was thrown into the water, but she was dead when she went in."

"No big surprises there." Kevin frowned. "Wong showed us the bruising on her neck."

"Right." Luis nodded. "Clothing removed from both victims shows tearing."

Donovan sat up. "You think he was trying to assault them, in a sexual way. And they were killed for resisting?"

Luis winked at him. "I knew this profiling stuff would sink into your brain eventually! In all seriousness though, we don't have enough information to say that yet. What we can say is that this guy seems like he wouldn't be above rape if a woman pissed him off enough. I'd be shocked—shocked—if he had male victims."

Kevin made a face at Luis. "What, you don't

think bisexuals can be serial killers?"

Luis laughed at him. "You can be anything your heart desires, Kevin. Truthfully though, it's got nothing to do with his sexuality. It's about power. The kind of personality this guy presents—from our whopping sample size of two victims, I'll admit—is showing a huge amount of rage against women. People who do that—of any sexuality—don't show the same behavior toward men. It's a thing. It gets back to hierarchies and power and place. Men can't step out of place, and trigger that rage, because they're already equals."

Donovan scratched his head. "This is from your sample size of two, right?"

Luis raised his eyebrows mildly. "And the five hundred fifty-seven rage killers I surveyed for an article I published last year in the *Journal of Criminal Psychology*, but who's counting?"

Donovan bowed his head. "Point taken. So you don't think there are male victims."

"I don't think this particular killer has male victims, no. This site has a history. If we dredge the bottom of that pond, I bet we'd find plenty of people who were all over the gender spectrum. Some of them are even real suicides." He looked down at the tablet again. "What do you think it would take to get them to survey the bottom of the quarry?"

"More than two floaters." Kevin sat back down. "You have no idea how much work it was to get them to do something about the Quincy Quarries site, and that was a known mob dump site for decades."

Luis acknowledged that with a nod of his head. "Okay. We'll just have to think of some other way. We're not going to find 'some angry dude who doesn't like women' in eastern Massachusetts with two dead bodies and a set of brass knuckles."

"And a ghost," Donovan added.

"And a ghost. Any way we could get the ghost to testify in court?" Kevin slumped in his seat. "There's legal precedent. One case, but it counts."

"I'll let you run that one by SSA Holcombe." Luis scanned through his tablet, like he could find the answers there. "Speaking of which, she says we should have the data from Angela's Tinder date's profile in a few hours. Once we had the warrant, they were very cooperative. Apparently, they wanted to make sure they weren't going to face a lawsuit, for privacy reasons, before they gave anything up." He looked up and shrugged. "I can understand. Plenty of people don't want others to know they use a hookup app or a dating site. You'd be surprised how many right-wing politicians and preachers use Mixr." He pulled his phone out.

"Check it out. Here's that guy who sued the Commonwealth of Massachusetts to end spousal benefits for same-sex couples, right here."

Donovan stopped breathing for a second. "Wait a minute, you still have a profile?"

Both Kevin and Luis gave him an odd look. Kevin took the phone from Luis and brought it closer to Donovan. "Yeah, he's got a profile. Look at it." He swiped over to find Luis' account. "It says he's inactive."

Luis stared at Donovan for a moment. Then he looked away, mouth tight. "I never used to exchange personal information, like phone numbers or whatever, with my hookups. I wasn't about that. If something happened, like a bad test result, this is the only way they can get in touch with me. It's responsible, for both me and for you." He got his phone back from Kevin. "I figured you would understand that."

"Sorry." Donovan gulped air in. "I just—it was a shock. You're right. It's the responsible thing to do." When Luis put it that way, it all made sense. He might have had a promiscuous lifestyle before, but he'd always been responsible about it. Keeping the Mixr account was just one more aspect of responsibility. It only made Donovan's skin crawl because of his own jealousy, because he'd never felt safe enough to put himself out there in that way.

They were together now. Donovan could relax.

Luis' smile looked a little forced, but he turned back to his tablet. "On that note, what do you say we send the crime scene team back to Freetown and see what else they can find?"

CHAPTER THREE

Luis got himself another cup of coffee and returned to the conference room. He'd normally have gone downstairs to the little coffee kiosk and sat at his desk with his work, but he didn't think that would be the best idea right now. For whatever reason—insecurity, indigestion, Mercury retrograde—Donovan was on some kind of jealous kick, and he'd almost certainly interpret it the wrong way.

It wasn't on Luis to manage Donovan's moods and insecurities, not even a little bit. At the same time, Luis loved Donovan. Whatever was going on with him, Luis wanted to make the man he loved feel more comfortable. If that meant sitting in uncomfortable conference room chairs while going over a list of missing women, then so be it.

Kevin and Donovan looked up when he walked back in. Donovan was on his phone, so Luis just waved and grabbed his seat. Thank God, or whoever, for electronic records and for spreadsheets. He'd be buried in paper otherwise, and that was only for the angle he was working. How much worse would it be for Kevin, who was dealing with the Tinder profile, or Donovan, who was working the Jane Doe side of things?

They'd drown in paper. In theory, that was supposed to be impossible, and they'd most likely just suffocate instead. Luis was willing to bet they'd drown. Maybe he was working too many serial killer cases, if he was getting pedantic about the method of death in a metaphor.

Donovan clenched his jaw. Luis resisted the urge to kiss it until Donovan relaxed. This was a workplace, after all, and Kevin was right there. "Dad, you're going to have to forgive me, but this just isn't a good time to play reunion. I'm just starting up a big case—"

Luis kept his eyes on his screen. Donovan didn't associate much with his father. They weren't technically estranged, but for Fred to have reached out to try to get together with Donovan was a big deal. Was he sick? Terminally sick, perhaps?

He created a report for the missing persons database. The Jane Doe had been between eighteen and thirty. Angela Kasperson had been twenty-two, and Jennifer had been close to the same age. It was hard to tell with ghosts, but if he had to guess, that's where he'd put her age. He filtered the missing persons reports to include women between eighteen and thirty, unmarried. Sure, it was possible that some of these women were stepping out on their husbands, but that wasn't the norm no matter what the more lurid murder porn TV shows liked to say. (Luis refused to admit he knew what those shows claimed. Only Donovan knew what he watched late at night, and Donovan wouldn't say a word. Donovan knew that *Luis* knew about his Great British Bake-Off fetish.)

Awesome. Still five thousand.

He added filters for a thirty-mile radius around the Freetown State Forest. That included a pretty good swath of Rhode Island as well as parts of Massachusetts that Luis had had the chance to explore during his forced leave of absence, such as Cape Cod. He didn't filter by race, even though the victims he knew about were all white, because he was going on a theory. These types of killers didn't often have a racial preference.

Limiting his geographical area cut his search to five hundred women. That was still a huge number. If there were five hundred victims, this serial killer would be one of the scariest guys out there. On the other hand, there were definitely five hundred missing women in that search radius. Something had to have happened.

"Dad, yes. I appreciate that you're my father. Now I need you to appreciate the fact that I'm a grown man with an actual job, a job that involves human lives. This is a murder investigation, the FBI is involved—"

Luis couldn't hear Fred's words, just the tinny sound of his voice. He was okay with that. He hadn't interacted with Fred since college, and he didn't feel compelled to change that at all.

He scanned the missing persons reports for people named Jennifer. There were four on his list. Two of them could have been his ghost.

"Dad, you were the first one to tell me police work comes first. Now you want to play the family card?"

Luis looked up and met Kevin's eyes, just for a second. Kevin grimaced and looked back down at his screen. The office wasn't the right place to air this sort of family drama, but Fred wasn't the sort of guy to take *no* or *later* for an answer.

"Fine. You know what? Fine. But you're coming up here, because I ain't fighting through Boston traffic to get to Southie at rush hour. And we're going to eat someplace around here, and I'm bringing my goddamn boyfriend. Which you will shut up and deal with, or so help me God, I'm chucking you into the harbor." Donovan hung up the phone. "Asshole."

Luis, who'd frozen in place as soon as Donovan mentioned bringing him somewhere, flinched. "Er, do you maybe want to run the plan by me? I only heard maybe forty percent of that conversation." Anything that involved putting Luis and Fred Carey in the same place wasn't likely to end well.

Donovan glared, and then he slumped. "I'm sorry. I shouldn't drag you into Carey bullshit. I just didn't want to go alone, and he was sitting there trying to force this stupid meet-up on me, and he kept trying to bring his priest into it . . ." He massaged his face. "I should have checked with you first. You have the right to say no to these things."

"I'm going to go talk to Holcombe about a couple of things," Kevin said, grabbing his tablet and making his escape.

"Sorry." Donovan grimaced as the door closed behind him. "That was unprofessional of me. I shouldn't let myself run your partner off."

Luis took Donovan's hand. Even this relatively minor touch was something they couldn't really allow themselves here, but this was a special occasion and they were in private. "Hey. How often have his family issues come up?"

Donovan managed to give him half a grin.

"Exactly." Luis brought Donovan's hand to his mouth and kissed it. He wanted to do so much more. He wanted to climb into his lap and kiss his lips, caress his face, and make a real mess out of the conference room. He gave Donovan's hand a squeeze instead and put it down. "I'll go with you to whatever you've got in mind. I want to help. Whatever's going on, I want to support and help you. I'm your boyfriend—your goddamn boyfriend—and I'm going to be here for you."

Donovan chuckled at the reference to his conversation with his father. "I know you will. Thank you, by the way. I appreciate it."

Luis' heart warmed as Donovan relaxed, and he got up to open the door. Kevin came back into the room, and they all got back to work.

It took Kevin all of ten minutes to figure out that the Tinder profile was fake. "Dude's a catfish, and not a very good one," he said in disgust. He turned his tablet around to show two pictures. "The one on the left is our boy's Tinder profile. He claims his name is Matt Monroe, he's twenty-eight, he likes the Sox, walking his dog, and home-baked cookies. He makes his home, ostensibly, in beautiful Lakeville, Massachusetts, where he works for Ocean Spray. Every last little bit of it is bullshit. Well, he might like the Sox. Everyone likes the Sox except for Luis, who's a heathen."

Luis yawned. "Baseball is boring. Real sports have more shin-kicking."

"Moving right along." Kevin smirked at him

and indicated the second picture, which was more or less identical to the first. "Meet 'Handsome White Man With Dog,' a stock image available for free when you sign up for a royalty-free image provider. Conveniently enough, it's also the image that came in the frame my son bought me at the school Secret Santa Market last winter, for fifty cents. It was made out of popsicle sticks."

"That's . . . creative." Luis stared for a long moment at Matt Monroe. "Did they make the frames in art class?"

"Focus, Luis." Donovan nudged him. "Are we able to trace anything about him?"

"We tried to trace payments, but they went through an anonymous provider. We know he's used the app mostly in Freetown, Fall River, and Rhode Island, but that's a lot of ground to cover." Kevin leaned back and put his feet up on the table. "He's been on the app for about a year, give or take."

"Okay. That eliminates about two hundred women from my victim pool, for one thing. Any complaints about him?" Luis cut the missing women from his list and pasted them into a different section of his spreadsheet. He'd come back to them at some point, when he had the time. They might not be relevant to his case right now, but they were still people. They still mattered. They deserved some follow-up.

"Um . . . yeah, actually. One woman contacted the company after meeting up with him to say he was a catfish, but the complaint didn't go anywhere. And another said he got violent, but she said she wasn't pressing charges and that's all she wrote." Kevin looked up. "He sent a few nasty messages to her before she blocked him, so he's obviously got a temper."

"What's her name?" Luis turned back to his spreadsheet.

"Florence Somogyi."

"She's not on this list, so she hasn't been reported missing. A name like that sticks out." Luis wrinkled his nose. "Let's see if we can get a couple of guys to go talk to her anyway. It was too much to hope for that our boy would leave a paper trail like that. Can you generate a list of all of his Tinder dates? I'm sure he didn't meet all of his victims on Tinder, but he met at least one of them that way. If we can show that other people who had dates with the same guy went missing, we might be able to get them to dredge the bottom of the pond."

"Let me see what I can do." Kevin turned to his laptop.

While Kevin handled the IT side of things, Luis and Donovan directed their attention to the Jane Doe.

Luis filtered for white brunettes with brown eyes, which didn't narrow down the search field much. "Tell me more about Jane," he urged. "What else do we know about her that would show up on a missing persons report? Any scars or tattoos?"

Donovan leaned closer. "She's got a C-section scar on her lower abdomen, and a small burn scar on her upper right thigh."

Luis filtered for scars in both places. He got six results, all with photos. He rejected one of the women because she'd been reported missing three months ago, and another because she'd only been reported missing yesterday and the body was several days old by the time it had been discovered. That left four.

Donovan studied the faces. "I think it's going to be this one," he said, pointing to Lisa Kilbride. "Twenty-five, from Fall River. Says the scar is from a house fire." He turned his head away. "We'll have to confirm the identity first."

"Dental records should do it." Luis hesitated, hands over his keyboard. "You want me to send the request?"

"No, no. It's okay. I'll do it, she's my case." He typed as fast as he could. "I kind of hope it's not her though. It says she's got two kids."

"She does." Luis bowed his head. "Even if it's not her, those kids would still have a missing mother."

"True." Donovan hit send, just in time for Kevin to finish making his list.

Luis took Kevin's list and compared it to his list of missing women. His mouth went dry, and he stared at his screen for a long few moments. "It never fails to amaze me," he said when he found his voice again, "that we don't find serial killers until they've killed a heap of women. In this case, he's got an average kill rate of a body a week."

He turned his computer around to show the others his list. Both paled when they saw his results.

"How does this happen?" Donovan stood up, shaking his head. "I know it's not on you guys. I'm not blaming you or anything. I just don't get it. For one thing, five thousand missing women and no one's saying 'Hey, something's wrong here?' "

"Right?" Kevin leaned his chair back. "There are a lot of reasons for it. For one thing, some of them are women escaping abuse. There's no law that says adults can't just leave. When local law enforcement suspects the women just took off, they don't tend to kick up a lot of fuss. For another, a lot of these missing women are from different jurisdictions. If nothing happens to bring in someone from outside to take a look at the cases and see the commonalities, then we wind up with this."

Luis tried to remember what he'd talked about with Father Geoffrey. "When I was a kid, no one would have cared when my mom went missing. My dad filed a missing persons report so he could get the legal stuff out of the way eventually, but no one blinked an eye until I proved she was dead." He licked his lips. "No one wants to believe they're talking to a killer, I guess. A few people tried to convince themselves she'd gotten away from my dad, but she'd never have left me with him."

He pushed the negative thoughts out of his head. They'd come back, but he was getting better at ignoring them. "All we can do now is try to stop Matt Monroe before he kills again."

Donovan found a microbrewery not too far from the FBI office where he could make his father meet them. He'd considered making his dad meet them at one of the small older more "neighborhood" places just to watch Fred squirm, but people in the neighborhood didn't deserve that. Luis could mutter under his breath about gentrification and yuppie microbrews all he wanted, but Donovan had a limited tolerance for Fred's shit today. He was taking his dad someplace with limited opportunities for outbursts, and that was all there was to it.

Besides, reviews for the brewery's food were good, and now Donovan could at least *recognize* how to say gentrification in Portuguese, Spanish, and Nheengatu. So it wasn't a complete loss.

They showed up a little early and asked for a table a little ways away from other diners. Donovan didn't know for sure that Fred was going to be disruptive, but why take the chance? He was going to be confronted with two of the things he liked least in the world, brown people and gay people.

Luis nudged his elbow. "If we'd had advanced warning, I could have worn one of my Pride shirts."

Donovan huffed out a little laugh in spite of himself. "You don't have Pride shirts."

"I most certainly do. I show up every year, if I'm not injured." Luis sipped his water. "I see your dad."

"Awesome." Donovan followed Luis' gaze to the restaurant entrance. Sure enough, there was Fred, with a red face and a Hawaiian-style shirt so loud they could probably hear it up in Maine. "Can you arrest him for that shirt? It's got to be a federal crime."

"If bad fashion sense was a federal crime,

every adult alive during the seventies would be locked up for life." Luis grinned, but he composed himself immediately as Fred approached their table.

Donovan thought of Luis' expression as his Fed Face, the standard blank expression that came with everyone involved with a federal investigation. They issued the face with the badge, on graduation from Quantico.

Fred sat down across from Donovan. His mustache made his sunburn look even worse than it was. "Donovan," he rumbled, picking up the menu. "It's good to see you. I heard you got hurt last spring."

"Just a scratch." Donovan could feel Luis tense beside him. He couldn't still be blaming himself, could he? "Nothing serious, nothing to worry about. So, how are you?"

"I'm good. I've been good. You know how it is." He shrugged and looked around. "Since when do they brew beer in Chelsea? This neighborhood's been shitty for decades. They're not using Deer Island water, are they?" He scowled at the menu.

"I'm sure they're using safe, sanitary water from the Quabbin Reservoir, just like everyplace else in Boston, Dad." Donovan forced a smile. "You remember Luis, right?"

Fred looked Luis over with a cool

expression. "Yeah. He's that dirty Brazilian kid you roomed with during college. You dragged him all the way up here for dinner to what, mess with me? You know I never liked that kid."

Luis snorted and leaned back in their booth. He didn't say anything, just left it for Donovan. It was exactly what Donovan would want him to do. Fred was Donovan's father, and he knew how to handle him. He didn't need for Luis to go blowing up at him, as satisfying as it might be. At the same time, he kind of did want Luis to blow up. It would be a great way to demonstrate solidarity, for one thing.

"Well, Luis was assigned to Boston earlier this year. He's a profiler with the FBI now." Donovan's palms had gone slick with sweat. "We worked a case together, and we started dating. Again." His chest felt too tight, but he couldn't let Fred see that.

"Oh, for fuck's sake, Donovan. We don't have queers in this family, and that's not what I called to talk to you about." He waved a hand in Luis' direction, like he was brushing him off. "I came to talk to you about your mother."

Donovan blinked. He didn't know what he'd expected, but that hadn't been it. Outright dismissal had not been on the list of possibilities. "Mom?"

"Yeah. Tall girl, blonde, runs a unit in Boston?" Fred rolled his eyes as their waitress approached. They ordered, with Fred and Donovan ordering beer as well as food. Fred scoffed at Luis. "I didn't think you spoke English. Anyway," he said, turning back to Donovan. "I've been trying to reach out to her and move back in, but she changed the locks and won't take my calls."

Donovan found himself stunned beyond words for the second time in five minutes. "I guess I'm a little surprised," he said when he found his voice again. "Are you sick?"

"No, I'm not sick." Fred made a face at him. "Are you nuts? I'm as healthy as a goddamn horse. I just think it's time. I get that she got a bee in her bonnet about something, but I'm her husband and she needs to deal with it."

Donovan pinched the bridge of his nose. "She didn't 'get a bee in her bonnet,' Dad. You got caught cheating, with a twenty-year-old. At work, I should add. A place where you both work."

Fred shrugged. "I'm a man. I have needs."

"You're a married man, not an unneutered tomcat." Donovan sipped from his beer. "You make choices. And what's-her-face, who was younger even than your youngest child, was not the first."

"I didn't call you here for you to sit there on

your high horse. I called you here to make your mom change the locks back." Fred showed no sign of having even registered Donovan's tomcat comment.

"I'm one hundred percent not getting involved. If you want Mom back, you'll have to do the work yourself." Donovan looked down at his empty place and looked back up at his father. "Also, locks don't work that way. It seems like someone who retired from the bomb squad should know that."

Beside him, Luis coughed into his hand. Donovan could only assume he was hiding laughter.

Their waitress appeared on the scene with their food. She set it out in front of them, winked at Luis, and wandered away again.

"You should go give her your number," Fred told Luis. "I think she's into you."

Luis kept his Fed Face on. "Martina had an issue at the office when I first got assigned to the Boston office. I was able to help get her child returned to her. She's not interested, and neither am I. Our relationship is purely professional, Mr. Carey."

Fred screwed up his face and mimicked Luis. " 'Our relationship is purely professional, Mr. Carey.' What, you're too stuck up to date a waitress?"

"Too gay, Mr. Carey."

Donovan had to swig from his beer to keep from laughing out loud. Well, Donovan had told Fred when he sat down.

"That's bullshit. They don't let queers into the FBI, for God's sake." Fred recoiled in disgust.

"Director Hoover hasn't been with the Bureau since 1972, Mr. Carey." Luis fixed him with a particularly penetrating stare. "Let's discuss why you asked Donovan here tonight. You say you want to reunite with your estranged wife. Why?"

Donovan took a bite of his pizza. This was going to be good. He hadn't had a chance to see Luis interview anyone before.

"What do you mean, why?" Fred pulled back and put his sandwich down. "The hell kind of question is that? We should live together because we're married."

Luis toyed with his own chicken sandwich. "It's interesting how you phrase that. We *should* live together because you're married. Not, say, I *want* to live with my wife, because I love her and I miss her. Just, *We should live together because we're married*. Tell me, Mr. Carey, did someone encourage you to start making overtures to your wife again?"

Fred stared at Luis in flabbergasted silence for a full fifteen seconds. "Are you stalking me?"

He turned to Donovan. "Is he stalking me?" He turned back to Luis, pointing. "You just keep your hands to yourself. I know this ass is mighty fine—"

"It's saggy, Mr. Carey. And considering the grooming habits I can observe from here, my guess is that it's otherwise not to my tastes." Luis managed to keep his smile tiny, almost undetectable, as Fred opened his mouth and closed it again like a fish on a deck. "And I'm very happily involved with someone else. Fidelity is important in a committed relationship, whether or not a legal commitment has been made." He ate a french fry and continued. "So, Mr. Carey, who put you up to trying to reunite with your wife?"

Carey shook his head. "I'm telling you, this is a serious overstepping of governmental authority. Are you watching me through my computer camera?" He paled, as much as he could with the sunburn. "Oh my God, you're watching me when I'm on my computer at night, aren't you? You Feds are everywhere."

"The capability exists. It would require several layers of warrant. Ask yourself this, Mr. Carey. What are you doing late at night on your computer that would make it worth the FBI's time to get a warrant to watch you watching porn?" He fell silent for a moment. "Now I am kind of curious. As a former law enforcement officer yourself, you know what it's like. When someone starts acting suspicious, you wonder what they're hiding."

Donovan hid his face in his hands. "Luis, I don't want to know what kind of porn my father's watching." His stomach gave a little lurch. "He's watching tentacle porn, isn't he? Oh my God, I'm going to be sick. Do they have any bourbon here?"

"Tentacle porn?" Fred squawked loud enough to turn a couple of heads. "What the hell is wrong with the two of you? I watch good old-fashioned American porn—"

"Mmm-mmm. You're watching gay porn." Luis' jaw tightened, and his eyes narrowed. "You keep glancing between me and Donovan, and the thing about someone looking at his roommate's father's ass is popular in some cheaply made productions."

"I'm so going to hurl." Donovan closed his eyes. "For real, Dad?"

"Wait a minute, I thought you needed a warrant!" Fred gaped.

"I would need a warrant to access your computer." Luis gave Fred a bored look. "I'm not a hacker or a surveillance specialist. I'm a profiler. I get paid to figure out what you're hiding. So. Back to the matter of Mrs. Carey—who put you up to trying to move back in with her?"

Donovan would cheerfully go and punch

whoever it was in the face. Everything he'd eaten curdled in his stomach. He hadn't known pizza crust could curdle, but here he was with a stomach full of curdled carbohydrates.

Fred looked away and slouched. "It was the priest," he muttered. "I went to Confession, and it's this new guy, and he wasn't content to let it stay with ten Hail Marys, you know?" He made a face. "Son of a bitch says I can't be absolved for watching that stuff until I move back in with Patricia. And the thing is, I didn't even watch much of it! It just came up because I'd been watching—"

Donovan held up a hand. "I'm going to have to put a great big 'shhh' on that. No one wants to know their dad's taste in porn. Or their mom's, for that matter."

Fred curled his lip. "Your mother doesn't watch porn. She's sixty-two, for God's sake. She's long past anything like that."

Luis pinched the bridge of his nose.

Donovan cleared his throat. "Look, Dad. However weirdly you came to the decision to try to make up with Mom, I can't help you until you admit you did something wrong in the first place, you know? I mean if you're not going to change how you behave or how you treat her, I can't sit there and tell her to let you back in. I don't know why she didn't call a lawyer after the thing with the doctor."

"We're good Catholics, Donovan. We don't do divorce." Fred stabbed a short finger at Donovan. "You should know that. We paid enough to send you to Catholic schools, for Christ's sake."

"And I still get to hold hands with this guy." Donovan smiled and grabbed Luis' hand.

"Cut that out," Fred snapped. "Catholics don't do that gay stuff either."

Donovan raised his eyebrows, but Luis just gave his hand a little squeeze. Catholics weren't supposed to cheat on their wives either, but here they were.

They finished their meals in a tense, creepy silence. When it was over, after what seemed like years, Luis got up to use the restroom.

As soon as he was out of earshot, Fred leaned in. "You got a lot of nerve bringing that sp—"

"Don't finish that," Donovan growled.

"That dirtbag in here. You knew I wanted to have a family meeting."

"And you knew I didn't. I told you I was bringing my boyfriend. I brought my boyfriend."

"And now you're pretending to be sleeping with him just to piss me off? I never figured you for such a mama's boy."

"I am sleeping with him, Dad. And I was in

college too. And I've slept with other guys. More than one. Luis, though—he's awesome." Donovan grinned at his father, sharp and vicious.

"That's disgusting. Don't get too attached. You know how it goes. These guys from down there? They don't like to be tied down. They don't think about family life the way we do."

Donovan recoiled. "This from a man who gave his wife an STI and tried to spread it around that she'd given it to him when she called him out on his shit! You have no call to be talking about family values, to anyone else. Maybe you should move someplace else. You'd still be a crap husband and a crap father, but I'm sure you can find someplace to live where they'd be a hell of a lot more tolerant of your racism."

"You don't get to talk to me like that." Fred pounded one fist on the table. "You know I'm right. You're just scared to admit it."

Donovan's phone pinged with an incoming text. It was from Luis. *We're all set with the check. I'm out by the car.*

Donovan got up to leave. "I've got to go. Take care of yourself, Dad."

He headed out to the parking lot. His father's words echoed in his head. He couldn't agree with Fred about the reasons, but he was right about one thing. Luis didn't think about family the same way other people did. He had his reasons, but that didn't change the fact that Luis just didn't have the same toolbox when it came to family.

He loved Luis, and he was pretty sure Luis loved him. But Luis hadn't even tried to have a serious relationship in years. Would they still be able to keep it together in the long term?

CHAPTER FOUR

Luis wished he could say he was surprised when the brass knuckles came back as a match to the injuries on Angela Kasperson. He wasn't, but he made the effort to fake it anyway.

Maxwell came up to the office in person to let him know other blood samples, in small quantities, had been found on the instrument. "I definitely think your boy tried to clean it up, but unless you really know what you're doing, it's hard to thoroughly clean the blood from something like this." He gave a little smirk. "Your guy's trying to cover his tracks, but he's not someone who knows true forensic countermeasures. He might've watched a TV show or two, but that's it."

"Well, that's something at least." Luis thumped the report Maxwell had given him onto his desk. The brass knuckles themselves were in the evidence room, where they could stay as far as he was concerned. They wouldn't be useful until they had someone's DNA to compare them to. "How many other blood samples were you able to get?"

"Three." Maxwell didn't hesitate. "And they were all too degraded to use to identify other victims. But that doesn't mean he's not responsible for more than four."

"No, no, I know. It just means he didn't use this particular weapon on the poor women. My guess is that these are a new purchase. Look, the shine isn't even worn away on the brass, but they broke from stress." He indicated the spot where they'd broken apart on the report.

Maxwell cringed away. "These weren't cheap. Can you imagine the sheer strength of his attack, that it would break metal like that? Have you ever seen something like that?"

"I haven't." Luis picked up a pen. He hadn't used a pen in years. Everything was electronic these days, so he could back it up. He just kept pens around to fidget with. "This is an *angry* man. He bought these because he wanted to hurt these women even more than he had before. He's disturbed, on a level even I don't see very often. He's not going to stop until we get him someplace far away from any women."

"There's a cheerful thought. I'm so glad I'm a dude." Maxwell shuddered. "I know I should be thinking of the victims first, and I'm doing everything in my power to help. I'm not a field agent. I'm a technician. This guy would snap me in half like a twig. He picks his victims up through Tinder, right?"

"So far, it looks that way. We might expand that—other online dating or hookup apps. He does seem to date women exclusively though." Luis flipped his pen over, caught it, and flipped it again.

"Good. I'd hate to run into that guy on Mixr." Maxwell made a face and tapped the table twice. "I'll see you." He left the conference room.

"Jeez, everyone's got a Mixr account." Donovan gave Luis a challenging look.

Luis blinked. Donovan had known exactly what he was getting with Luis. He'd said he understood. He'd said it didn't bother him. What did he think he was trying to do with a comment like that? Luis had justified keeping the inactive account, and Donovan had admitted the wisdom of it.

Kevin, bless him, stepped in. "Not everyone has the luxury of stepping into a committed relationship right away. Some of us have to work hard to find someone, you know?" He checked his watch. "Okay, well, this is my weekend with the kids. For real this time, so I'd better get going. Give me a call if you need anything, okay?"

Luis waved goodbye. Something was clearly going on with Donovan, and Luis didn't need to access his psychology degree or experience to know it had something to do with his dad. And because it was Fred, Luis would be of limited use in making things better.

You've never made anything better in your life. Even your job just cleans up after the scum of society, like a scavenger. Or bacteria.

Luis pushed his father's voice away and put a hand on Donovan's shoulder. "You okay?"

Donovan tensed, and then he smiled a little. "Yeah. Yeah, I've just got a lot on my mind. I told Mom about Dad's little outing."

Luis winced. He and Patricia had been getting along well lately. She'd gone out of her way to welcome him into the family circle. He couldn't quite forget everything that had come before, but he was learning to forgive. Patricia could be a force of nature, for good or for ill. Right now, she was using her powers for good, and Luis didn't mind succumbing. "I'm sure that was exciting."

"The scary thing is, if she decided to burn his house down, she could get away with it. She's just that good. I'm a little iffy on the Church. I'd call myself agnostic, if I had to put a label on it. But I'm glad she has a moral code she believes in, because damn." Donovan grimaced. "I thought I was going to have to take her keys away. Needless to say, she was distinctly uninterested in returning my father's so-called overtures."

"I don't think I'd be all that interested either." Luis glanced at the time. They had plans this evening. He felt an obligation to stay here and work on the case, but given how twitchy Donovan had been acting lately, he didn't think that would be the best idea. Plus, Luis liked going to Donovan's cousin's place. "If we want to get to hang out with Nick at all, we should hit the road. Getting to Waltham is a nightmare this time of day."

"Yeah, you're right." He glanced over at Luis. "Let me guess. You're bringing work home with you."

"I always do." Luis grinned, even though he wasn't feeling it. "This guy's prolific. The sooner we get rid of him, the more comfortable I'll feel, you know?"

"Oh, I know." Donovan stood up. "Here, let's pack up." They gathered their things and inched their way out to Donovan's cousin Alicia's place in Waltham.

Alicia lived with her son in a small house on a generous lot in a popular suburb. Nick's birthday party was tomorrow, and she was throwing the best possible shindig she could for the little guy. Donovan and Luis were coming out to help decorate and set up, and Luis found himself looking forward to the task.

His own family life had been pretty screwed up, even before his mom's murder. None of this suburban stuff had ever been part of his experience, and being around Donovan's giant extended family usually set Luis on edge. He liked Alicia though, and he and Nick got along like a house on fire. Patricia, before finding out Luis was gay, had tried to fix Luis and Alicia up just to have a positive male role model in Nick's life. She'd gotten that part of her wish, at least.

As they pulled up to the bright-yellow house, Luis found himself grinning. He'd played a lot of catch over the summer. He hadn't had much better to do, and Nick had been a patient teacher. He was here to do work, not play, but maybe Alicia would let him and Nick sneak off a little bit.

Alicia hugged them both, and Nick threw his arms around Luis like his life depended on it.

"I missed you!" the little boy told him, looking up with a huge grin on his face.

"I missed you too, little buddy." Luis ruffled Nick's hair. "How was your first week of second grade?" Luis had called him on the first day of school, of course, but these things were important to little kids.

"It was okay. Math is boring. We're doing baby math. I like the workbooks you brought better." Nick pouted, but then he brightened up. "And one of the boys in my class is from Brazil. His name is Joao, but everyone just calls him Joe."

"Is he nice?" Luis asked, getting down so he could be more on Nick's level.

"Yeah! We're best friends now. He's coming to my party tomorrow. Come on! Let's put up the streamers!" Nick grabbed Luis' hand and dragged him off to the kitchen.

The quartet worked to put up streamers, cutouts, and balloons for hours, stopping only for pizza. According to Nick, pizza was a rare treat in the Kennedy household. "Mom doesn't like to get pizza because she says it's not good for growing boys. And she says it slows her reflexes."

"Once in a while is fine," Alicia hurried to add. "But eating it as often as you want to would make it hard for me to do my job, and then where would we be?" Alicia, like pretty much everyone in Donovan's family, was a cop. Unlike most of the other people in Donovan's family, Alicia was part of the Mass State Police's SWAT team.

"Okay, but, Mom, pizza has all of the food groups. It's got protein and dairy and carbohydrates and vegetables." Nick pointed them out as he made his case, right there on his pizza. He stumbled a little over "carbohydrates," but he clearly knew what the word meant. The Waltham schools must be doing something right. "And you can run around while you eat it, and you don't have to get a bunch of forks and knives dirty."

Luis leaned over to Donovan. "He's not going to be a cop," he whispered. "That kid's going to be a lawyer, and a scary one at that."

Donovan chuckled but didn't argue.

After Nick went to bed—tucked in by Luis, at his insistence—the grown-ups sat out back on the patio and relaxed.

"I'll be so glad when this party is over." Alicia yawned and slouched in her chair. "It's his birthday, and I'm happy, but this place is going to be packed tomorrow. And I mean packed."

"Between all the kids and then all the family coming by after, it's going to be a lot." Donovan nodded in sympathy. "It's intense. We'll be here to help, of course. Don't worry about that."

Luis nodded. They had a lot of work to do to catch the Freetown killer, but family was also important. They could do both. They'd make the time for it. "What can we do to make it easier for you?"

"Don't interrogate anyone about their porn choices," she replied promptly, and laughed. "Oh my God, I heard that from Uncle Fred, and it was all I could do to keep a straight face. That was precious!"

Donovan buried his head in his arms, right there on the patio table. "Oh my God. Who goes around and talks to his niece about porn?"

"I think he forgets the family connection." She sipped from her lemonade. She looked so feminine and delicate out here, it was hard to imagine her getting grimy on SWAT. "At least he doesn't hit on me. Small favors, I guess. I hate to say it, but he's gotten downright gross since he and Aunt Patricia split up."

"He was most likely gross before." Donovan picked his head up just enough to look over his arms, like a sad Kilroy. "He's just finally gotten the bandwidth to express himself. What I want to know is how he doesn't see the contradiction in going from hitting on anything in a dress and watching porn all the livelong, to walking right into Confession with the full intent of doing it all again as soon as he walks out of Mass?"

Luis squirmed. It wasn't right for him to criticize his boyfriend's father, even if it had been fun to analyze him at the brewery the other day. At the same time, he did have a contribution to make here. "He comes from a different era, and in that era, men expected to have a lot of leeway with their sexual proclivities. Sure, it all had to be heterosexual, but infidelity was still considered to be the wife's fault for a long time. It was considered almost normal, in some cultures, for a man to have at least one mistress. That was the norm for centuries."

Alicia curled her lip. "Disgusting. All that, but if a woman had an affair, her life was over. Sometimes literally."

Luis snorted. His father had drunkenly accused his mother of infidelity the day he killed her. "I didn't say it was good. I just said it was normal. Anyway, he truthfully doesn't see a problem with it. And until he does, his behavior isn't going to change."

Donovan groaned and buried his face in his arms again. "So why can't he just leave her alone?"

"The priest told him not to." Luis shrugged. "He told him to reconnect with Patricia, so he has to do that. He didn't tell him to find his respect for Patricia or their marriage, so he won't."

"Well, they'll both be here tomorrow, so fun times!" Alicia sat up straighter and smiled brightly. "I think just having you two here will be enough."

Luis smiled. He wasn't sure how to identify this weird, warm feeling in his chest, but he kind of liked it.

Nick's party was everything Donovan had thought it would be. The early part of it was packed with children, so much so that Alicia's one bathroom was overloaded and two little boys had to borrow pants from Nick. Nick himself didn't care, as long as he could show off his uncles to the world. He was keen to show off "Uncle" Luis, who was a "superhero" with the FBI and caught "really bad guys like you see on the news."

"God, I hope these kids' parents don't let them see news about the kind of bad guys Uncle Luis catches," Patricia muttered in Donovan's ear. They were standing on the patio watching Luis preside over a soccer game on Alicia's lawn. Donovan had seen Luis going into the woods in the dark to fight a serial killer, and he hadn't looked as scared as he looked now. He was holding his own with the kids, though, who seemed to adore him. "He's doing well. I thought he didn't 'do' kids."

"He doesn't," Donovan told her. "He's been holding out on me."

"Well, don't take it to heart." Patricia patted his arm and smiled. "He just didn't know. He hasn't had a lot of opportunity. I know Nick thinks he hung the moon."

"Tell me about it." Donovan sighed. "I just wish I'd noticed Alicia and Luis getting close enough for Nick to have any interest in him. It's . . . I don't know. It's disconcerting, I guess. It's weird. I'm glad, of course. I love him, and I'm glad he's making connections with people outside of me, but it's weird to see him hanging around with my family. I'll get used to it."

"You're just jealous." Patricia grinned. "It's not exactly surprising. Just try not to let him know. He needs it, and Nicky enjoys it. And of course, it's a huge relief to Alicia. Nicky needs a consistent male role model, you know. She does the best she can, but she can't be a dad."

"I know. I know. Let's just not put that kind of pressure on Luis yet, okay? Not by telling him, anyway. He'd be uncomfortable." Donovan softened as he saw Luis explaining something very quietly to Nick's friend Joao. Given that Joao had been running circles around the other kids, it almost certainly had something to do with sportsmanship and how American kids didn't have as much familiarity with soccer as Brazilian kids.

Joao nodded and went back out to the other kids. His English wasn't great, but he explained slowly and with a lot of demonstration how to do a head shot. The kids were suitably impressed and all wanted to learn how. Joao got to show off and improve the quality of play, Nick got to be proud of and happy for his friend, and all the kids got to learn a new trick and bonk themselves in the head with a ball.

Family members started showing up as the

kids' party ended, which made for a bit of a traffic jam, but whatever. Luis reappeared at Donovan's side, with Nick firmly attached as usual.

"Uncle Luis just got to meet Joao's parents!" he announced, eyes wide. "It was awesome! They're going to talk on the phone and everything!"

Donovan felt a pang. He was glad Luis was getting out and about, of course. He needed that, and Luis had always liked being around other Brazilians. Wouldn't Luis find someone more appealing than Donovan if he got out there into the wider community though?

Patricia swatted his elbow, behind his back where Luis and Nick couldn't see. It was like she was reading his mind.

"That's great," he said, remembering himself. What the hell was getting into him lately? "Fantastic. It'll be good for you to have someone around to speak Portuguese with."

"His mom speaks Nheengatu too." Luis slipped his hand into Donovan's, just long enough to squeeze his hand. "I almost never get the chance to speak that one with someone face-to-face. So that'll be good."

"Luis has been teaching me Portuguese." Nick stood up a little bit straighter, all but glowing with pride. "I'm going to speak a hundred languages when I get big, just like Uncle Luis."

Luis blushed. "There's nothing you can't do if you set your mind to it, buddy." He ruffled Nick's hair. "I think your mom's looking for you!"

Nick pouted. "She wants me to go get my cheek pinched by some more relatives."

"Well, they are all bringing you presents, buddy," Donovan told him with an easy grin. "How about this. You can go and tell them hello and thank them for the present, but you don't have to let them pinch your cheeks. Deal?" He held out his hand for a high five.

Nick gave it, and gladly. "I don't like the pinching. It hurts. And I don't want to go see Uncle Fred. He smells bad."

"That's fair enough." Patricia smiled gracefully. "How about if I take you around to go see people? Uncle Fred won't go near you if you're with me."

Donovan had to admire her aplomb. No one would ever suspect any anger or bitterness. As Patricia and Nick walked away to greet the rest of the extended family, Donovan turned to Luis. "Look at you, Mr. Soccer Coach."

"It's football," Luis told him in a deadpan voice, and then he relaxed into a grin. "One of the fathers asked if I'd coach in the league this spring. Can you imagine?" He paled just mentioning it, and Donovan laughed.

"I think you'd do just fine, except for the part where you'd disappear on short notice because someone up in northern Maine decided to start planting people like potatoes."

Luis brightened at the thought. "Just the eyes, then? Because I'm curious about the forensics involved there. Those wouldn't last long in the soil—"

Donovan buried his face in Luis' shoulder, muffling his laughter. He knew he was drawing stares, but he'd decided not to care a while ago. It had been hard to get used to not worrying about people's reactions, but once he'd gotten through the initial fear, his world felt so much better. A few family members were upset by it. He wouldn't pretend they weren't. It just felt so good to be able to show his affection, or take some comfort, that it was all worth it.

Luis put his arms around him for just a second, and then he let Donovan go. It was funny—Luis had always been out, but public displays of affection were more difficult for him. "I love you," he murmured. "And your father's on your six."

Donovan stiffened and turned around. Just as Luis had warned him, Fred was storming toward him from a knot of relatives to the rear. "Great," Donovan muttered, and then he plastered a smile on his face. No reason to antagonize the old goat. "Dad, you made it!"

"Donovan." Fred nodded and scowled over at Luis. "I hear he's been here corrupting the youth all day."

"It's called soccer, Dad." Donovan's smile felt tight.

"Football," Luis corrected with a vicious little smile. "I'll go see if Alicia needs anything." He patted Donovan's shoulder and headed off toward the kitchen.

Donovan and Fred watched him go.

"You've got to be kidding me." Fred turned back to Donovan. "They let him hang around kids? What the hell is wrong with you?"

"The kids picked him, Dad." Donovan tried to remember how to keep his temper. "And he was good at it. Believe it or not, he was good at it."

"Yeah, well, I've been doing some poking around into his background. If you're going to insist on this charade of being gay just to piss me off, I mean I should at least know who's messing around with my son. Right?"

"I'm not some delicate and virginal flower, Dad. I've been gay my whole life. He's not the only guy I've been with." Donovan rolled his eyes. "Are you kidding me? Why would you do that?"

"What kind of father would I be if I didn't?"

Fred put a hand on his chest and pretended to look affronted. "I'm telling you, Donovan, the kid's no good. You know his father's in jail for murder, right?"

"No, Dad, his father being a murderer is something that never came up before. Yes. I'm aware." Donovan glanced over toward the house. Luis emerged, carrying three cases of beer like they were boxes of marshmallows. He smiled softly. Luis was something else.

Fred followed his gaze. "You know he's got a reputation, right?"

"I know he wasn't pining when we split up. What's it to you?"

"There's 'pining,' and there's spreading himself around like a man whore." Fred pointed over at Luis, who was putting the beer into coolers. "And his Mixr profile says specifically no white guys. You, in case you haven't looked into a mirror recently, are very white. You can't think this is going to last. There's no way he's going to stick with you. He doesn't stick with anyone, he doesn't like white people, and he's a whore."

Donovan turned to face his father. "You don't know him. You don't want to know him, and your racist self couldn't have anything constructive to say about him even if you bothered to get to know him. We've talked about his past, I know about his Mixr profile, it's fine. Did you have a purpose in coming over here and bothering me, or are you just having a bad day and looking to spread it around?"

Fred curled his lip. "I wanted to warn you about the skank you're sleeping with, but fine. Don't listen to your old man. When he winds up running off with some migrant worker, don't come sobbing on my shoulder." He tugged at his collar. "Did you talk to your mother for me?"

"I told her the truth. I told her your priest wants you to try to reconcile." Donovan refused to look at his father. His gaze followed Luis instead. Luis was talking to Alicia, and Nick had once again firmly attached himself to Luis' leg. It was a great image of family.

It didn't include Donovan.

"Did you try to convince her?" Fred pushed closer to Donovan's space. "Because I've got to tell you, she ain't looking too conciliatory."

Donovan pressed his lips together. "Dad, I think you've got a lot of nerve casting aspersions on anyone else having a lot of partners when you brought an STI home to your wife. No, I didn't try to convince her. I told her your priest is an idiot, and you're an idiot if you think someone like Mom is going to welcome you back into her life after everything you've done. The first thing you should do, before you even think about going *near* my mother again, is figure out what it is you think makes you entitled to cheat on her. Then kill that thing with fire because she deserves respect." Donovan walked away from Fred and joined Luis and Alicia.

Luis seemed happy to see him. He put an arm around Donovan's waist for a moment and grabbed a beer for him. It said a lot that Luis didn't drink but remembered what kinds of beer Donovan liked and even made sure he stocked them for when Donovan came over. That was important, right? It spoke volumes about Luis' feelings, even more than when Luis just said *I love you*.

Then again, Fred used to buy Patricia some lovely jewelry.

"So, Donovan, Luis is going to be an assistant coach in the kids' league in the spring." Alicia beamed at them. "He can't be a full coach because, you're right, his duties with the Bureau won't allow it, but I think he could do some assistant coaching. I think he'll be good at it, don't you?"

"I haven't found anything Luis isn't good at yet." Donovan gave Luis a long, measuring look. He didn't want to believe anything his father said. It was Fred, for God's sake. But then again, it was Fred. If anyone could be said to be an expert on infidelity, it was Fred. "You'd tell me if something was wrong, right, Luis?"

Luis chuckled. "Have you ever known me to shut up about anything on my mind?" He looked over at Alicia. "I'm nervous, but I'm willing to give it a shot."

Donovan tried to force himself to relax. Luis wouldn't volunteer for something like that if he wasn't committing to family life, right?

CHAPTER FIVE

Luis stayed at Donovan's place on Saturday night. They were both exhausted from the party, Luis in particular, and sleeping together was more of a matter of expedience than sexuality at that point. Luis would have slept on Donovan's couch if he'd had to. Donovan didn't ask it of him. They slept together in the same bed, wrapped up in each other's arms and breathing one another's scents.

They might have slept late on Sunday morning. They might have even felt frisky enough for sex as the morning sun drifted through the sheer curtains. Even through his exhaustion, Luis would have welcomed the chance to touch and be touched. Donovan clearly had something on his mind, and Luis wanted to be able to give him reassurance. He wanted to reassure himself too and to ground himself.

But their phones both went off at the same time, seven o'clock in the morning, and that could only mean one thing. There had been another killing down in Freetown.

They showered and dressed quickly and drove down to Freetown together. Donovan was quiet as they headed down Rt. 495. There wasn't too much traffic at this time of day, which was a nice change from the usual.

"You okay?" Luis asked finally. He couldn't show his concern and his love the way he was most comfortable with, so he'd have to go with words.

Donovan grunted. "Yeah, I'm fine." He screwed up his face in disgust. "Sorry. I've been distant, haven't I?"

"You've seemed to have something weighing on you." Luis chose his words carefully. He didn't want to piss Donovan off or seem judgmental. Not that Donovan would get violent, but he wanted Donovan to feel comfortable speaking. If he felt like he'd be judged, Donovan would lock down tighter than the Pentagon. "If you want to talk about it, I'm here. It's a long car ride, is all I'm saying."

Donovan took a sip of his coffee. "It's my dad," he said after a second.

"I saw the two of you speaking yesterday." Luis carefully kept his voice neutral. He knew Fred was high on Donovan's shit list right now. He couldn't understand why Donovan would sit around and entertain a damn thing Fred had to say, but he'd be the first to admit he didn't understand how families were supposed to work. "I take it the conversation didn't go well."

"You could say that." Donovan sighed. "You already know he's not a fan."

Luis set his jaw. "Yeah. Yeah, I got the memo."

"Well, he did some poking into your background, to try to find some dirt to try to break us up." Donovan's grip on the wheel tightened, and Luis narrowed his eyes.

"I've always been an open book, Donovan. You know that. I've never tried to hide anything from you."

"Other than the occasional injury."

Now what the hell was that supposed to mean? "Valid," Luis said. His heart sped up, just like it might if he was getting ready for a fight. His adrenaline shouldn't be kicking in for a conversation with Donovan, for crying out loud. Why would all of his instincts be screaming about dangerous territory when he was with the man he loved?

"You'd tell me if you were bored, right?" Donovan didn't look at Luis.

"Of course I would." Luis snorted. "I'm not bored. I'm in love, with you. I'm so in love with you I volunteered to be an assistant coach for your nephew's football team." Where was this going?

"Soccer," Donovan corrected. "And yeah, I know you did. You seemed to be having a pretty good time with all those kids."

Luis had to laugh. "With the exception of Nick and Joao, I thought they were going to eat me alive. You know that. I'm still not sure some of the parents won't. Four different mothers tried to give me their phone numbers, one of them right in front of her husband!"

"They might have wanted a threesome." Donovan's voice was carefully neutral, and Luis recognized what he was after.

He rested his head against the car window. "I don't appreciate being tested, Donovan. I get that your father was trying to give you ideas or whatever, but you know damn well that I'm not interested in women. Never have been, never will be. And random threesomes were fine when I was on my own and substituting sex for affection. I don't have to do that anymore. I'd rather spend a night in bed with you, even if we're too tired to do more than snore in one another's general direction, than make a big sweaty mess with a pile of strangers. Okay?"

Donovan's cheeks got red, and he set his jaw. "I know. I mean, I know that in my head. It's just . . . well, I mean, he did find your Mixr profile."

"Oh, the one that states clearly that I'm inactive and the profile is for past contact info only?" Luis crossed his arms over his chest. He felt oddly cold, and it wasn't because of the air conditioner.

"I know, I know!" Donovan thumped his head lightly against the headrest. "It's just—never mind. I'm being irrational. He really is putting thoughts in my head, things that I don't really think. And I tell him so when he says them, but then they bounce around in there after I've walked away and it's like they just get louder. It's stupid, and it's frustrating as hell."

The psychologist in Luis wanted to point out that Fred couldn't put thoughts into Donovan's head if they didn't find fertile ground to land on. The lover in Luis wanted to reassure Donovan, and himself, that things would be okay. He'd spent a decade catering to the psychologist and the cop in himself. It was time to honor the lover. Luis liked him better anyway.

He put a hand on Donovan's tense arm. "Hey," he said. "It's okay, you know? We're both still new to this. We'll get there. Just remember, we love each other."

Donovan's smile looked a little forced to Luis, but he figured he was just being paranoid. He pushed past it and took his hand back. They were almost to the Freetown exit, and he needed to get his game face on. No one at a crime scene wanted to hear from lovey-dovey agents.

When they pulled in, Wong was already on-site. So was Maxwell, whose hair was all but standing on end as he argued with the pathologist about evidence. Ruben Noguera looked on from the shore, by turns amused and repulsed. State troopers were doing their best to shield a pair of witnesses from the scene—they looked like a couple of middle-aged women with dogs, but Luis didn't take much time to look at them. He was too busy trying to get between the two technicians.

"How many times do you need to be told that your jurisdiction ends with the body itself?" Maxwell shouted. "The body is not on the shore. You have no right to put your gross little corpse hands on these sunglasses. None!"

"Those sunglasses might have belonged to the victim!" Wong screeched.

"Oh my God," Luis muttered. He thrust his arms out to keep the two scientists apart, just as Maxwell took a swing at Wong.

"He just tried to punch me!" Wong tried to jump back, aghast.

"If I'd tried to punch you, motherfucker, you'd fucking know it!" Maxwell told him.

For a second, the briefest of moments, Luis

thought he saw a glimpse of something purple. He couldn't put his finger on it, other than to describe it as a haze. "Maxwell, go cool off. Over there, in the shade." Luis pointed. "Wong—do you have a plan for getting the floater out, or nah?"

Wong screwed up his face. *"Wong, do you have a plan for getting the floater out, or nah?"* He pointed one finger at Luis, with the finger ending just shy of his nose. It took every last bit of Luis' patience to keep from moving the finger with force. "I do these things on my schedule, Gomes, not yours. Go ahead, call my brother and tattle, I don't care. It's not going to get your corpse out of the water any faster."

Luis took a deep breath. "It's early on a Sunday morning, and I know we're all tired and cranky. So let's sit back and think about why you'd certainly never want to come off as though you were obstructing a federal investigation for personal reasons, Dr. Wong." Luis used his Fed Voice, the one he knew made him sound like a soulless robot.

"I would never." Wong recoiled at the hint of accusation. "How could you even suggest it?"

"Because there's still a corpse floating in the water, and you're here poking at sunglasses instead of out there retrieving the body." Luis straightened up. He used all of his height, and his bulk as well, to convey his message to the pathologist.

Wong was maladjusted from a social perspective, but he wasn't stupid. He pouted, but he waved to the two assistants waiting nearby. "Grab the rowboat," he snarled, and stomped off to where the rowboat waited for him.

Ruben approached him. "That was pretty impressive," he said, with a little smile on his face. "You were these guys' daddy, before most guys are even out of bed."

Luis kept himself from blushing, only because he couldn't conceive of the idea of sex with Wong. "I'll be honest, it's early for me on a Sunday too." He made himself grin. Ruben surely didn't mean anything gross by his comment. "And while Wong has his quirks, Maxwell can be a little highly strung too. It is what it is. Let's just hope poor Donovan can convince the witnesses this is normal." He grimaced and looked over at his boyfriend, who'd jogged over to the two women with the dogs.

Ruben stepped into Luis' view. A few moments later, a crime scene tech walked near the space where he'd been. Ruben's move, his excessive proximity, almost seemed reasonable in light of the sudden appearance of the tech. The only problem was that Ruben had moved in a little too far in advance of the tech to push it off as getting out of the way.

Luis frowned. He was just being paranoid. "Those women found the body?"

"They did," Ruben confirmed. "They're here every morning, walking their dogs rain or shine. They don't always come out to the Ledge, but they're in various parts of the Forest. They saw the deceased floating there, and they called the ranger station for help."

"And you've got the night shift."

"I do have the night shift." Ruben chuckled. The newborn sun seemed to glint off his perfect teeth. "You've got a good memory."

Luis smiled, just a little bit. Of course he had a good memory. He was a profiler, damn it. He fought the urge to lash out. It was too early for any of this. Just once, he wanted to deal with a killer who took the needs of night owls into consideration.

"Were there any other reports of any unusual activity around here last night? Cars where there shouldn't be, people walking where they wouldn't be walking most days . . ."

Behind them, Wong and his assistants got the rowboat into the water. One of the assistants got stuck rowing out to the corpse. He didn't seem to be incompetent at it because the soft splash of the oars was rhythmic instead of chaotic.

"No, nothing." Ruben smirked. "Not that anyone would necessarily notice. It's a big park, you know? I spent most of my time up by Profile Rock. It's not a huge section of the park, but a bunch of kids from the high school thought it would be a grand idea to throw a bonfire party up there. It happens. Kids are going to be kids, no matter what."

"You're not wrong about that." Luis made a mental note to verify Ruben's alibi. He didn't think Ruben was involved with the killings, but he was still the only person who'd been around when all of the victims had been discovered. "Did you get contact info from any of the kids? One of them might have seen something."

"I got something from a few of 'em. That doesn't mean it's accurate, but I got something." Ruben winked. "I mean, I've got contact information for fifty-seven seniors from Apponequet Regional High School seniors named Charles U. Farley, but I got something."

Just then, Donovan made his way over to the pair. He glowered at Ruben, who seemed unfazed by Donovan's display of jealousy.

"Anyway, I'd better be escorting the ladies back to their cars. I'd hate for anything to happen to them."

"Yeah, that's a good idea. Thanks, Ruben."

Donovan smiled tightly at their host as Ruben turned to go. As soon as he was out of earshot, he turned to Luis. "Dude, I was trying to get your attention for like three minutes!"

"Sorry." Luis slumped. "Ruben stood right between us. He seemed to be trying to get out of the techs' way, and I can't really complain about that but . . ."

"But he's trouble. Mark my words, he's trouble." He tightened his jaw and looked around. "The dog walkers said they saw her right there, just like that. They didn't see anyone else either."

"Nah, I wouldn't expect that they had." Luis bowed his head. "My guess is he brings them here around sunset. She'd have been here since then. We won't know for sure until Wong pulls her out of the lake."

In the water, the ME's office techs were struggling to get a picture of the body as she lay in situ.

"Think it's going to be a while?" Donovan asked, and yawned.

"You know it's going to be a while." Luis made a face.

"You guys totally need an intern," Donovan told him. "You could send them out on a coffee run."

Luis grinned. "You know, I'll have to see

about getting the budget for that."

It took Wong and his techs forever to wrestle the body into the rowboat. Some of their slow pace was reasonable because they had to take photos and do their best not to damage the remains further in their attempt to remove her from the water. They also capsized the boat once. Wong fell in twice besides that, and he accidentally threw in one of his assistants too. It turned out that the assistant in question couldn't swim, which was briefly entertaining to watch even if Luis had to jump in and save him.

Donovan would normally appreciate that more, particularly as Luis stood there in his soaking-wet tee shirt and dress pants. The shirt clung to him in ways that truly blew Donovan's mind. Unfortunately, Donovan couldn't help but notice Ruben Freaking Noguera appreciating the view too. He wasn't even being subtle. That soured his mood right away.

Luis was able to help the techs get the body into the boat, since he was out there already, and he even rowed them back to shore amid Wong's shrill insistence that none of this changed the rules and Luis didn't get to handle bodies without his sign-off, damn it. Luis ignored him and stalked off to the car to change. Ruben, damn the man, tried to follow. Donovan had to block him, which prevented him from going to get a better view of his own. Ruben didn't say anything, just sneered in this knowing way that made Donovan want to wash his own skin down with bleach.

The day was turning out worse and worse.

While all the drama with the boat and the body was happening, Maxwell had gotten his team together to process the rest of the scene. Given that Wong was otherwise occupied, and safely contained, he was able to gather up all the other evidence readily available to the naked eye. "I don't like it out here," he admitted to Donovan, while his team packed up to go home. "It feels like there's something watching you."

"What, like ghosts?" Donovan gave him the side-eye. Was Donovan the only person around here who didn't see ghosts? He knew he was being ridiculous and pouting because of the whole thing with Ruben. Maybe he'd feel better with some coffee.

"Sure, I guess. I'm a scientist. We don't do ghosts." Maxwell shrugged. "I was thinking more like . . . I don't even know what I was thinking of. It's just creepy. You know it's a popular spot for suicides, right?"

"I'm sure this is just another one." Ruben

popped up from somewhere. Donovan hadn't even noticed him approaching. "It's sad, but it does happen. Not much you can do about it, I'm afraid."

"It does happen," Maxwell told him, narrowing his eyes at Ruben, "but not like it does here. I've read some interviews with people who survived their attempts. They said they had no history of depression, no prior attempts. They just had a sudden overwhelming grief, so terrible they couldn't live with it. And once they were off the Ledge, they were over it."

Ruben rolled his eyes. "Buddy, I've heard it all. Every last little bit of it. Believe me. Who do you think tackles them to the ground before they can jump, or fishes them out of the drink like your handsome, buff friend over there?" He jerked his head toward Luis, who'd dressed in the casual clothes he'd packed for today. "Damn, you can dress him up or down, he still looks good."

Donovan wondered if Luis would get mad if he decked Ruben. "A lot of people do claim they've felt something watching," he said to Maxwell, ignoring his rival. "But I wonder how much of that just comes from the reputation this place has. You know, people hear about it and everything that's happened here, they get to thinking about it, that kind of thing."

Maxwell gave Ruben a look of unmistakable

distaste. "Yes, possibly. Whatever. I'm not here to prove or disprove. For all I know, it's just a rabid raccoon. All I know is it's uncomfortable here. I'm going to get back to the lab and start processing. I'll leave you guys with a kit. I assume you're sticking around?"

"You know it." Donovan grinned at Maxwell. "I'll see you around, okay?"

"You bet." Maxwell took off, just in time for Luis to join them.

Luis was still shaking his head. "If I know I can't do something, I don't volunteer to go do something that requires me to do the thing. You know, like rowing out to the middle of a deep quarry to retrieve a dead body when I can't freaking swim."

Donovan snorted. "Oh, come on. Do you think Dr. Charming gave him the chance to say no?"

Ruben laughed and laughed into a burst of rapid-fire Spanish. It was too fast for Donovan to follow. He spoke some Spanish, enough to get by, but not like this. He thought he picked up on the word for milk. And was that bull? Whatever it was, Luis' eyes bulged and he burst out laughing.

Donovan couldn't make Luis laugh like that. He looked so beautiful, smiling wide and practically glowing. Donovan balled his hands into fists. It wasn't hard to see what Ruben had that he didn't. The big question was, what did he have to offer that Ruben didn't?

Donovan couldn't think of a single thing.

Luis glanced over at Donovan and straightened up. "Anyway, we need to get to work. Sorry you had to see all that." He shook his head, eyes closed. "It was unprofessional, all of it, and you shouldn't have been exposed to it."

Ruben said something else in Spanish. Donovan didn't need to know those words to know it was inappropriate. Luis' cheeks darkened, and Ruben's teasing, purring tone told him enough. He opened his mouth to say something angry, but Ruben's radio squawked at him just in time.

"Noguera, come back to the station. The Feds have been here often enough they ain't going to get lost, and I'm not paying you overtime to hang out with them."

Ruben gritted his teeth, and then he waved. "I guess that's my cue. It was good to see you both again, even under circumstances like this."

"Likewise." Luis' smile was cool and professional, but Donovan had to wonder if there wasn't more to it than that. He had to have encouraged Ruben, if the guy felt comfortable hitting on him so blatantly. Right?

They poked around on the side of the pond

for a few minutes. Luis seemed reluctant to say anything to Donovan. Was it the sign of a guilty conscience?

"So. He's friendly," Donovan tried.

"Yeah. He is." Luis glanced over at Donovan for a second. "It's not appropriate for him to sit there and make jokes in Spanish in front of you, but maybe he thinks you speak Spanish?"

Donovan bit down on the inside of his cheek. Did Luis think he was stupid? "People don't switch languages like that unless they want to exclude someone."

Luis sighed. "Or unless they just don't know the English, but you're right. And Ruben was born here."

"How do you know?" Donovan scoffed.

"I did run a check on him." Luis side-eyed him. "I do know how to do my job, Donovan. I get that you don't like him, but give me a little credit. He spends all of his time wandering around in the woods. People in that profession don't always have the most polished social skills. What's he going to do, smooth-talk the badgers?"

Donovan chuckled, more or less against his inclination. "Okay, you've got a point." They'd gotten a little farther up the trail. "Is it me, or does it seem like the brush here is disrupted?"

"Like someone was running through and

not being overly careful where they went?" Luis gestured to a small flag left behind by the crime scene team. "Yeah. I don't think our victim was a suicide."

Then Luis froze. He focused on something, a little circle of sunlight breaking through the tree cover. Even when Donovan strained his eyes, he couldn't see anything more than a few dust motes. Luis was seeing something though. And Donovan couldn't pretend he was faking it either. He could smell the distinct scent of rotting meat if he breathed deep enough.

"Jennifer," Luis said, addressing the sun spot.

Donovan looked away. Sure, he was jealous. He didn't understand why Luis got to see and interact with the spirit world and he didn't. If he thought about it logically, he knew Luis would rather not have this "gift," but that just made it worse.

"Okay. That's good to know. Thank you. We'll see what we can do about getting your remains up from the bottom. And thank you for telling us what you saw. We appreciate it."

He relaxed and turned to Donovan. "She says her body is at the bottom of the water. And today's victim got away from the killer. She tried to run, but he was too fast. He knew where he was going, and it was already dark. He knocked her down, and she hit her head. Jennifer didn't see what happened after that."

Donovan scoffed. "She couldn't have stuck around and at least given us a description?" He knew he was being petty, but they were dealing with a serial killer here. He figured he had a right to be petty.

Luis did a double take. "What's gotten into you today? Would you ask a living survivor of violence, sexual or otherwise, to stand there and watch someone else be victimized just so they could be a witness?" He shook his head and started back down the trail.

"Where are you going?" Donovan asked, chasing after him. "And come on, Luis. She's not living."

"Which brings me to my second point." Luis pushed his still-damp hair out of his face. "What is it you want me to do, put a ghost on the stand? For real? Retraumatize a crime victim for evidence we can't use?" He took a fork in the trail, one that headed up. "I'm going on a hunch. If our guy is as strong as I think he is—and he did break those brass knuckles—he's certainly strong enough to throw a woman off the Ledge."

Getting up to the top of the Ledge took time, and Donovan's thighs burned by the time they got to the top. He was in good shape, and he'd always prided himself on his condition, but he hadn't been training for this kind of hike. Luis, of course, wasn't even breathing heavy, despite having just come back from a serious injury to his lungs.

The view from the top was stunning. Donovan could see for miles over the tops of the trees. Fall River was close, and it was an urban center, but Donovan could almost believe they were on untouched land from up here.

That was, he could believe he was on untouched land until he looked down. The Ledge itself was covered in graffiti. Bright colors marked the place with traditional street tagging, song lyrics, creative art, anatomical improbabilities, and a bright-yellow exhortation to "JUMP," complete with arrows. He stared at the word, which seemed to grow the longer he looked at it.

Why not? The voice in his head wasn't his own. It didn't belong to anyone he knew. It slithered, wrapping itself around his consciousness like a boa constrictor. *You know if Luis isn't doing the ranger, he will be soon. Your dad already hates you, you've broken your mother's heart, your career is stalling—*

Luis grabbed the back of Donovan's collar and jerked him away from the Ledge. He didn't let go, or stop pulling, until they were off the rock and back among the tree line. Just like that, the voice left Donovan. He could breathe again.

"What the hell was that?" Donovan gasped. He clutched at his chest. "It was like—I don't even know. I've never seen or felt anything like that."

Luis nodded. His skin had gone sallow, and his eyes were sunken. "I know." His voice was quiet. "Believe me."

"What, you read minds now?"

Luis' jaw twitched, but he kept his temper. "No. I was hearing something similar. And I do have certain advantages." He gave a little laugh. "When I started getting those intrusive thoughts, I could *see* they weren't my own. And I could see you were being bombarded too." He rolled his shoulders. "There was a bloodstain on the rock, relatively fresh. I got a swab. Hopefully, it will be a match to our victim. Let's get it to Maxwell."

"Anything to get the hell out of this place." Donovan shuddered and grabbed at Luis' hand. "Hey. Thanks for saving my life."

Luis dropped a quick kiss on Donovan's lips. "Any time. You're important to me."

They hiked back down to the car and told the troopers to secure the Ledge itself. Then they headed back to Chelsea. Donovan had Luis drive. He could still hear the intrusive thoughts echoing in his head.

CHAPTER SIX

Luis rode home with Donovan, just as he'd ridden out with Donovan. It took him by surprise that he'd started thinking of Donovan's place as "home." Sure, they'd lived together once before. Maybe that was why it felt natural to think that way, as natural as breathing. They weren't *there* yet though, and he couldn't let himself get complacent.

The way Donovan had been acting the past few days, they'd never get there. Had it only been a few days ago, or a week ago, that Luis told Donovan he didn't mind a little jealousy? *Little* had been the operative word. He wanted to know he was wanted, he was someone important to Donovan. What he was getting from Donovan wasn't that.

Luis couldn't remember Donovan having been all that jealous when they'd been together last time, but he was seeing a lot of things from that era with rose-colored glasses. They'd been happy together, but nothing could have been as good as he remembered it. Had there been any moments then that should seem like red flags to Luis now, with his training and experience?

He couldn't think of any. That didn't mean they didn't exist.

He sighed, and Donovan glanced over at him with a hard set to his jaw. "Thinking about Ruben?"

Luis looked up at the ceiling. "Thinking about the case." It wasn't a lie. The case in question just happened to be where in the name of God this jealous streak in Donovan had popped up from. "Another floater in the same space, along with a long list of missing persons, should be enough to get them to let us dredge the quarry, but I don't want to make assumptions."

"Getting dredging equipment in there would be a pain," Donovan agreed after a few seconds' hesitation. The hesitation lasted just long enough for Luis to understand his lover was struggling with something, most likely Luis' lie. Was Luis that obvious? He supposed he must be, but he didn't want to think of himself that way. "I can see why the powers that be would be reluctant on both sides—law enforcement and the Department of Conservation."

"Right?" Luis forced himself to relax, just a little bit. At least they could talk about the case, right? "Maybe if we sent divers in, it would work better. I don't know." He managed a little laugh. "I mean, they'd have to put up with Wong screaming about not touching the bodies, but there's not a lot of options."

"Hm. How the hell did you get Wong's brother to help you out?" Donovan looked straight ahead and gripped the wheel even tighter. "With Wong, I mean."

Luis did a double take. "Are you for real right now? His brother is *straight*. And I didn't find out about the brother until after we were together. I asked his brother for help, and he said okay. What is with you today, Donovan? You're acting like I've gone off and done something wrong, when you know damn well I've been loyal since we got together."

"You were pretty friendly with Ruben." Donovan still wouldn't look at him.

"Oh, for fuck's sake." Luis curled his lip. "I can't believe I'm having this conversation. I conversed with Ruben, sure. I was polite with him. And sure, he's friendly. He's a little overfriendly. Are you planning to be one of those guys who gets angry because other guys find me attractive? Because that's going to get real old, real fast, let me tell you."

Donovan bowed his head. "I'm sorry. I

know I'm being ridiculous." He took a deep breath and smiled tightly. "So. Divers. I don't suppose the Bureau has them?"

"I think we do have an underwater recovery team, but not in the Boston office. We'd have to send for them from Quantico. Which we can do, but the state police have divers closer to home." Luis didn't trust Donovan's sudden shift, but he didn't make an issue of it. He didn't want to sit around and fight. He just wanted to get through the case. Everything would be fine once they got through this case.

Because that always worked.

He wanted to understand what was going on with Donovan too. He just wanted to do it without having to get into a big fight about it. Couldn't he figure it out like any other case, through profiling and detective work? That made sense. These veiled accusations and the need to defend himself all the time did not.

Luis messaged Kevin and asked him to put in a request for divers. Then he drummed his fingers against his leg. "So our killer has an issue with women," he mused aloud. "That's not exactly news. A lot of serial killers have issues with women. He's meeting them through dating sites, but he's not using his real picture or profile. So he's definitely seeking victims, hunting, not becoming enraged and losing his temper."

"Is he killing all of his dates?" Donovan had hesitated before asking.

Luis couldn't tell if he was pausing because he didn't trust Luis' profile or because he was still mad about Luis chatting with Ruben.

"No way to tell yet. We need to finish going through the data Tinder sent. I don't mind telling you, I'm a little creeped out by that part." Luis kept his eyes forward and his body loose, but he carefully observed Donovan's response.

Donovan scoffed. "You, who won't even delete his Mixr account, are creeped out by looking at someone else's Tinder data?"

Luis couldn't resist a little smirk there. Okay, so Donovan was still angry about that. Good to know. "Maybe it's because of my Mixr account. Going through all of that data feels like I'm breaching someone's privacy in the worst way, you know? I'm super uncomfortable with it. I hate it. I get that there's no help for it, it's the only way, but if I got a welfare check call from law enforcement because of my online dating profile, I'd be super uncomfortable. Wouldn't you?"

"No. Because I don't have an online dating profile." He glared. "I'm faithful." For a second, Luis thought he saw a purplish glint come into Donovan's dark eyes, but he had to be imagining it.

He was looking for an excuse that wasn't there.

Luis didn't rise to the bait. Instead, he turned his mind to trying to solve the problem at hand. Donovan was feeling insecure about Luis' fidelity. Luis hadn't so much as thought about another guy in a sexual way since they'd gotten together, but he needed to find a way to prove it to Donovan. Could he?

He wanted to go home when they pulled into Donovan's driveway. They had a fresh body, and they had a lot of work ahead of them. Donovan was important though. Luis' relationship with Donovan was important. Luis needed to prove both of those things to Donovan. When they got out of the car, he caressed Donovan's stubbled face. "You know I love you, right?"

"Yeah." Donovan wouldn't look him in the eye. "I know you do."

Luis' insides quaked, but he guided Donovan's face toward him. "Hey. I mean it." He kissed Donovan then. Words hadn't been their friends today, but he might get somewhere with action.

Donovan, bless him, kissed back. He licked into Luis' mouth like his life depended on it, gripping his shoulders tight. The sun had just started its descent, and they stood in the waning light exploring one another's mouths like it was the first time.

Donovan pulled back for a moment. "Are you coming in?" He fumbled in his pocket for his keys.

Luis nodded. "If you want me to."

"I want you to." Donovan unlocked his door and led the way into his condo. They didn't waste time with crap like stopping for food or pretending to watch TV. They headed straight for the bedroom after locking the door behind them.

Luis was tugging at his clothes before he even got to the bedroom. He just wanted them off. He wanted to rid himself of the day and the taint of Freetown. He wanted Donovan to see *him*, not this case or Ruben or ghosts or whatever else was chasing around in his head. He was nude by the time Donovan closed the bedroom door.

Donovan grabbed him and claimed his mouth in a rough, passionate kiss. He was usually more gentle than this, and Luis knew his lips would be sore afterward. Right now, he didn't care. He just wanted Donovan's attention and affection, any way he could get it. He slid his hands up underneath Donovan's shirt, relishing the warmth of his body.

Donovan took his shirt off as fast as he could and got rid of the rest of his clothes too. He was already hard, and that was a good thing, right? That had to mean he still loved Luis. A part of him understood that bodies didn't work like that, people got hard for any number of reasons to include a good stiff breeze, but he shushed that part up. He needed to believe Donovan still loved him right now, and he'd grasp at any straws he could to justify that belief.

Luis wasn't there yet, not even close. He'd get there. He always did.

He let Donovan manhandle him as much as he wanted and luxuriated in every nibble, scratch, and bite. Donovan held onto him a little too tightly, hard enough to bruise sometimes, but he didn't mind. It couldn't bother him, if Donovan loved him enough to lose control of himself like that, right?

Donovan laid him down on the bed, mouthing at his chest like he could actually eat him. He cried out at the pleasure mixed with just a little bit of pain, but Donovan didn't seem to notice. On the contrary, he had left actual marks on Luis' skin. Luis was no stranger to getting a little rough here and there, but it wasn't something he usually encountered with Donovan.

He let go and just went with it. He didn't object to it most of the time, and if this was what Donovan needed tonight, then he could have it. When Donovan started to prep him, Luis let it happen, even though he wasn't quite ready yet, and when Donovan slid into him, he made himself relax into the stretch.

Sometimes love was giving of yourself, after all. Something was bothering Donovan, and Luis was going to give him whatever he needed to get it out of his system.

Donovan didn't draw it out. He set a fast, demanding pace, and Luis struggled to keep up with him. When Donovan came, he came hard, seeming to surprise himself, and he pulled out only seconds after finishing. He got rid of the condom and disappeared into the bathroom, as though he was eager to wash the stain of sex away from himself.

Luis sat up. He couldn't remember feeling dirty after sex before now. It wasn't a great feeling.

Donovan took his time coming back into the bedroom. He wouldn't look Luis in the eye. "So. Who were you thinking of, just now?"

Luis felt like he'd just been stabbed. He jumped out of bed and threw his clothes on, not caring that his pants wound up inside out and his shirt backwards. "I can't believe you'd ask me that. After everything, I can't believe you would ask me that." He jammed his feet into his shoes and stormed toward the door.

Donovan grabbed at Luis' arm. "It's a legitimate question, Luis! I mean, come on, Ruben was all over you."

"The hell he was. He was flirtatious, sure. That's not my fault. And, you know, he's not a jealous dick. So there's that." Luis shook his boyfriend's hand off him. It would be easy to remove it in such a way that Donovan never tried to put it back, but he didn't want to hurt Donovan.

"Luis, we need to talk about this." Donovan scowled.

"Get your head out of your ass, stop being a jealous prick, and we can talk all you want. I am appalled. I'm just appalled." He left the condo, got into his car, and drove back toward Medford.

His stomach quailed, but he refused to pull over. Maybe he'd handled Donovan wrong, but he couldn't believe the accusation in his lover's tone. Did Donovan really believe Luis was cheating on him, or ever would cheat on him? How could he ever think of such a thing? After everything they'd gone through to get back together, cheating was the last thing on Luis' mind. It should be the last thing on Donovan's.

Luis couldn't think of a reasonable explanation. There had been that purple glimmer in his eye, but Luis had almost certainly imagined it. Maybe it wasn't about cheating at all though. Maybe it had more to do with Donovan being sick of Luis. Maybe he was tired of Luis' drama and wanted to be rid of him but had hesitated to do anything about it while Luis had still been recuperating.

No, his jealousy had been real. It didn't make sense, but it had been real. Men flirted with Luis all the time. Women were more likely to flirt with Donovan, and maybe that was why Luis didn't get jealous. No, he didn't get jealous because he figured Donovan would tell him if he wanted to be with someone else.

Luis needed to get help. This wasn't a problem he could solve on his own. The only problem was that he couldn't go to the people who knew Donovan best—his family—and ask for help. Even if they didn't have issues with Donovan's sexuality, it would be weird.

He got to his own condo and washed up. A good hot shower could help soothe away the hurt feelings. When he finished, he crawled into bed. Obsessing about it, as Father Geoffrey told him, wouldn't solve anything. He'd sleep on it and focus on the case in the morning. Maybe they were both just made tense by the case.

Donovan replayed the trip out to Freetown all night as he lay alone in his bed. He hadn't counted on sleeping alone, but Luis had gone storming off in a snit and Donovan didn't have much choice. All Donovan had done had been to call him out on his infidelity. He felt justified in having done so too, given the way he'd been behaving with Ruben Freaking Noguera.

The thing was, it seemed to have come out of nowhere. They'd been fine when it had just been them, while Luis was convalescing. Of course, Luis had plenty of time alone. Donovan hadn't had to see him with anyone else. Maybe he'd been that flirtatious with everyone. Maybe Luis had a harem of guys just hanging on his every word.

He probably did. It wasn't like Luis was used to monogamy. Luis hadn't even pretended to be monogamous in over a decade. Maybe it wasn't reasonable of him to expect a guy who'd been out playing the field for years to just suddenly restrict himself to one man, and a man who was busy at that. The poor guy had to be going into withdrawal.

He couldn't fall asleep that night. What if Luis had driven right back down to Freetown, right into Ruben's arms? There was no way he could keep Luis' affection. He'd already lost him. He couldn't make himself give up the ghost though. What if he could somehow induce him to stay by his side? Surely, there must be something he had to offer, something Luis wanted.

He went to work the next day even more

exhausted than when he'd lain down that night. Luis looked as fresh and as crisp as ever. He was beautiful. He was wasting away here. He should have been a model, but then he'd have even more men flinging themselves at him. He greeted Donovan with a nod of his head. The only sign he was still angry was the tightness of his jaw.

What did he have to be angry about? All Donovan had done had been to call him on his bullshit.

Kevin must have picked up on the tension because he stood up and glanced between the two. He didn't say anything though, just bit his lip before moving on. "Okay," he said slowly. "Not my circus and all that. We have an ID on yesterday's floater. Meet Macy Wilkerson, twenty-three, administrative assistant at an advertising firm in Boston. She lived in Avon but accepted a Tinder date with our mystery man on Friday night." He pressed a button on his laptop, and a pretty if suggestive profile picture popped up on the screen on the wall.

Donovan stared. So did Luis. Donovan tried not to notice, but it was hard not to pick up on it when he was right there, with that intense look on his face. Would he ever look at Donovan with that same kind of intensity again?

Kevin spread his hands wide. "Guys, I

worked my ass off to set this up. The least you could do is give me an 'attaboy, Kev.' "

"Attaboy, Kev." Donovan didn't change expressions at all.

Luis, however, got even more intense. "Kevin, can you put the profile pictures of the other victims up?"

"Sure. No problem." Kevin pressed a few keys. "Want me to add the women who are confirmed to have had dates with this guy, but who are still unaccounted for?"

"Please." Luis scratched at his jawline.

Fifty faces filled the screen. "They're all under thirty-five," Donovan commented. He still couldn't make himself look directly at Luis, but he had to speak. "Other than that, there's nothing in common between them."

Luis snorted. "There's one thing."

Donovan gestured at the screen. "They come from different racial and ethnic backgrounds. They come from different economic backgrounds. They come from three different states. They have a hundred different jobs, family backgrounds, whatever. Some have kids, some don't. What do you see that I don't?"

"Kevin, I'll defer to you since you have a sexual appreciation for women. Would you describe those profile pictures as suggestive or adventurous?" Luis' tone stayed even and neutral, but his hand clenched into a fist at his side.

Kevin scoffed. "One of them's in full-on bondage gear, dude. That's not a matter of orientation. That's not subtle."

"They're all in suggestive photos in their profile pictures." Luis sat down and took a long, loud sip of his coffee.

Donovan watched his throat work as he drank. Then he shook himself out of it. "Okay, sure, but it's a dating site. Your profile picture is your bare abs and chest, without your face."

"It was, when I was unattached. Now it's a much more sedate and professional picture. I've even got a tie on. With a shirt underneath." Luis' smile lacked warmth. "Your profile picture is your first chance to tell a potential match something about you, and what you're telling him is why you're there. If you're looking for a relationship and romance, your picture will be a little more clothed than it will be if you're looking for a hookup or a sexual situation."

Donovan pressed his mouth closed for a second. He didn't want to fight in front of Kevin, or at work. "And you think these girls were all to blame for their own deaths because they dressed skimpy for their profile pictures?"

"Get over yourself, Donovan. That's not

what I said. I said that's what they have in common. We know our guy is killing women, we know he's meeting them through Tinder. What we don't know is how he's choosing his victims. Does he have a problem with all women or just some women? Kevin, can we get pictures of some of the women he's had Tinder dates with who we can account for—women he's chosen not to kill?"

Kevin cleared his throat uncomfortably and typed the parameters into the system, and the women in suggestive clothing and poses were replaced by women in more restrained clothing, in more candid shots.

"Bingo." Luis snapped his fingers. "A lot of misogynistic serial killers have strong feelings about women who are sexually liberated or enthusiastic. That's not an endorsement, for the record, it's just a fact. A lot of them prey on sex workers, but they'll also prey on women they view as the equivalent. I can get into Madonna/whore complexes, the effect of patriarchal systems on masculine psyches—"

"We get it," Kevin said, in a long-suffering tone. "Remind me never to watch a football game with you. The guy's a pig. So what, he decides a woman is too slutty to live and then he kills her?"

"That remains to be seen, but that's usually how it works. Ordinarily, I'd say he'd come on to her, and if she was receptive, he'd choose to kill her then. The fact that he's setting up dates with these women, knowing they're people who enjoy sex, makes me suspect they'd be doomed from the moment they accepted his invite." He rubbed at his face. "To some extent, the whole hookup app culture phenomenon makes our job easier, and to some extent, it changes the game. Once upon a time, these guys would have to go cruise for their victims. They'd have to hit the singles bars, the pickup spots, all the fun stuff. Now they just have to swipe right."

"My God." Kevin shuddered. "Macha's never going to date. And I'm taking her phone away." He rolled his shoulders. "I'm not serious, of course. That's so archaic it's positively feudal. I *will* be having a good long talk with her about keeping safe though."

"I'd have a talk with all of them." Donovan shrugged. "But, hey, what do I know?"

"You know enough," Kevin sighed. "It's not like you're a cop or anything. Let's test this hypothesis. Let's see if we can track down the ladies on his list who aren't accounted for yet. Some of them might have escaped. I want to track down some of the people he went out with and didn't kill, too. They'll almost certainly have some insights. And, Donovan, let's see if you can't pester the state police to give us some divers. If he's disposing of the remains in that old quarry, we need to figure out how many there are."

Somehow it seemed like a better plan coming from Kevin than it had coming from Luis. Donovan didn't want to think too hard about why that should be the case. He knew he was overreacting when he couldn't prove Luis was stepping out, but he was nowhere near ready to examine his own behavior yet.

He got on the phone with Lt. Power, who conferenced him in with a few other people. Thankfully, the results of that phone call got him summoned back to Framingham for a meeting. On the one hand, that got him excused from having to sit in the conference room with Luis. On the other hand, he wasn't able to work things out with Luis on Monday, and that disturbed him. It disturbed him, too, that he felt being excused from sitting in a room with Luis was a good thing.

He stayed in Framingham for the rest of the day, making his case for divers. It wasn't easy, and he wondered if maybe they shouldn't have had one of the Feds come and do this. They had a lot more clout than he did, after all, and he had to think the higher-ups would put a lot more stock in what the FBI had to say than in the words of a mere detective.

He got a call from his father toward the end of the day, to put a lousy cap on a lousy day. It wasn't as out of place as he wanted it to be. Fred was an ass, and he'd always be an ass, but he was also someone who wasn't in Luis' fan club and Donovan needed that right now. He answered, instead of letting it go straight to voice mail as he had been.

"Hello?"

"Donovan! It's your dad!"

Donovan rolled his eyes. He recognized his own father's voice, for crying out loud, and he had caller ID. "Hi, Dad. What's going on?"

"Not a whole lot. I just wanted to check in and see how you were doing. See if you maybe wanted to get together for dinner or something."

Donovan hesitated. He didn't want to get together. His father had nothing useful to say to him. Donovan had lost more respect for his father with each passing day. At the same time, he didn't think being alone with his own jealousy and dark thoughts was the best idea. "Yeah, okay. I can do that. Where do you want to meet up?"

"I don't know. What's okay with you and the dark horse candidate?"

Donovan bit the inside of his cheek. It was a racist statement. It was probably the least racist thing Fred had said about Luis since they'd met.

"He'll be on his own tonight."

"Oh really?" Fred's surprise was entirely feigned, and it didn't take a profiler to figure it out. "Is there trouble in rainbow paradise?"

Donovan bristled. "We're fine. Everything's fine. We've only been back together for a few months, Dad. We don't live together. Where do you want to get together?"

Fred hesitated. His voice sounded a lot warmer when he replied, "Let's get together at one of the restaurants in the Natick Mall. Sound good?"

"Yeah, let's do it." All the energy flowed out of Donovan at that point. It would be a miserable night with Fred, but at least he wouldn't be alone.

"So what's Louie Louie doing with himself tonight?"

Donovan shrugged, even though his father couldn't see it. "I have no idea. I'm going to assume he's working on the case. That's what he does, most of the time. Why?" Oh, he'd be working on the case all right. He'd be working on the case with Ruben. Muscular, handsome, Latin Ruben.

"Huh. You know his Mixr profile is still on there. It says inactive, but you know that doesn't mean anything."

Donovan pretended it didn't hurt. "Dad, I swear to God if you don't stop searching Mixr, I'm going to start telling people about your account."

Fred chuckled. "I'll see you tonight, son."

CHAPTER SEVEN

Luis pulled into the parking lot and parked his car as far out of sight as he could. He was taking a huge chance, and he knew it. He'd taken one of the Bureau vehicles, on the grounds that it would be less likely to get towed. Most people, even law enforcement, saw those government plates and steered clear. Of course, the government plates were a pretty clear signal that someone was on the scene and hadn't checked in at the ranger station.

That was just bad protocol.

In all seriousness, Luis didn't want to offend the rangers, certainly not at this early date. He didn't want to attract their attention either. He hadn't run this visit by SSA Holcombe. He hadn't mentioned it to Kevin, and he hadn't mentioned it to Donovan either. Both of them knew about his ability to see and interact with ghosts, but he still didn't enjoy talking about it with them.

Plus, if he brought up a visit to Freetown to Donovan, he'd have to hear about Ruben. Ruben was a nice-enough guy, he guessed, but Luis wasn't in the market for a guy and he was 90 percent sure Ruben was straight. He was flirtatious, but in a weird way that told Luis he was all talk and no action. Luis wouldn't have been interested even if Ruben was into guys. All Luis wanted was to convince Donovan he was faithful and to get back to building a real relationship.

Scratch that. All Luis wanted was to not *have* to convince Donovan he was faithful, which was an entirely different animal. And he'd be pleased as punch to figure out what a real relationship was too. He was pretty sure constant tests of his fidelity weren't on the menu, but he could stand to do some research. And if he looked at things objectively—the way he would at any other case—he could admit the fidelity tests weren't constant. They might have become frequent, but they weren't constant.

Unfortunately, Luis needed answers. The ghosts might not give him anything that would be admissible in court, but they'd give him some direction in terms of places to look. Every time he came back to this site, he could feel them pulling at him, demanding his attention, and he couldn't ignore them anymore.

Jennifer found him as soon as he stepped into the woods. He was getting used to the rotten smell that came with the dead, although few of them smelled quite as bad as Captain Lightfoot. Jennifer had a vaguely soggy scent to her, like stuff that had been floating on the top of a pond.

She grinned at him when she saw him, the rictus exceptionally terrible in the light of the full moon. "I wondered if you'd come back without an audience."

"It's not as easy as it sounds," he told her. "With the FBI, someone's supposed to be able to account for your whereabouts every minute of every day." *More so lately.* That could apply to geopolitics or to the life of one disgraced agent.

"In particular if they happen to see ghosts?" She raised an eyebrow and laughed, peals of laughter incongruous with her deceased state. "I'm sorry. I'm sure it's not funny to you. I just don't get a chance to laugh anymore."

"I can't imagine you do." He frowned and followed her deeper into the woods. "Do you get to talk to other ghosts?"

"I can, if I want. Most of them don't have a lot to say. A lot of them are just echoes. Which is great for them, you know? They're not really here. Like them, over there." She pointed.

Luis followed her gaze and saw a pair of Native men suited up for war moving quickly down a path that didn't exist. "Residual, then?"

"Precisely. That's the word. You'd never know I'd been an English teacher." She scoffed, maybe a little sadly. "Even most of the girls he kills don't stick around. I wouldn't either."

"Most people don't." Luis could at least explain that much. He hated not knowing. He hated his own ignorance even more when he couldn't give a little comfort to someone who had nothing at all, not even a body. "A—well, a friend, I guess, explained it to me. He's been dead two hundred years, and he hasn't figured it out yet either."

"There's likely not any logic to it." She turned to face him. Moonlight passed through her for a second. "I grew up going to Catholic school. Do you think that's why I stayed like this, maybe? Because I left the Church?"

Luis huffed out a gentle laugh and held out a hand to her. "No," he told her, not hiding anything. "Not even a little bit. I had the questionable fortune of chatting with a nun in your condition, from when they burned the Ursuline convent in Boston. Trust me, there is no rhyme or reason to how someone ends up a ghost. I'm sorry."

"I guess that's some comfort. And hey, at least I'm still conscious, right?" She managed a weak smile and took his hand. By now, he was prepared for the painful, almost burning cold of her touch. "Why did I die?"

Luis looked intently at her. It wasn't easy to remember he was supposed to be here as a cop, not as a psychic or a friend. "You don't remember?"

"I remember dying. I remember falling, and I remember the water rushing in. But I don't remember getting to this place. I don't remember the one who did it. I wouldn't have jumped. I wouldn't!" She fizzled out for a second as she got more insistent. She popped back in an instant. "You have to believe me."

"I believe you." He gave her hand a squeeze. "Again, it's the trauma. I came out here tonight to talk with you some more and to try to figure out together some of what happened."

"Some of the people here jumped." She pulled into herself a little. "Brad!"

A burly athlete type of guy slipped out of the trees. His eyes were empty black sockets. "Jen." He stuffed his hands into his pockets, which squelched as water was forced out of his soggy jeans. His voice gurgled.

"This is Luis. He's trying to figure out what happened to those of us who didn't jump." She glared at him.

Brad's sigh sounded like bubbles. "I didn't show up meaning to jump, you know. I heard about the place and wanted to see what all the fuss was about."

Luis nodded slowly. The air around him was perfectly still. He couldn't hear anything moving, not even the nocturnal critters that populated the woods. "Let me guess. You went up on the Ledge, and there was this overwhelming feeling of grief, despair, loathing, that came up on you all of a sudden."

Brad straightened up. "Were you there?"

"Not when it was you. I've been up there though. And yeah. It was bad. Brad, what happened to you wasn't natural. There's some kind of force, I'm not sure what, that influences people that way." Luis offered the ghost a tentative smile. He didn't know if it would be any kind of comfort at all, considering that the guy was still dead no matter what the cause. Still, maybe it would give him something to hold on to.

"I was murdered, then?" Brad brightened up. He seemed to glow, and his skin became more solid. The scent of decay left him then.

Luis didn't know if he'd call it murder. He didn't know if the force up at the top of the Ledge was intelligent or just malevolent, but it was definitely evil. He wasn't going to sit here and quibble with Brad over semantics though. He didn't know what was happening, but he could see whatever was happening to Brad was *big*. "Yeah,

Brad. You were killed."

"Thank you." The voice, no longer a gurgle, was just a whisper. Brad's glow had expanded until it encompassed his entire body. It was as bright as the sun itself, and just as warm. Then it faded, taking Brad with it.

"Do you think that'll ever be me?" Jennifer asked, after a moment's silence.

"I don't know." Luis swallowed hard. He wasn't a religious guy. He didn't do gods, or anything like that. What he'd just witnessed had been as close to proof of the divine as anything he'd ever seen. "I'm still pretty new at this so I couldn't say. With him, I think he was a ghost because his guilt over suicide was holding him back." Luis turned to fully face Jennifer again. "What do you think is holding you back, Jennifer?"

She sat down on a nearby boulder, one of many in the area. New England was the world's own rock garden, and that was the truth. "I don't know," she confessed, in a small voice. "I know I don't know how I got here. Maybe if I figure it all out, what I did to deserve it, I can move on?"

Luis put his hand on her icy shoulder. "Jennifer, you didn't do anything to deserve it. Okay? The only person at fault for what happened to you is the person who killed you. That's all. That's it. No one else. He is the only person responsible for his choices. Am I being clear here?"

She ducked her head. She couldn't blush, but Luis recognized the look. "Yeah. I guess. Thanks." She straightened her shoulders. "I remember I had a date. Not really a date, just a hookup. Maybe I was a little wild. Do you think that's why? Because I was kind of a slut?"

Luis huffed out a little laugh. "I'm the last person to be casting stones, okay? There is absolutely nothing wrong with enjoying what your body has to offer, as long as you're safe about it. Before I got together with my boyfriend, I absolutely refused to settle down or even be with the same guy twice. That doesn't mean I deserved violence. You and I had our reasons, okay?"

"It's different for guys," she said, shoulders curling down again.

"No. It isn't. Maybe some people think it is, but at the end of the day, it's okay for all of us. What's good for the goose is good for the gander and all that. Your body belongs to you, and no one else gets to decide what you get to do with it." He grinned. "So you were on a date, for a hookup. Was it through an app?"

"Yeah. Tinder. No judging, okay?" She glared.

He held his hands up. "Like I said before, I'm the last person entitled to judge you. I was a

Mixr guy myself. That one's more oriented toward men. So, you showed up for this hookup. Was it someone you'd been with before?"

She shook her head. "No. And it wasn't who I thought I was showing up to see, either. I thought I was meeting a white guy, but he was Mexican or something." She glanced at him. "Not that there's anything wrong with that, but when you're looking for a redheaded guy named Monroe and you see a dark-skinned guy named . . ." She winked out for another second. "I don't remember, but it totally ended with a Z."

Luis smiled. He understood what she was getting at. "It's okay. It would have been a fake name even if you had seen an ID or something, so it's not that important. And I'm guessing that, yeah, it would have thrown you for a loop, right?"

She gave him a look of pure relief. "Exactly. Like, I didn't reject guys because of their background, but he said he got a lot of people swiping left because of the name alone. Which—well, I can believe it. I mean it sucks, but it's a reality. I was a little pissed off at the bait and switch, but he was hot so I stuck around. I mean, what the hell? You're only young once." She looked around with a look of unmitigated disgust. "And not even for very long, I guess."

Luis grimaced and shifted on his feet. She'd

been an open-minded, bright young woman whose life had been taken too soon. Then he paused. Someone was coming. He heard rustling on the trail.

"It's that ranger," Jennifer told him. "Come on, I'll help you get out of here before he finds you."

Luis ran along the trail back to his car. He'd been worried that Ruben would find him chatting up ghosts. He hadn't realized Jennifer would be able to mask his escape, but he learned something new every day. She hid the sounds of his passage while guiding him back to the parking lot.

"Thank you," he whispered, just before he got back into the black SUV and sped back toward Medford.

He looked down at his silenced phone. He had six messages from Donovan. All of them were the same, just with different degrees of anger. *WHERE ARE YOU?*

He sighed and called Donovan back. He didn't want to deal with this by text. "Hey," he said. "I headed down to Freetown to try to talk to Jennifer."

"Jennifer or Ruben?" Donovan bit out the words.

Luis sighed. It was too late for this, and he was too tired. He'd seen something beautiful tonight, and he'd gotten some useful information.

He'd love to be able to share it with his partner, but Donovan wasn't in a place to be able to deal with that like an adult right now. "I got some good information—from Jennifer. I'll give you the details in the morning, but I just can't deal with the jealousy trip tonight. I don't have the energy to sit here and prove myself again. I'll see you in the morning. I love you." He hung up the phone and tried to ignore the hollow feeling in his chest when he did.

All of this tension with Luis was killing Donovan. His teeth hurt from grinding them. His jaw hurt. His shoulders ached from keeping them so stiff, and his hands throbbed because he kept balling them into fists. Was this what real love was supposed to be like? This constant state of unease, distrust, and anxiety?

Luis had gone to Freetown last night, alone and unsupervised. He knew Donovan was uncomfortable with the way he behaved around Ruben, yet he'd gone out to Freetown when he knew Ruben was on duty and patrolling. That gave them hundreds, thousands, of acres to have their trysts with no one the wiser. He could spin whatever BS he wanted about chatting with ghosts, and who was going to contradict him?

Luis knew he needed to be kept on a short leash. He'd been so promiscuous, even within the past year, that no one in their right mind would trust him. Donovan hated to admit it, but his father had been right about that much. Fred might be a cheat and a liar, but that just meant he knew about cheats and liars, damn it.

And now Donovan had saddled himself with one.

He buried his face in his hands as he looked down at the data in front of him. Kevin, over on his side of the table, cleared his throat. "You got something you want to share with the class, ace?"

Donovan picked his head up. Luis' head was still buried in his own work, face bathed in the light of his monitor. He looked downright angelic. Of course, Lucifer had been an angel once. "Yeah," he said slowly, scrambling for cover. "No, not really. It's just kind of overwhelming. I mean this guy killed maybe as many as fifty-two people in a year, and it's been entirely under our radar. How does that even happen?" There had been more than fifty-two people unaccounted for when they'd gone through that account's Tinder dates, but it wasn't likely that all of them were victims of this serial killer. Serial killers didn't often clear out their victims' belongings from their homes, and at least three of them had.

Luis finally picked his head up. "Same way it always happens. Different jurisdictions, no one happens to talk to the right person in the other jurisdiction to pick up on the similarities. It's just the way it is, you know? It sucks, and if I could build a web bot to crawl around the country looking for crimes with similar characteristics, I'd get in trouble for overstepping my jurisdiction. Oddly enough, a lot of people don't like the Feds coming into investigations. Can't figure out why though."

Kevin snorted. "Someone might think you're getting bitter in your old age, Luis." He picked up his report. "So. What did the dearly departed tell you?"

Luis closed his eyes for a second. He hated dealing with ghosts, and he hated any mention of them in a professional setting. That gave him a plausible reason for not having disclosed his having ventured out last night. If it weren't for Ruben, with his perfect body and dark good looks, Donovan might almost believe it.

"Jennifer said she'd made a date to hook up with a guy from Tinder. She said she was expecting to hook up with a redheaded guy named Monroe, which is consistent with our boy's fake Tinder profile. What she wound up meeting with was a guy who 'looked Mexican.' " His mouth tightened when he spoke. "She said she was irritated by the deception, but when he explained most people didn't get past the *Z* on the end of his last name, she gave him a pass. She didn't care about his background, she said, just about the lying, and he was hot."

Donovan smirked. "Well, I guess there's a downside to hookup apps after all, huh?" He gave Luis a triumphant glower.

"So far, the only downside I've found has been self-righteous assholes who think they've got something to say about what people choose to do with their own bodies when said assholes aren't involved with them, but hey. What do I know? I only deal with serial killers for a living. It's not like I've got a little experience with this sort of thing or anything." Luis kept his face impassive and cracked his knuckles. His posture seemed to say *Bring it.*

Donovan's blood boiled, but Kevin shut him down before he could react verbally. "Not the time or place, either of you," he snapped. "Luis, did she say anything else? Like the killer's actual name?"

"No. We picked up on someone else in the area, and I bolted."

"What's the matter, didn't want your precious ranger to catch you communing with the spirits?" Donovan knew it was uncalled for, and he knew it was unprofessional of him to even bring it up. It had just slipped out of him.

Luis gave him a look of such profound disgust it physically hurt. "Donovan, maybe you should go take the rest of the day off. Something about this case is obviously getting to you. Go home, relax, have a nice cold beer or something, and get your head on straight."

"I have to agree with Luis." Kevin got up and walked over to Donovan. He handed Donovan his jacket. "We all want this case closed, and we're all feeling frustrated by the lack of movement. Come back in a couple of days when you're feeling a little better." His words were conciliatory, and he wasn't making noise about telling Donovan's superiors, but he also wasn't going to let Donovan tell him no without making a scene.

Donovan didn't have to be graceful about it. He grabbed his things and left without another word, storming out of FBI headquarters.

He went to the gym, intent on taking his issues out on the equipment. The exercise at least calmed him down, or maybe it was being out of proximity to Luis that did the trick. He needed to talk to someone about this, and he knew it. He shouldn't have to be apart from the man he loved in order to get perspective.

There was only one person he could take this

to. His dad had plenty to say about Luis, but none of it was anything Donovan thought would be at all useful. His mother, on the other hand, might be able to give him some good advice. After all, she knew all about being the victim of a cheater.

He sent her a text to see if she wanted to get together for dinner, and she did. They agreed to meet up in Brookline, since it was mutually inconvenient, and grabbed dinner at a fake-Irish pub that made Donovan want to cringe. Sometimes, he wanted to go to the people who decorated these places, shake them by the shoulders, and scream, *Ireland has more counties than Kerry!*

He never did. It would be assault.

Patricia showed up maybe five minutes after he did, and they settled in quickly. "Such a day," Patricia grumbled. "I swear, one of these days, I'm going to grab a nightstick and remind some of these cops who's boss. They *hate* reporting to a woman. I actually had one of them tell me he didn't have to follow my orders because Saint Paul claimed God put men above women. Can you believe that man?"

Donovan had to laugh as the server brought their drinks. "I can't believe the balls on him," he laughed. "What did you do?"

"I suspended him without pay. When he comes back—if he comes back, depending on how things go with the union—we'll have to see if he gets reassigned or if he gets to spend the rest of his career managing paperwork." She curled her lip and wrinkled her nose. "I'm telling you, I just don't have time for shenanigans like that. I've worked too hard and come too far to let a turd like that stop me."

"Damn straight you have." Donovan raised his glass to Patricia. "I'm damn proud of you, Mom."

"You're a good boy, Donovan." She patted his free hand. "Now talk to me. When you texted me, you said you needed advice about something big. What was it?"

Donovan took a deep breath. Could he say the words out loud, to a third party? "I think Luis is cheating on me." He pushed them out as fast as he could. They tasted sour in his mouth, like bad beer.

Patricia put her beer down and took Donovan's hand. "Oh, Donovan. I wouldn't wish that kind of pain on anyone. What made you think so?"

"There's this ranger, at the crime scene where we're working. He's tall, he's good looking. He's not Brazilian but he is Latino, and he and Luis are always conspiring in Spanish together." He clenched his fists at the memory. "He makes Luis laugh, all the time. And Luis even sneaked over to the crime scene late Monday night!"

"I thought Luis spoke Portuguese." Patricia scratched her head and sipped her beer.

"He also speaks Spanish. His foster dad was Puerto Rican. I'm just . . . He said he didn't date white guys anymore, so I'm not sure why he broke that rule for me. And now this hot guy who's more his speed is right there. And you know how promiscuous he is—well, he'd say *was*." Donovan wiped his hands on his jeans. His stomach turned itself in knots just thinking about Luis and Ruben.

Patricia looked at him with an impossibly grave expression on her face. "Have you talked about this with Luis?"

"Of course. We're adults, and we try to behave like adults. But he tells me I've got nothing to worry about, like I'm not an actual detective who can figure things out for himself. And he's getting nastier and nastier about it too. Called me a self-righteous asshole when I brought up his online dating profile, which Dad told me is still up."

Patricia sat up a little straighter, eyes blazing. "You've talked about this with your father."

Donovan held his hands up. "Not because I brought it up. Dad's the one who came to me after meeting Luis and told me he'd found Luis' profile on that Mixr site. He said it was set to inactive, but come on. That has to be code or something."

Patricia leaned back, eyes narrow. "I need you to think about this very carefully, Donnie. Your father isn't open to homosexuality, and he's not going to be at all comfortable with the idea of a gay son."

Donovan scoffed. "No. He's not. But he's not going to be comfortable with the idea of a son who's getting cheated on either. And let's face it, the guy definitely knows what to look for."

Patricia's mouth tightened, but she let the comment pass. "So if your father was going onto a gay hookup app . . ."

"It would only be because he was looking out for his son." Donovan looked down into his beer glass.

"Mmm." Patricia took another drink. "It wouldn't have anything to do with the fact that he's still trying to move back into my house, would it?"

"No, why?" Donovan bit his lip. He couldn't stop tapping his foot. He knew his father often did things with ulterior motives, but what motive could he possibly have for trying to interfere with Donovan's relationship? "He just wants what's best for me."

"Fred Carey wants what's best for Fred Carey." Patricia looked at him over the top of her pint glass. "I know it sounds like sour grapes, and you can tell yourself it's sour grapes if it makes you feel better. Lord knows, I've got enough to be sour about. But, Donnie, listen to me. Your father picked up on your insecurity in your relationship with Luis and is using that to try to break you up."

Donovan pulled back. "Why would my own father do that to me? I get what he did to you was wrong—evil, even. But there's no way someone would do something like that to his own son."

Patricia smirked. "You can go right on thinking that. You'd be wrong, but you can go right on believing it if it makes you feel better. Don't go throwing away your relationship with Luis—which you fought so hard for—because of it. If you can't bring yourself to believe Luis' word, get counseling. His former behavior didn't bother you when the two of you got together. I think you need to sit down and figure out what changed."

"Ruben changed." Donovan crossed his arms over his chest. "That's what changed. If he'd just stay the hell away from Ruben like I told him—"

Patricia was having none of it. "Nope. He's an FBI agent. He's going to travel, he's going to meet all kinds of people. Some of them will be good looking. You don't get to demand he drop parts of his job. And while I'm sympathetic, I haven't seen any evidence that he's cheating. I've seen evidence you're feeling insecure. Take care of you, and the relationship should sort itself out."

Donovan forced a smile and let the issue drop. Patricia had been on his side until he'd brought his father into it. That had been his big mistake. Luis was cheating, and he needed to figure out how to handle it.

CHAPTER EIGHT

When the weekend rolled around, Donovan still didn't want to talk to Luis. Luis had made a few attempts, but all he'd gotten in return were a few grunts and one-word answers. He sent a few texts, but the responses were equally disappointing. Luis hadn't realized it was possible to grunt via text, but Donovan managed, and it frustrated Luis to no end.

Luis hadn't done anything to deserve that kind of treatment. He could cut a lot of slack because dealing with his father had always bothered Donovan to some extent, but Luis' patience had limits. He wasn't obligated to put up with this crap. He didn't want to lose Donovan, but he was worth more than this. *They* were worth more than this, and if he had to force the issue with his lover, he would.

He slept in on Saturday morning, alone, and went for a run to clear his head. After he got back, he got a text from Donovan's cousin Alicia. *Hey, Nick's been asking to see you. Are you free to stop by?*

Luis scratched his head at that. It all felt odd to him. Alicia knew he was as gay as the day was long, so she wouldn't be making a move on him. Why else would she reach out to him?

I'm not sure what Donovan's got planned today. That should be polite enough. Not that he didn't want to hang out with her, because he liked Alicia a lot. It just didn't make much sense for her to want to see him.

He's off with Uncle Fred. SO NOT someone I want Nick around. Are you around?

Luis did a double take. He liked Nick. Nick was a good kid, and Luis wouldn't deny him anything in his power if he didn't have to. *Sure, let me know when.*

He has a game that starts at noon. If you can make it, he'd be over the moon.

I'll do my best. Luis couldn't make much sense out of that, but he couldn't deny that he and Nick got along pretty well. Maybe he would like someone at his soccer game.

He washed up as fast as he could, got dressed, and drove out to the soccer field Alicia had mentioned. He stopped at Dunkin' Donuts to pick up coffee for both of them and a donut for Nick. When he got there, he found she'd brought two folding chairs with her, so he had somewhere to sit and watch. Nick startled him with a hug before he ran out to join the rest of his team, and Alicia accepted her coffee with a smile.

They made small talk as they waited for the game to start. Her unit with the SWAT team had taken on a bank robber this week, which had been some unwelcome excitement. Luis told her a little bit about the case down in Fall River, since it had been occupying all of his time. "And get this, all of the women met the suspect on Tinder." He felt comfortable telling her that much, since she'd never be put on a jury.

"Oh my God." She rolled her eyes, and a little blush came into her cheeks. "Believe it or not, I still had a Tinder account up until about fourteen months ago. My divorce wasn't finalized yet, but he'd taken off a long time before."

"Really?" Luis sipped from his coffee to hide his grin. He couldn't imagine her going the online route. "There's nothing wrong with that."

"Of course not." She scoffed and tossed her hair. "I mean, some people are always going to have a bug up their butt about it. My eternally charming cousin, for example. But, no, I'm not really ashamed of it. I stopped using it when I decided I wasn't going to pretend to be interested in guys anymore. I mean, I'm still not out, to my family, but I'm not faking it anymore, you know? Screw it. I blow shit up and knock down walls for a living, I don't have to fake anything anymore."

"I really like that attitude." He lifted his cup in a kind of toast.

"Thanks." She let out a little sigh that sounded relieved and relaxed her shoulders. "It feels good to say it out loud, you know? My last Tinder date was a guy named Ruben. Although he was a total catfish."

Luis' gut clenched. On the one hand, Ruben couldn't be their suspect. Their suspect was—well, okay, there was no reason he *couldn't* be their suspect. Ruben had theoretical alibis for the nights of the confirmed killings, but his alibis were that he'd been at work.

At the crime scene.

No one had checked to make sure he'd been on-site during his entire shift, and there wasn't likely any way to confirm it for certain. It wasn't like they had bar codes for rangers to scan or anything.

"Ruben Noguera?" he tried, hoping it was wrong.

She snapped her fingers. "That's the guy! Oh my God, do you know him?"

"He's one of the rangers helping us on our case." Luis forced his body to relax. "Why do you say he was catfishing?"

She curled her lip. "The profile I clicked on

said his name was George Murphy, his profile picture was blond, and he said he liked long walks in the woods. When I met him, he was this big buff Latin guy. Which, I mean, the guy had nothing to be ashamed of. He was more attractive than the fake pic, you know? Not that he's the only one who did that, but whatever. You don't look surprised."

"I've seen the same thing come up before." Luis gave a nervous little laugh. He couldn't tell her why he'd heard about the catfishing. Let her think it was about his days on Mixr. She wasn't in on the secret about the ghosts, and how he'd have heard about Ruben's particular scheme.

"Well, I called him on it, and he said most girls swiped left just because of his background. And I told him the background wasn't what bothered me, the lying was." She ran her free hand through her hair and shook her head. "Anyway, he asked if I was there for a hookup or if I was looking for a serious relationship. I told him I was a mother, I don't have time for hookups. That seemed to satisfy him. He didn't try to put any moves on me or anything, but when he found out I'm a cop, he got real nervous. We didn't get together again, and I am not heartbroken about it." She rolled her eyes. "The next two times I saw that same alias came up were for different guys, too. It's like they've got a club."

"No. I wouldn't be either." Luis' chest ran cold. "Hang on for a second." He pulled out his phone and sent a text to Kevin. *Hey. Where are you?*

Chaperoning a Girl Scout trip to an alpaca farm. How's your day going?

Luis stared at his phone for a long moment and thanked whatever gods might be listening that cis men couldn't get pregnant. Then again, he'd just volunteered to coach a youth football team, so maybe he hadn't dodged the "weird kid activities" bullet after all. *I need you to do some deep digging into our ranger friend, Ruben. And I need you to keep quiet about it.* He paused for a second. *Also, check out any accounts under the George Murphy alias.*

The secrecy makes me uncomfortable. Kevin didn't hesitate.

Every time he hears Ruben's name from my mouth or in my presence, he loses his mind. This case is too important to waste time on jealousy. Luis' cheeks burned. He shouldn't have to go around Donovan, damn it. Donovan should be right here, by his side, already looking for the warrant.

You're right. But the two of you need to handle your shit.

I'm trying.

Try harder.

Luis allowed himself a single long sigh before turning back to Alicia with a smile. "Sorry about that."

"Hey, it's the job. I come from a long line of cops. No one gets it more than I do, you know?" She leaned in closer, hair falling into her face to shield her words. "Do you think Ruben is involved with your case?"

Luis looked around before lowering his voice even more and continuing. "I think we need to cover all of our bases, and some of his behavior is too similar to ignore. But we'll look into it, and with any luck, you just had a bad date and didn't dodge a bullet. I mean, like you said, there were three other guys who used the same alias."

She looked down and away. "So things with you and Donovan have hit a rough patch, huh?"

Luis stiffened. "He's a great guy, and I love him more than anything."

Alicia put a hand on his arm. "Something else no one gets better than I do is that sometimes it takes a little more than love to make it work. Aunt Patricia and I got to talking. She said he's been spending more time with his dad, and ever since he started with that, he's been making some jealous noise about you."

Luis gritted his teeth. He wasn't going to trash Donovan to his relatives, but Alicia had brought it up. "Yeah. On both counts. And he's super jealous of Ruben." She'd already figured everything out, so why hide it? "And he's got his reasons. Before we got together, I didn't do relationships. I did one-night stands. I wasn't real particular either, but Ruben would've been just my type."

Alicia snorted. "So? You committed to Donovan, right?"

"Yeah. Yeah, I did."

"Have you done anything to make him doubt you?" She tilted her head.

"I don't think so. I set my profile on Mixr to inactive, so if anyone I hooked up with needed to reach out for health reasons, they could, but I told him that. We talked about it at the time, for crying out loud. Not that he remembered ten seconds later. But I haven't even looked at anyone else since we got together." He set his shoulders. "I've tried talking to him, pointing out that he's the one I love, but he doesn't want to hear it. And now it's bleeding through into the job.

"I'll be the first to admit I've got some serious workaholic tendencies," he said, watching as Nick scored a goal with the same technique Luis had taught him at his birthday party. "I think it kind of comes with the badge."

"Right?" Alicia clapped and cheered for Nick and then turned to face Luis again.

"I don't want to sell my relationship with

Donovan short. Something's eating away at him, and this is the way he's expressing it. At the same time, I—we both—have a responsibility to these victims. We need to be able to stop these killings, as fast as we can. And because there are women's lives at stake, we have to make sure those lives come first, before personal issues."

"Well, you're not going to get an argument from me." She put a hand on Luis' shoulder. "I don't know what's going on with him, Luis. You're the psychologist. I'm going to defer to your judgment, about the psychology behind it. What do you think you can do about it?"

"I don't know. Right now, not a lot." He balled his hands into fists and then forced them to relax. "I can't force him to talk to me, and I feel like trying while we're working on this case is just making things worse. Once we solve the case, and the trigger that is Ruben is out of his face, maybe we can sit down and discuss it like civilized human beings."

Luis wasn't as confident as he sounded. When Donovan called halfway through an impromptu soccer clinic in the backyard demanding to know where the hell Luis had gone off to and who he was screwing now, he became even less sanguine about it.

Alicia took the phone from him, before he

could say something he'd regret. "Donovan, if you think he's cheating *with me* you've gotten hit on the head or you're drunk. You need to sober up, get your head on straight, and figure out what it is that you're trying to do here. Because if you keep on going the way you have been, buddy, you're going to end up losing the best thing that ever came into your life."

She handed the phone back to Luis. Luis wasn't expecting an apology. He wasn't expecting his lover to growl, "Now you're turning my family against me? This is just too much, Luis. I expected better from you, but I probably shouldn't have. You were never anything but—"

Luis hung up the phone. "I didn't need to hear the rest of that sentence," he told Alicia, and went back to the soccer lesson.

Donovan hadn't intended to blow up at Luis. He'd been confused and hurt when he realized Luis wasn't at home. He'd assumed the worst, and given that Donovan had been so reluctant to sit down and talk, he supposed he probably deserved the worst too. Having his father right there, egging him on, hadn't helped.

Fred just shook his head after Luis hung up on Donovan. "I'm sure you kids today do things differently, but if a woman treated me the way Luis treats you, I'd kick her to the curb faster than you can say no-good whore."

Donovan clenched the steering wheel. "He's not a whore. Or a woman."

"I don't need the intimate details of your sex life. But one of you has to—"

"Stop, Dad. Just stop. You're being gross." Donovan's insides twisted. Luis wasn't a whore, but he'd been promiscuous for years. How stupid could Donovan have been to think he could satisfy Luis' needs now? He probably hadn't even been able to satisfy Luis back in college.

"Okay, okay, fair enough. I thought I was being sensitive." Fred chuckled and scratched at his stomach. "I can tell you one thing. Someone hangs up on you like that? They don't respect you, and they sure as hell don't love you. I never would have put up with that kind of crap from your mother, or from any of my girlfriends either. You have every right to question where he is when he's not where he's supposed to be. Be a man and either straighten his ass out or cut him loose."

Donovan changed lanes to avoid a Volvo. "Dad, what the hell is this 'straighten his ass out' crap? You're not suggesting I hit him, are you?" Violence wouldn't get him anywhere with Luis. For one thing, it was wrong. For another, Luis could kick his ass, and Donovan wasn't a slouch when it came to hand-to-hand combat.

"You might have to raise your voice a little, Donnie. I know you queers don't like to do that, but you have got to remind him of his place or he's going to keep walking all over you. You know it, I know it, everyone in creation freaking knows it, okay?"

Donovan bit his tongue. He wasn't going to get into it with Fred about Luis' "place." Fred wouldn't listen, and Donovan was angry enough. He didn't need to add to his rage pool. Instead, he said, "He's over at Alicia's."

"Oh, I'm sure." Fred scoffed and waved his hand, like he was brushing smoke out of the air. "Maybe they're seeing the same guy. How do you know?"

Donovan pulled over to the side of the road as soon as he could. He threw the door open and barely got his head out before throwing up onto the shoulder. He heaved until he had nothing left to give.

He didn't think Luis would be cheating with Alicia. Luis was as gay as they came. But Alicia, she was another story. She might be into women—she hadn't come out yet—but Donovan had his suspicions. That didn't mean she wasn't also into men. She could be part of a threesome with Luis and Ruben. She could be covering for an affair too.

Why else would his boyfriend be hanging out with Donovan's cousin, without Donovan?

He wiped his mouth on his sleeve as Fred patted his back. "It's okay, son. I know it's rough. A guy like Luis, he's just not capable of being loyal. It's not his fault. It's just his culture, it's the way he was raised. Come on. Drop me off at home, and I'll let you get back to your evening."

Donovan finished driving his father home in silence. Then he raced back home and hurried to bed, despite the early hour. He wasn't up for anything else. Luis never called to apologize for hanging up on him, and that nagged at a little corner of Donovan's mind too. What had he really interrupted when he'd called? Some kind of kinky threesome, or *more*some? Had Luis and Alicia stowed Nick with some neighbor and gone off to enjoy some wild orgy with Ruben?

Or was it nothing more than Luis and Alicia being friendly? Even in his current jealous state, which Donovan could admit was about as rational as an overcaffeinated toddler presented with a pound of candy, Donovan understood how much Nick adored Luis. Maybe she'd just reached out to him to see if he'd hang around with Nick a little bit.

Cheater or not, sometimes these things did happen.

Sleep came eventually, but not quickly. It didn't come quickly enough for him to be anything other than sleep deprived when his phone rang at six o'clock. He groaned and grabbed for it, intending to send it to voice mail when he saw the caller ID.

He sat up. "Hey, Kevin."

"You guys should just start setting Sunday alarms for this creep." Kevin sounded exhausted. "I guess Saturday night is date night."

"Christ, are you kidding me?" He yawned. "What the hell is wrong with me that I'm just yawning instead of jumping up and running out the door?"

"Well, hell, Donovan, it's not like she's going to get any deader. I'll see you at the scene, okay? I've got the kids this weekend, so they'll be hanging around in the ranger station."

Donovan grimaced. He could sympathize with the kids. He'd been the kid who had to go to scenes himself. "Want me to bring anything for them?" Not that he had anything kid-related in his house, but he felt he should offer.

"Nah, they've got it down to a science at this point. Just bring your own sweet self, and it should be okay."

Donovan grimaced. He hadn't felt all that sweet these days. "Have you notified Luis?" That was a good neutral way to bring him up, right?

"He notified me. And he, in turn, was notified by Ranger Ruben Noguera, once the body was discovered. This time, the remains were found on land, so there shouldn't be any stupidity with the boat." Kevin's voice didn't shift at all, giving no indication of judgment of any kind. "I'll see you soon. I'll be picking Luis up on the way."

So Luis hadn't been with Ruben. He'd been home—well, that made sense, since Ruben worked nights. Unless Kevin was in on the plot, which wasn't unlikely.

Christ, he was getting paranoid in his old age now.

He drove down to Freetown, stopping for coffee on the way. He almost bought Luis a cup as a peace offering, and then he decided against it. Fred might have a lot of issues, and might not be someone he should be taking advice from, but he'd gotten one thing right. Luis shouldn't have hung up on him. It had been hugely disrespectful, and Donovan needed to nip that stuff in the bud.

Luis didn't seem very remorseful when he and Kevin pulled into the parking lot. He met Donovan's eyes with a look of pure defiance, but he didn't speak. When Maxwell approached, Luis gave him his full attention, which earned them all a sneer from Wong.

"Trouble in paradise, I see." Wong snorted. "You shouldn't date anyone you have to work with. It's bad policy. It makes everything awkward for those of us who have to be around you, whether we have to be around you when things are going bad or going well."

"Thanks for the support, Doctor." Donovan gave him a thin little smile. "What've we got?"

Wong curled his lip. "I can't say anything until I get her back to the lab, you know that. Not anything definitive. I can tell you she did go into the water because her clothes are still damp. And no, that's not enough to give us time of death."

Donovan counted to ten, to avoid losing his temper.

Kevin interrupted. "Of course. Can you maybe hazard a guess as to background and approximate age though?"

Wong sighed, as though he'd just been asked to handle all of their paperwork himself for the next three years. "Come with me," he groused.

He led them over to the body, which had been bagged up already. That seemed to have been too quick to Donovan, and he said as much, but Wong had a ready and almost polite defense.

"More dog walkers," he said. "They're just dogs, they can't help it. I didn't want the dogs to do more damage to the body than they already had, so we moved quickly. Everything was done properly and with perfect documentation, I can assure you."

Two cases in the past year had been tossed for imperfect documentation of the remains, to include one of Wong's. Donovan was going to hope that Wong had learned from the incident. He looked into the bag to see the battered remains of a slim young blonde. She'd been very pretty, right before the beating.

"It's a lot of bruising there on the throat." Donovan pointed to the ring of bruises, like a grim necklace.

"Remarkably astute of you." Wong sniffed and zipped the bag closed again. "Don't touch. I'll be in my lab."

He waved his hand imperiously to his assistants, who got the body loaded into the van and took off. Donovan watched him go and shook his head before turning to Kevin. "I have to grateful, I guess. No matter how rough some things get, at least I don't have to work for him."

"It's true." Kevin made a face. "Let's go see if Luis and Maxwell have gotten anywhere with Ruben."

Donovan restrained a growl. He could just bet Luis would get somewhere with Ruben, or with Maxwell. Or with Maxwell and Ruben. Goddamn it.

Kevin just snorted and headed over to where Luis and Maxwell were talking to the ranger. Luis gave him a cool nod in greeting. Maxwell grinned slightly. Ruben, though, Ruben gave Donovan a long wolfish grin. What kind of a sick bastard was he anyway? Who sat there grinning like a coyote at a crime scene?

Kevin elbowed Donovan, just a little bit. "So. What've we got here?"

Ruben made a comment in Spanish that made Luis choke. Donovan didn't know if he was choking with laughter, shock, or a combination of the two, but he was definitely turning an awesome shade of red.

"Ruben told us that the body was found by a pair of dog walkers, a man and a woman. He called us as soon as he heard from them—"

"That's not what he said just now." Donovan stepped a little closer to Luis. "I don't speak Spanish well, but I know enough to know that's not what he said."

Luis wasn't intimidated by Donovan's display. Donovan hadn't really expected him to be.

"I didn't translate that. This isn't the time or place, Donovan. It's a crime scene. With *witnesses*," he added, inclining his head toward where the dog walkers in question were staring at them. "We're professionals."

"This isn't over." Donovan shook a finger at Luis, then recoiled in horror at himself. He didn't go shaking fingers at people. He'd seen his father do it a time or two. That thing where he'd tried to crowd Luis, that was straight out of Fred's playbook too.

"Maxwell's crew is doing their thing. They've found a couple of good leads. Thanks for your help, Ruben, I think we can take it from here." Luis smiled over at Ruben, who smirked at Donovan before making his goodbyes to Luis—again in Spanish.

Donovan started forward again, but Kevin put a hand on his arm. "Let it go, man. Just let it go."

Donovan took a deep breath. He'd never been the kind of guy to just "let it go." But Kevin was right. This wasn't the time or place to get into it, not with Ruben and not with Luis. "All right. I'll handle the dog walkers. Kevin, care to join me? Luis, you can go and do whatever."

Luis narrowed his eyes at him, but he didn't argue. He turned on his heel and stalked off. Donovan took a deep breath and walked toward the dog walkers. His stomach was roiling, but Luis was right. They were professionals. It was time for them to act like it, Donovan in particular.

CHAPTER NINE

Luis' whole body trembled with rage, and he walked into the conference room like a coiled spring ready to go off. He wanted to go off, all right. He'd never been one of those guys who exploded and punched walls to express his anger. It was more his father's thing than his own, but right now, he could understand the urge. He had to let all this energy out somehow, or something inside of him was going to break.

It might be his heart.

Kevin reached out to him. "Whatever's going on, I'm sure it's just . . . you know." He jerked his hand back when Luis rounded on him.

Eventually, Luis would likely feel bad about making Kevin feel like that, but right now, he couldn't make himself care. Right now, it was just time to rage.

He took a deep breath. He was a professional. He was going to act like it, damn it. "Sorry," he snapped. *Keep it cool, keep it calm. You're still on thin ice here.* "I shouldn't let it get to me. We're supposed to be better than that."

Kevin shrugged and sat down in his usual spot. "You're totally justified. He tried to pick a fight with you in front of witnesses, and a suspect, at a crime scene. What are your thoughts about reading him in, by the way?"

"About Ruben?" Luis ran both hands through his loose curls. "I still don't think it's a good idea. On the one hand, he's a coinvestigator in this case and it feels wrong to be working an angle without keeping him in the loop."

"You're telling me." Kevin cracked his knuckles and winced. "On the other hand, he's irrational where Ruben's concerned. I don't trust him not to go and confront Ruben right now, and we just can't have that."

"No. And that's the problem." Some of the rage inside of Luis moved to the side, letting him feel the profound sadness underneath. He loved Donovan. He'd always loved Donovan, but he'd known from the start they shouldn't try to be together. There were too many obstacles. Granted, no part of Luis had suspected psychotic, jealous rages would be one of them, but in the end, it didn't matter. Obstacles were obstacles, and the end results were the same. "It's wrong to keep information back from a colleague, but we shouldn't have to either."

"Exactly." Footsteps reached them from down the hall. The office was otherwise empty on a Sunday morning, so Luis knew there was only one person it could possibly be. Kevin straightened up, so Luis knew he'd heard them too. "Oh good. With any luck, he'll be ready to buckle down and get to work."

Luis hoped so too, but he wasn't going to count on it.

The conference room door flew open, smashing into the wall hard enough to leave a dent. "How long have you been fucking him?" Donovan had two big red spots coloring his cheeks. Luis saw that purple glint again, but he still couldn't bring himself to believe it was anything but his own imagination.

Luis stared.

Kevin gaped in shock. "You get this is an office, right? A workplace?"

Luis' cheeks burned in shame. Kevin shouldn't have to put up with this crap at the office, not when his kids were stuck in the conference room right next door. Oh God, they could probably hear every word. Donovan wasn't even trying to keep his voice down.

He knew on some level that this wasn't his own fault. Donovan made his own choices, and

Luis couldn't control him. The small part of him that still spoke with his father's voice couldn't help but point out how he could have stopped all of this in its tracks if he'd just been better and proven his loyalty to Donovan.

"Oh, I get this is an office, all right. It's an office where we work, as detectives. And I might not be Mr. High-and-Mighty FBI Guy, but I'm actually pretty damn good at my job. Luis, you've been fucking Ruben since you met him, haven't you?" Donovan stepped even closer to Luis.

Luis had seen this kind of behavior a thousand times. A guy stepped into someone else's personal space to try to intimidate him, try to crowd him. Donovan might not be aware he was doing it, but it was also the second time he'd done it today.

"You've lost your mind," he told Donovan. He didn't raise his voice, even though he wanted to. He didn't ball his hands into fists, even though it would give him such an amazing excuse. He knew how to deescalate a situation.

If Donovan did attack though, he'd have every excuse to let all this anger and grief and pain out.

Since when had he ever been afraid of Donovan? He'd been angry with Donovan. He'd been resentful. He'd never been worried that

Donovan might take things to a physical extreme.

"You're full of shit. You wouldn't constantly be joking with him in a language I can't understand. You wouldn't be sneaking off to the site all alone, in the middle of the night, if you weren't fucking him. He wouldn't call you first if you weren't fucking him."

"Why?" Luis smirked. "Because he should be calling one of the white cops first?"

Way to deescalate, his father's voice told him.

Donovan threw his hands up in the air. "Why does everything always have to come down to race with you? Could it be an excuse to cover up the fact that you're about as capable of being faithful as the average tomcat?"

Kevin walked around the table to stand by Luis' side. "Look, Donovan, he's been nothing but faithful to you. You know this. I don't know what's come over you, but you haven't been like this the whole time I've known you. It's really out of character."

"Nah. You know what?" Luis shook his head. His mouth went dry, but he couldn't make himself keep the words back. "A lot of guys turn into their fathers as they get older. I can't be surprised it's happening now. I love you, Donovan, and I love what we had, but I can't be with you."

Donovan poked Luis in the shoulder. It was

hard enough to bruise, and everything in Luis rose up to strike back, but he held off. He wasn't going to be the one to get them both fired, damn it. He wasn't going to let Donovan cost him his career. He loved Donovan, and he understood that Donovan was going through something right now, but he wasn't about to let Donovan do that to him.

"Are you breaking up with me because I called you on your shit?" Donovan sputtered.

"I'm breaking up with you, Donovan, because you don't trust me. I'm too old, and too busy, to spend my time looking over my shoulder or arranging my work life to try to please someone who's already decided I'm unfaithful. We'd been over the thing with the Mixr account, we'd discussed my history, you said you understood that it was history. Know what that tells me? It tells me you're a liar and that I can't trust *you*."

"I can't believe you'd try to twist it around like this. I should though. Cheaters never take responsibility." Donovan's face had gone pure white, except for those two spots of red.

"Just ask your dad, right?" Luis gave a bitter little laugh. "You've been spending a lot of time with him, and all of a sudden, here we are."

"He's a better man than you'll ever be." Donovan stabbed at Luis' shoulder again, hitting the same spot.

Kevin opened his mouth to speak, but Luis interrupted him.

"Donovan, it's over. If you touch me again, it's assault. You can bring anything I left at your house with you to work tomorrow. That's all there is to say about it. You may feel your dad is a better man than I'll ever be, and that's your prerogative, but I'll never know. Because you and me are no longer a thing, and when this case is over, we'll never see or hear from each other again. In the meantime, you no longer have to worry your jealousy-filled little head about who I am or am not sleeping with because it's none of your fucking business from this point on. Am I clear?"

Donovan staggered back. Luis hadn't had to hit him with his fists. His words had done just fine. "You're serious."

"Hell yes, I'm serious. What did you think I was going to do, throw myself at your feet and kill myself trying to prove myself after you accused me of cheating on you? No. Hell no. I might not be worth much, but I'm worth more than that. Get away from me, Donovan Carey. I love you, but it's over." Luis went to his usual seat.

Donovan gaped at him. "You're really leaving."

"Excuse me. We have a serial killer to catch. I've tried—repeatedly—to work this out with you like adults, in private. You couldn't have that. Either sit down and get to work, like the professional I know you are, or maybe go home and sleep it off. Whatever's going on with you, we've got a guy who's murdering a woman every single week. And no one else is going to catch him if we don't."

Donovan stared at him in open, naked shock. Then he turned on his heel and walked out the door.

Luis hung his head for a long moment. His chest burned, and for a second, he flashed back to the time when he'd been shot. He couldn't afford to sit here and wallow. He had work to do, but he could allow himself a few seconds to grieve.

"You okay?" Kevin asked in a quiet tone.

"No." Luis considered lying and saying he was fine. He knew it wouldn't help, and it would only hurt things between him and Kevin. At least his time with Father Geoffrey had been well spent. "But it was the only thing I could do. I couldn't keep going on like that. And he . . . I don't know what's gotten into him, but I can't fix it either. Whatever it is, I can't fix it."

Kevin nodded, looking down. "For what it's worth, I'm sorry. I didn't expect it to go down like this."

Luis licked his lips. "I should have. I mean

not like this. The jealousy thing is new. But I should have known something would come up. I knew I shouldn't get too comfortable. I never was good at relationships."

Kevin hesitated for a few seconds. "I'm pretty sure what just happened had nothing to do with you, dude. That was all him."

Luis shook his head. "If I'd been better, or whatever, I'd have been able to do something about that before it got so far. He'd never have had a reason to worry about me with anyone else. He'd have been perfectly secure in our relationship. I thought I'd been good about not flirting, not looking, not any of that. Maybe he's right, maybe I am about as capable of fidelity as a tomcat."

"That's shit." Kevin pounded his fist on the table. "I've never seen you be at all inappropriate on the job. You've never flirted with a suspect or a witness, you sure as hell never flirted with Ruben Noguera. Luis, I get the way you grew up was a little unconventional. You had to rely on yourself, which meant you had all the responsibility for everything.

"But seriously, he needs to own his own shit. Something's making him insecure, something that most likely has nothing to do with you. Should you be expected to deal with it or manage it? No. It's his job. Don't set fire to yourself to keep someone else warm, even if you love them. I'd tell any one of my kids the same exact thing."

Luis huffed out a little laugh. "It sounds like you know something about that."

Kevin gave a wry grin. "When I came out as bi, my wife was furious. She had all the reactions you'd expect—I must be cheating, bi folks aren't capable of fidelity, my mere existence is spreading disease, you name it. She was willing to take me back if and only if I went to conversion therapy."

Luis recoiled. "Good God."

"Right? So we split. I still love her, but I wasn't about to stay with someone who couldn't love all of me. I've got your back, Luis. I know I haven't always, but I've got your back."

Luis managed to smile. He'd grieve later, but at least he knew he wasn't alone. "Thanks, Kevin. Let's see if we can get an ID on our victim today."

Donovan felt completely empty, like a hollowed-out pumpkin, as he walked back to his car. He couldn't hear the cars on the street, and he couldn't hear any birds in the trees. All he could hear was the static in his head, like a radio in-between stations. He'd confronted Luis about his cheating, just like he'd planned. And instead of confessing, Luis turned it right back around on Donovan.

He hadn't even tried to defend himself. He'd acted like he had nothing to defend, which felt worse somehow than it would have if he'd confessed. Instead, he'd said Donovan was the one who couldn't be trusted.

None of that made sense in Donovan's mind, but right now, he didn't think anything was going to make sense. He was lost, adrift, and he couldn't find his way back to sanity. He needed help. He fumbled for his keys and drove back to Framingham.

Luis hadn't just dumped him. Luis had dismissed him from the investigation—okay, just for the day, but still. Donovan hadn't been in the habit of taking advice from his father for a long time, so maybe he should have expected this discussion to crash and burn, but he still didn't think it should have gone quite so badly. After all, Dad had been around a long time and he'd had more than a few relationships. He should have known what he was talking about.

He let himself into his condo, which still had plenty of reminders of Luis just sitting around. They hadn't lived together, not yet, but most of their time together was spent at Donovan's place. His bed was sized for two, for one thing, and his apartment looked less like a flophouse. The throw blanket on the back of the couch was an afghan Luis had picked out, during his convalescence. He'd sneaked out to do it, since he was supposed to still be resting, but he'd wanted to get out and do something, and Donovan was too touched and charmed to object.

He stalked through the living room to the kitchen, refusing to look. He should be safe there from any reminders of his cheating lover or everything he'd just lost. It wasn't like Luis cooked. Even there though, Luis' stamp was everywhere. When Donovan opened the fridge to grab a beer, he found bottles of Luis' favorite weird Brazilian soft drinks. When he rummaged through the cabinets to find a snack, he found the adorable sticky notes Luis had left for him ages ago just to make him smile.

Love you!

Your badge is in your top drawer. You left it on your pants again. Donovan had to laugh at that note because it could have been left at any time. Luis had put it in the coffee cabinet, on a level with Donovan's eyes.

Don't forget your cuffs today!

He sat down on the floor, curled up into a corner, and cried. He'd been willing to hear Luis out on the cheating. Sure, cheating was bad and he was angry about it. He was angry as hell, in fact. If Luis had just owned up to what he'd done, asked for forgiveness and maybe for help, Donovan would have welcomed him with open arms.

Luis hadn't been looking for forgiveness. He'd been firm about that. The mere accusation had been enough for Luis to close the door on everything they'd had. Calling Luis out on cheating had been enough to make Luis declare Donovan untrustworthy. How did that even work? What was Donovan supposed to do with that?

He dried his eyes after a while. He didn't know how much time had passed, and he knew he'd get to crying again before too long. He needed to get some things done before he got there though. He took a swig from his beer, which was working its way to room temperature, and sent Alicia a text. Surely she'd want to back away from Luis now that they weren't dating anymore.

Unless, of course, she'd been part of a weird cover-up or threesome.

Then he called his mother. Patricia, at least, was above suspicion.

She picked up the phone on the second ring. "Donovan, how are you?" She sounded as warm as always. "I was thinking of you. I just got back from Mass."

Donovan smiled a little. Patricia always

brought that out in him, especially now that he'd come out. "Hey." He swallowed hard. "Um. Luis and I split up."

"Hang on, let me get outside." Her voice went soft with sympathy, and he heard her moving through the house.

Who was indoors with her that she had to go outside to talk? The detective in him wanted to know. The son in him just wanted his privacy.

She must have gotten out into the backyard, because she made a little sound in the back of her throat. "Okay, sweetheart. First of all, I'm so sorry. You sound devastated."

"I am." It wasn't hard to admit it. He wanted to scream to the sky, but the creepy neighbor might call the police. Donovan was the police, but it still got awkward. "I confronted him about his cheating, and he didn't take too kindly to that." He sniffed and took another swig of his beer.

"I can't imagine he did." Patricia sighed, a tiny sound that spoke volumes. "We spoke about this, my love. Do you think that maybe, just maybe, he might not have been cheating at all?"

"No. He was a hundred percent cheating. It's what he does." Donovan slammed his fist against the floor. It stung. The floor had no give at all. It was laminate over concrete, and he had to bite back a curse. "I mean, you should see the way he was with this ranger. The guy's always flirting with him, he's always gabbing with him in Spanish because they both know I don't speak it. He didn't even bother to deny it."

Patricia let his words sink in for a moment. "So far, you've only talked about how this other man has behaved, not about how Luis behaved. And when I've been accused of cheating, I didn't bother to deny it either. I knew your father wasn't interested in the truth. He was interested in baseless accusations."

"Dad accused you of cheating?" Donovan had to laugh at that one. He let his head thunk against the cabinet door. "That's ridiculous. You'd never cheat."

"That's kind of my point, love. He accused me of cheating because I stopped having sex with him, or even sleeping in the same room, after he passed on a dose of syphilis. Which seems like a reasonable response to me, to this day. And since obviously no reasonable woman can live without dick, I must have been cheating."

Donovan almost choked on his own tongue. Patricia hadn't ever talked about sex in front of him. She'd told him what Fred had done to her, but she hadn't gone into details. He took another swig of beer to wash down his shock. "That's insane!"

"That's your father. Of course, he made his

accusation in an open police station, full of our colleagues. At least you made yours in private." Patricia sipped from whatever she had on her end.

Donovan cleared his throat noisily. "Er, not so much."

The sound of her disappointment only needed two words to become a physical thing. "Oh, Donnie."

"It was only Kevin, his partner. There wasn't anyone else in the office. I mean, I started to lose it a little bit at a crime scene this morning, but he got me to calm down—rightly—by pointing out that it wasn't the right place. But I just kept thinking about it, all the way back to Chelsea. And I couldn't stop. It was like Ruben—the ranger—was so goddamn smug, you know? He's everything Luis has ever gone for. There's no way he's going to keep it—" He stopped himself and reevaluated his phrasing. "There's no way he's going to be faithful with Ruben dangling catnip right there."

Patricia went silent for a long moment. "Well, I can see why he wouldn't trust you, I guess. And you clearly don't trust him. This is his first case since he got back from medical leave, right?"

"So what?" Donovan scoffed and took another swig of his beer. It was empty now. How had that happened? "What has that got to do with anything?"

"Luis wasn't in a position where you had to see him around other men or how other men reacted to him. He's a very handsome man, Donovan. It's only reasonable that people who are interested in men would show their attraction."

"But he doesn't have to act on it." Donovan scooted over to the fridge. He didn't care enough to stand, but he wanted another beer.

"And he doesn't. At least you haven't shown me that he does." Patricia's tone was still sympathetic, but she'd added an undercurrent of steel. "All you've shown me was a man with a lot of insecurities."

"Ma, I'm a detective. My whole job is figuring things out when people don't want me to know them." He opened his beer and ground his teeth before drinking from the bottle.

"And I'm a veteran cop who raised four children, all of whom became cops, thank you very much. I'll thank you to remember that, and to remember who it was that tracked down twenty fugitives for the City of Boston. Don't go thinking you got every brain cell in this family, boyo, just because your father didn't." Patricia took a deep breath.

You may feel your dad is a better man than I'll ever be, and that's your prerogative, but I'll never know. Because you and me are no longer a thing, and when this case is over, we'll never see or hear from each other again. Luis had spoken those words to him, and Donovan had earned them.

"Oh God," he said, and clutched at his stomach.

"What is it?" The anger faded from Patricia's voice as suddenly as it had come, replaced with only maternal concern.

"I told Luis Dad was a better man than he'd ever be." Donovan held his cold beer bottle to his forehead.

Patricia hissed. "You said that?"

"The discussion got heated." Donovan went fetal again. "All I wanted was for him to admit what he'd done. He wouldn't do it. He just said we couldn't trust each other, and it was over. He loved me but it was over. And now he's gone." He sniffed as the tears returned.

Patricia sounded like she was close to tears too. "Oh, honey. I'm so sorry. I wish it could have gone some other way, I do. But I think he's right."

"What do you mean?" Donovan wiped his nose on his sleeve.

"Well, honey, you've said in the past you understood why he was so, er . . ."

"Promiscuous?" All those men who'd gotten to be with Luis, when Donovan hadn't. All the men who now would get to be with Luis, when

Donovan couldn't. His gorge rose, and he drove it back with more beer.

"Yes. You said you understood, and it didn't bother you, but anyone can see it does and you clearly still hold it against him. Luis isn't doing anything, from what you've said. And if this ranger is giving you smug looks, then maybe there's another reason for it. All I know is that Luis looked at you like the sun rose and set around you, and now he's had to cut you loose."

"He could have apologized. He could have asked for help." Donovan wiped at his eyes.

"He didn't do anything wrong!" Patricia roared her words so loudly Donovan had to pull the phone back from his ear. "Donovan, you're my son and I'm always going to love you, but I think you need to take a good hard look at yourself. Ask yourself why you don't believe Luis *could have been faithful* to you, and get help. Because this will be a problem for you in every relationship you have with a man, until you solve it."

"I love you, Mom." Donovan tried to get control of himself as the tears flowed down his face.

"I love you too, Donovan. Do you want me to come over?"

"Maybe."

"I'll be there in about an hour."

Donovan hung up and buried his face on his

knees, just like he had when he was a small boy.

CHAPTER TEN

Luis made it through the next couple of days at work more or less on autopilot. Kevin ran interference for him with the rest of the office, and Donovan had the good sense to work from home or from the state police office in Framingham or from whatever pit of hell the demon possessing him had crawled out of.

They got the ID on their victim pretty quickly. Sonia Hibbert had been on the young side for their suspect, and she hadn't been reported missing yet. She was a sophomore at UMass Dartmouth majoring in Women's and Gender Studies, and she was originally from Athol.

Donovan, communicating via group chat, agreed to head out to speak to her parents while Luis and Kevin headed down to Dartmouth to speak with her teachers and her roommate. In the meantime, Maxwell was working with Tinder to get a record of her dates and with her phone company to try and get a record of her calls and whereabouts.

Sonia's roommate, Priya, told them some details, but on the whole, it wasn't anything they didn't already know. "Sonia had a date, but she was . . ." Priya blushed deeply. "She didn't date like normal people. She didn't like to date the same guy twice, you know? She didn't want that from men. She wanted to be . . . She only wanted sex from men. She'd hook up with them when she wanted it and then leave them alone. She didn't want romance, she didn't want a boyfriend, and if you talked to her about marriage or starting a family someday, she would laugh in your face. 'That's fine for some people,' she'd say, 'but it's nowhere on my radar. I'm here to smash the patriarchy, not hold it up.' And that was her, in a nutshell." She pulled her sweater closer, like it could somehow protect her.

Luis could sympathize, with Priya and with Sonia. He'd felt that way once, at least about relationships. He'd let himself get sucked into one, let himself want one, and look how well it had turned out for him. Maybe Sonia had it right. Of course, it hadn't done her much good either. "That's good to know," he told Priya with a little smile. "Did she say anything about the guys she met up with?"

Priya shook her head. "Not usually. She

always thought using the app kept her safe, you know? That it would leave a record of who she was with and when. I tried to tell her it didn't work like that, but she just laughed at me. She thought because I'm a virgin, and because I don't do hookup culture, that I don't understand how it works." She snorted and then looked down. "I shouldn't speak ill of the dead."

Kevin sat down on the edge of Sonia's bed. It was neatly made, and Luis wondered if that was standard for her.

"It's okay," Kevin told Priya. "You have to tell us the truth, you know? We don't have any real suspects at this point. The only way we can find one is to get to know Sonia—the nice and the, er, not so nice." He smirked. "Once we know her, we can understand who she'd have been with, and then we can find him that way. It's not that we're being judgmental of her, that's not our place."

Luis saw the doubt in Priya's eyes. "I get where it can seem that way sometimes. Not only are we asking some uncomfortable questions, we're pretty much tearing through someone's life and going down to some pretty difficult details while their loved ones are grieving. It can come off as pretty insensitive, and we can *be* kind of insensitive. We get kind of inured to it, I think, in the kind of units we're in. Maybe in Art Crimes they don't, I guess, but when you deal with the kind of violent crimes we do, you just kind of get used to getting into some details that other people would just cringe away from."

"I can see that, I guess." Priya relaxed a little bit.

"Believe me when I tell you there's almost nothing at least one of us hasn't seen before." Kevin nodded toward Luis. "This guy in particular. He's not going to judge anyone."

Priya nodded and took a deep breath. "Okay. She was a good person, don't get me wrong, but she wasn't always great at listening to other people. And she knew it, you know? She was working on it, trying to get better. She was trying to move beyond her privilege and uplift other voices, but it's not so easy when you're used to being deferred to. She didn't mind being reminded, up to a point. But with some things, you couldn't tell her anything."

"Like about using hookup apps." Luis made a note of her comment.

"Right. It was like . . . like a trigger for her, or something. It was like she thought you were trying to control her or shame her. If you even brought it up, you were a tool of the patriarchy and needed to go out and educate yourself on sexual liberation. I mean, I pointed out the whole thing with bodies being found in Freetown, and she still got mad at me." Priya twirled her long dark hair around her finger.

She lapsed into silence for a moment, and then she spoke up again. "I can't believe she's dead," she said, "but I'm not surprised either. That doesn't make sense, but the way she carried on and the things she did, it's just the plain truth. Whoever is killing women—the news people say he's targeting promiscuous women, right?"

Luis let out a little growl. "I'm really starting to hate that word. The killer has issues with women. Most serial killers do. The women he's targeting do seem to have a certain lack of regard for patriarchal norms. There is absolutely nothing wrong with a sexually liberated lifestyle, so long as they're taking adequate precautions and so long as everything they're doing is consensual. Just like there's nothing wrong with avoiding sex, so long as it's your choice."

Kevin put a hand on Luis' shoulder, and Luis calmed a little.

"Our suspect doesn't feel that way, but that doesn't mean women should change their behavior to accommodate him." Kevin leaned forward a little. "He's the bad guy here. These women shouldn't be punished for making choices about their own bodies, and we're going to track him down and bring him to justice. Okay?"

She nodded. "If I find anything or think of anything, I'll give you a call."

They left the dorm and went to speak to Sonia's advisors, but they didn't have any more details. According to them, Sonia avoided men entirely, at least if they were straight.

As they left the dorm to head out to the car, Luis hummed to himself. "So he's not terribly picky about the type of woman he's going after."

Kevin did a double take. "What do you mean? He's still going after women who, er, wallow in their sexuality."

Luis managed half a grin. He couldn't offer anything more. It was a cute euphemism, but his heart still wasn't in it. "Jennifer, the ghost I've been speaking with at Freetown, doesn't seem to identify very strongly as a feminist. And the last victim we ID'd wasn't a feminist at all, she just really liked sex. A couple of the women we picked out of the missing list who'd had dates with our guy had histories of prostitution. Sonia here was clearly only using men to satisfy physical needs and had no use for them otherwise. The only thing that seems to set him off is a woman's sexuality—whether or not she embraces sex enthusiastically and quickly or takes things slowly and with more restraint. That's unusual."

Kevin opened up the car, and they both got in. "Does it mean something?"

"Probably. He might have been cheated on by a promiscuous girlfriend or someone he just thought was cheating on him." Luis curled his lip a little there. He was still bitter. He supposed he'd be bitter for a while. "He might have picked up a disease somewhere along the way and blamed it on a woman. He could come from a rigid religious or patriarchal background and twisted it in his mind. It's someone who knows Assonet Ledge, I can tell you that much, because he's been getting away with his crimes by having them classified as suicides."

"It's not looking good for old Ruben, is it?" Kevin headed back north toward Chelsea. "I don't know anything about his upbringing, but he knows all there is to know about the damn Ledge, doesn't he?"

"That he does." Luis sighed. "What've you been able to find out about him? Or those other guys Alicia listed?"

"Not too much. The other guys checked out. One of them moved to Oklahoma halfway through our boy's active period. The other one wound up in jail for fraud. Ruben's single, he's been working here for about eighteen months. Before that, he was a ranger out in California." Kevin passed a tractor trailer as they picked up speed. "He shows up on time to work. There was a slight uptick in suicides and lost campers at the state park where he worked in California, but nothing so significant it caused alarm."

"Yeah, well, it was a rough time, economically speaking. Those were easily explained. Any history of domestic violence?" Luis tapped his fingers against the armrest for a few seconds.

"There's no recorded history of him having lived with a woman. Interestingly, his purchasing habits do show a fondness for self-help gurus." Kevin raised his eyebrows and let himself grin, just a little bit.

"Self-help gurus." Luis tried to process that one. It was a new one for him. He'd never met a serial killer who was into self-help. Maybe that exonerated Ruben, leaving him guilty of nothing more than being maliciously socially awkward.

"Right. Like Dale Carnegie or Stephen Covey. But not all of them are quite so benign. You've got quite a few of them who aren't very friendly toward women, and it looks like Noguera has been to see a few of them. He's gone to see the guy who talks about how 'risky' it is to hire women now that they're talking about sexual assault and harassment, for example."

"Charming." And Donovan truly believed Luis would sleep with someone like that? It made him want to run home and scrub until his skin came off. What was it about Luis that made Donovan think he didn't have standards?

"Oh, and something like fifteen pickup artist 'teachers.' " Kevin chuckled. "Quite the charmer, our little Ruben."

Luis turned his face away. "He shouldn't need that crap if he's a decent guy. Which I suppose leads to the conclusion . . ."

"Where there's smoke, there's fire. He got into one more absolutely wretched self-help guy maybe fourteen months ago, a few months before his date with Alicia Kennedy. That would be the 'Clean Your Room' guy." Kevin couldn't wipe the smirk from his face this time.

Luis' was more of a sneer or a grimace. "Isn't that the guy with all the lobsters?"

"That's the one!" Kevin laughed and patted the steering wheel. "What is with the lobsters?"

"Ugh. Apparently, they have dominance hierarchies. Which is somehow fascinating to the same kind of guy who views women as beneath men and different races as beneath white. Why we should be taking our cues from a giant sea cockroach, I have no clue." Luis slammed his head against the headrest. "I had to sort through this guy's bullshit on a risk assessment."

Kevin sputtered. "How could you deem him low-risk? He's obsessed with lobsters! Lobsters! Giant sea cockroaches, Luis!"

"Right? I didn't deem him low-risk. I deemed him a scary motherfucker and recommended he be closely monitored like any other hate speech–mouthing fool. That's about all you can do. And by the way, the word *lobster* is typically pronounced with an *R* on the end." Luis closed his eyes against the headache brewing there.

"Lob-*stah,*" Kevin said, stabbing one of his fingers toward Luis. "Get used to it, buddy, or I'm dragging you out for lobster rolls tonight."

"Yuck. Giant sea cockroaches with extra mayo." Luis shuddered. "No one needs that in their lives. All of those things justify some extra digging, but they're not evidence. They don't hold up in a court of law. A judge is going to look at that and say, 'Well, he made some bad life choices and maybe he should avoid the Clean Your Room guy, but that doesn't mean he's throwing girls off a cliff.' "

"We'll just have to find a way to connect him to that account." Kevin grinned. Then he sobered. "We still can't bring Donovan in on the thing with Ruben. I'd love to be able to read him in, but I don't think we can trust him yet."

Luis didn't open his eyes. His headache was full-blown now. "No. I would have hoped breaking up would help with that, but he hasn't . . . he's still insistent that me and Ruben are a thing."

"As near as we can tell, Ruben is straight." Kevin scratched at his jaw. "But he's definitely trying to flirt with you. Why do you think that is?"

Luis groaned. "I have a few ideas, but none of them are good. And we can't prove any of them yet. So let's just . . . not."

"Good plan." Kevin kept driving, and Luis tried to push Donovan out of his thoughts.

Donovan couldn't make himself physically be near Luis again for the rest of the week after they split up. He knew it raised a few eyebrows, but no one said anything to him. He had to be grateful. When the call came in about a new body at Freetown, on Saturday morning this time, he couldn't avoid it anymore. He got dressed and drove down to the state park as slow as he could. At least he was spared having to sit through a miserable Saturday-night stakeout, as they'd planned before the breakup. Donovan would be grateful for the small things because that was what he had now.

He knew it was wrong. Someone, a living human being, had been murdered, and Donovan shouldn't let his own personal grief and anger get in the way of investigating the killer. He just couldn't make himself drive any faster. Every mile that passed brought him closer to the man who'd cheated on him. Probably. No, certainly. Luis had absolutely cheated on him, there could be no doubt at all about that. Hadn't Fred himself clued him in? If anyone was scientifically incapable of fidelity, it was Fred. He would absolutely recognize the signs in someone else.

When Donovan pulled up to the site, he frowned. Wong and his band of unhappy souls were there, of course. So were Maxwell and his team, and Kevin. Something wasn't right though. It took Donovan a second to figure it out.

He crept over to Kevin. "Is it me, or is this the second body we've found in a row that wasn't in the water?"

Kevin pursed his lips and nodded. "The killer is either getting bolder or getting angrier. Could be both," he added with a shrug. "He's got a ton of rage. Wong won't say for sure, but it's not like this is my first battered body. Either he threw her from the cliff down onto the rocks instead of into the water, which would mean he overshot his mark and just left her there, or he beat her so badly it just looks like she got thrown off a cliff."

Donovan let out a low whistle. "With this

guy, it could go either way."

"Precisely." Wong rose from his position beside the remains. "Which is why I'm not going to make a declaration which one is the cause of death until I get back to the lab and do a proper examination. If I have to wait for tox screens and other analyses, like I did with the last one, it can take weeks. And there's not a damn thing you, or I, or even the pope can do about it." He wagged his finger at Kevin. "Speculation is completely improper and not allowed." He gestured to his assistants, who zipped up the body bag and bore the remains away.

"Is there no other medical examiner we could work with?" Kevin asked, with a plaintive sigh.

"Unfortunately, there are only three. And no one in the state's ME office likes the Feds, so he gets stuck with you all." Donovan stuffed his hands in his pockets. "Who found the body?"

Kevin grimaced and scratched at his mustache. "A priest."

Donovan raised his eyebrows. "A priest?"

"An eighty-year-old priest out walking, trying to meditate and talk to God. The guy's at the ranger station with Luis right now, giving a statement. He'll be going to the hospital after that. Believe me when I tell you, he'll need it. He was not in good shape when we got here."

Donovan flinched at Luis' name. Kevin couldn't have missed it, but he didn't say anything.

"Any sign of her clothes?" Donovan asked after a second.

"Nope. But she was blindfolded, and there are no signs of ligature marks. None that I could see, not that Dr. Charming there let me get a good look. We'll find out more, but it's possible she was killed during voluntary sexual activity." Kevin opened up his tablet and made a note. "It wouldn't be the first time."

"Jesus Christ, your work is grim." Donovan shuddered. Maybe he should have been more lenient with Luis. A guy who spent his career trawling through serial killers' heads was bound to develop a few quirks. Then again, plenty of guys worked in homicide or even chased serial killers and managed to be faithful.

He heard a motor in the distance.

"Sure it's grim." Kevin met Donovan's eyes as the motor drew closer. "Someone's got to do it, might as well be guys with the stomach for it, right? And hey, it's not like either one of us has anyone at home to worry about."

"Was that really necessary?" Donovan took a step back.

"I think it was." Kevin smiled blandly and

then looked over at the entrance to the area around the quarry pool. "Hey, guys. How'd the interview with the priest go?"

Donovan wasn't ready to see Luis. He sure as hell wasn't ready to see Luis sitting on the passenger side of the ranger service's ATV in his suit and tie, gripping the roll bar for dear life, with Ruben Noguera behind the wheel. His vision went red for a second, but he pulled himself back. Of course Luis was with Ruben. He'd been with Ruben all along.

Ruben stopped the ATV, and Luis hopped out like he was wearing a freaking leotard and not dress pants. "Thanks for the ride," he said with a smile. Was he batting his eyelashes at Ruben? He was, wasn't he? He might be hiding it behind those standard-issue FBI sunglasses he always wore, but hell if he wasn't gazing adoringly over at Ruben.

"No problem. I'm happy to wait around if you guys need anything." Ruben smirked over at Donovan. "Why, Detective Carey, what a pleasant surprise."

"Ranger." Donovan shoved his hands into his pockets, to keep them away from his gun.

"Thanks, Ruben, but we'll take it from here. We'll give a shout if we have any issues. I know your boss was making noise about overtime." Luis' easy grin showed no acknowledgment of Donovan, or of his pain.

"Yeah, he says that all the time. You're likely right though. Well, I'll see you next time." He waved and drove off.

Donovan looked at Kevin, who looked over at Luis. Even a few of the crime scene techs exchanged glances.

"I'll see you next time?" Kevin repeated. "What the hell?"

Luis shrugged and looked down. He already looked thinner. Maybe he regretted letting Donovan get away. Well, it was too late now. "It's not like it hasn't been happening on the regular, like freaking clockwork. Maybe he's getting jaded."

"Maybe he's just an asshole." Donovan spoke through gritted teeth. "Have you thought of that yet, genius?"

"I've considered all of the possibilities for assholery, thank you." Luis picked his head back up. "So. What've we got?" His eyes were sunken, and it was obvious he wasn't eating or sleeping right, but he wasn't about to give Donovan the satisfaction of a confession. Well, fine.

Maxwell stepped into the tense little knot of people, sliding between Luis and Donovan with ease. Was he sleeping with Luis too? "We've got the path they took, up to a certain point. I think they came from a car. She absolutely ran from the car, to the spot where she was found."

"So there goes the theory about being thrown from the cliff." Kevin snapped his fingers.

"Yeah, no, there's no sign of anyone having been up on the cliff last night. And our vic was bleeding from the time she got out of the car. Based on direction and the size of the drops, I'd say the cut wouldn't have been big." Maxwell made a pinching gesture on his arm, to show a rough size of a cut that could have accounted for the blood drops. "Could have been from a rock or a physical altercation, there's no way to know."

"What did you learn from the priest?" Kevin asked Luis.

Luis looked up at the changing leaves. "Let's see. First, I learned that God will have mercy on her soul, and the killer's soul, because God is merciful. Then I learned about the guy's bad knees and how he'd come out here as a penance and how if you pray the rosary on the ninth day of the ninth week or something like that, you'll get your wish."

"What you're saying is that he's not a reliable witness," Kevin interrupted, wiping his face with one hand.

"Not at all. I'm sure when he's calmed down a little, he'll be able to give the basics, which is all we'll need from him. He saw the poor woman lying on the ground and checked for a pulse, but not only was there no pulse to be found, she was cold to the touch. Also, the quantity of blood lying around her was a pretty big clue. He said he called the police, who sent Ruben to come and get him. He didn't touch anything but her neck, to check for a pulse, and I believe him. There wasn't enough blood on him for him to have done anything else."

"So he didn't take anything else from her." Donovan knew Luis would have mentioned it if the priest had, or if Luis had any reason to be suspicious, but he had to get that dig in. Maybe Luis was right and he was turning into his father.

"Yes, Donovan, he emptied all of her viscera into his priestly pockets and made rosary beads out of her phalanges." Luis' voice stayed perfectly deadpan. "How could it have slipped my mind? Moving on."

Maxwell grimaced and inched away from him. "Dude. Gross."

"I've seen it." One corner of Luis' mouth quirked up. "I'll send you pictures if you want."

"Can I use them in my presentation at Northeastern next month?"

"Knock yourself out."

They were losing focus. Donovan cleared his throat. "And did it really take that long to interview the priest, or were you off canoodling with Ruben while we were out here working?"

"Doesn't matter if I was or wasn't. I'm a single man, and once my job is done, I can canoodle with whomsoever I choose." Luis cracked the knuckles on his right hand.

Kevin scoffed. "Donovan, you have no idea how long it took him, since you got here five minutes ago. This isn't the time or place to hassle your ex. Luis, did the witness have anything else to say?"

Luis narrowed his eyes. "Yes. He'll be praying for me. And you. And Ruben and Ruben's boss . . . it got wordy, man." He yawned. "I shouldn't be dismissive, I'm glad it brings him comfort, but it was a little intense."

"I can believe it. The poor guy was a wreck." Kevin shook his head. "Well, let's head back to headquarters and get to work. Maxwell, are you guys going to be okay here?"

"Yeah, sure, just so long as there aren't any pukwudgies or anything." Maxwell glanced around and pulled his FBI jacket a little closer to himself.

"If you see one, you're a federal agent. You're entitled to demand it stay the hell of your crime scene." Luis grinned, somewhat wanly, and looked over at Kevin. "Shall we get rolling?"

Donovan blinked back tears. Up until last week, Luis would have ridden with him. "Hey, wait a minute." He chased after them. "Can we talk for a minute?"

Kevin bit his lip but then nodded. "I'll be at the car."

Luis looked outraged, but he stayed with Donovan for the moment. "What?" he snapped. "Now you want to talk? When everything's in the trash, now you want to talk? I don't have a damn thing to say to you, Donovan."

"Are you ready to tell me what Ruben has that I don't have?" Donovan crossed his arms over his chest. He hadn't known what he'd say if he got Luis to speak to him. The words flew out of his mouth, like someone else had put them there. Donovan knew they were his own, he just hadn't meant to say them out loud.

Luis just scoffed at him. "The only thing Ruben has that you don't is a job with DCR. I was never with him. I made a commitment to you, and I didn't so much as think about anyone else while we were together."

"Then why did you dump me, huh? Why didn't you try to make me believe?" Donovan put his hand on Luis' upper arm, feeling the warm, solid muscle underneath.

Luis barely moved, and suddenly, Donovan was on the soft forest ground. Donovan had no idea what he did. He felt Luis' arm move, and then hands. There might have been a leg or a foot, but everything happened in less than a second. All Donovan knew was that he was flying. "You even think about putting your hands on me again, Donovan, and I'll knock your ass out and leave you here for the crows." Luis' face froze over, and he turned on his heel.

Donovan stayed on the trail, right where Luis had left him, until he couldn't see Luis anymore. Only then did he get up and make his way slowly back to his car.

CHAPTER ELEVEN

Luis had to be grateful for Sunday. He wasn't usually a big "day of rest" guy, but he needed the break. He needed to pull back from the adrenaline of having to knock Donovan down. He needed to wash the feeling of Donovan's hand on his arm from his mind. Even through his jacket and his dress shirt, Donovan's touch had burned.

He'd gotten to such a good point, back before he got assigned to the Lightfoot case and saw Donovan again. Okay, it hadn't *really* been a good point. His colleagues hated him, his career was in a downward spiral he couldn't stop no matter how good his record was, and he'd had to accept his own inability to relate to other people a long time ago. But he *had* accepted it, for better or for worse. Then Donovan came back into his life. Donovan had come back, and all of Luis' carefully built acceptance went right out the window. It took his equilibrium with it.

His spiraling career tanked. He almost lost

his job, the one thing in his life that gave him any meaning or purpose. He'd been so miserable about the way things had been with Donovan he hadn't cared either. And then, in the end, Donovan had *wanted* him. Donovan had chosen him, the only person ever to do so, and he'd essentially forced the rest of his unit to tolerate him too. Donovan's family had welcomed him—parts of it, anyway—and life had started to look up. For the first time since college, Luis had something outside of work.

Luis missed Donovan for himself. He also quaked with grief for the loss of everything that had come with their relationship.

He didn't expect to hear from any of Donovan's family ever again. Some of them had been more accepting of him than others, but they were all Donovan's family first. They would never, not in a million years, choose to stay friendly with Luis.

So when Alicia's text came in on Sunday morning, it caught him completely off guard. *Hey, Luis, are you around?*

Luis stared at his phone for a long minute. *I am. I don't know if you've heard, but Donovan and I decided to go our separate ways.* That sounded a lot more gentle than it had been, both in the initial action and Luis throwing Donovan onto his ass.

I know. I hope that doesn't mean you don't want

to see me and Nick anymore.

Luis rubbed his eyes. He couldn't be seeing what he was seeing. *I do want to keep seeing you guys if you'll still have me.*

She sent him three angry-faced emojis. *My cousin being an ass isn't contagious, I promise. Or genetic—on the Kennedy side at least.*

Ah. So she too believed Donovan's father had more to do with what had happened than anyone wanted to acknowledge. *What time do you want to see me?*

They made plans to meet up at Nick's favorite restaurant in Waltham for lunch, and Luis got up to get ready to start his day. He'd been looking forward to hiding in his bed and pretending the world didn't exist, but he knew that wasn't a healthy response. And if he didn't have to lose everything when he lost Donovan, well, that was the best possible outcome, wasn't it?

Both Alicia and Nick hugged him tight when he got to the restaurant, a Buffalo Wild Wings.

"Aunt Patty says Uncle Donovan's being a butt," Nick told him, "except she didn't say butt. She said another word that I'm not supposed to say until I graduate from the academy."

Luis had to laugh at that. He ruffled Nick's hair and sat down. "Well, I'd do what your mom and aunt say. They're pretty smart, and they have guns."

Nick nodded glumly. "I know. I'm not supposed to touch those until I've gone to the academy either. I'll be totally old by then, but that's okay. I don't really want to touch guns. I just want to play soccer and hang out with my friends."

"That's a good thing to want to do." Luis grinned and relaxed into the meal. He still didn't have much of an appetite, but he never did when he was upset or when he was on a complex case. It would come back.

After lunch, they went back to Alicia's house. Nick's little friend Joao came over, and they played in the yard while Alicia and Luis sat at the patio table and watched. Alicia told him about a hostage situation she'd been called to, a domestic dispute in Wilmington. There had been children involved, so the rescue had been delicate. They'd wound up blaring one of those Viking death metal bands at the house to distract the father and hide any sounds from the entry team and sending people in to rescue the children. Only then was it safe to deal with the father, who was barricaded into the ground floor with the mother. They even managed to get the pets out before the father caught wind of what was going on.

Luis grinned. "That was pretty clever. I like it. I might have to steal it sometime." He sipped from his lemonade. Alicia was drinking a beer, and if Luis didn't have the voice of his father still in his head, he might have thought about reaching for one himself. It had been a rough week.

"So." Alicia toyed with the label on her bottle. "Do you want to talk about it?"

Luis almost told her no. He was so used to assuming—*knowing*—no one cared, he didn't know how to react when someone did. He took a deep breath. "He was great all while I was getting better, you know? But then we got this case, and all of a sudden, he's Mr. Jealous." He bowed his head. "It still feels like I got T-boned by a freight train when there weren't even any tracks."

Alicia snorted. "Oh, I know. It's bizarre behavior. But to be honest, it didn't start until he started hanging around with his dad."

Luis considered. "It did a little bit. Not this full-blown insecure mess stuff, where he's absolutely convinced I'm cheating right that minute even in front of his face. It's . . ." He waved his hand, unable to find the right words. "It was more nuanced than that, I guess. More subtle. More about this other guy, Ruben, than about me. And then, yeah, he started hanging around with Fred, and it was all over."

"Fred is not your friend." She made a face and took a long swig from her beer. "He doesn't like folks like us."

"And he doesn't like the tan." Luis bit his tongue for a second, and then he decided to go for it. He didn't have much to lose. Donovan was already gone, and Alicia loathed Fred Carey. "I can't help but wonder if he hasn't been doing it on purpose, and not just because I'm a scary brown gay guy."

"What, encouraging Donovan to be suspicious?" Alicia opened her mouth, and then she closed it again. "I don't want to think that of anyone, but you know what? He always was a manipulative little shit." She covered her mouth with one hand and looked out at the boys in the yard. Neither of them seemed to have heard her.

"That's just right. A guy can change in thirteen years, but he's not going to change *that* much. Donovan was trying to intimidate me, and he's never done that before. It was stuff Fred *has* done, not that it worked. I just . . ." Luis massaged his temples for a second. "It doesn't really matter anymore. I mean, it's over. I can't trust him, and you can't have a relationship where the two people involved can't trust each other. But I'm worried about him too."

She gave him a sad little smile. "Because he'll be with someone eventually, and Fred will pull the same stunt."

"Right." He snapped his fingers. "And Donovan does deserve to be happy. He deserves to not have his father sitting there pulling his strings." He clenched his hand into a fist, and then he hid it under the table. He didn't want to scare the kids, and he wasn't about to go and confront Fred Carey. For one thing, it wouldn't get him anywhere. For another, Fred wouldn't be moved one inch.

"I don't know what to do. I know Patty tried to suggest, gently, that he might be getting a little too much guidance from his father. It didn't go over well." Alicia turned the bottle around in her fingertips.

Luis sighed. "It's not important, I guess. There's not a lot I can do. If Donovan wouldn't listen to me before, and I certainly don't have any proof, he's not going to listen to me now. He tried to show me up and call me a liar on a crime scene yesterday."

"That's not okay." Alicia turned to face him fully, eyes blazing. "You need to get him removed from the case. He's already unreliable enough that you have to hide case information from him, and now he's pulling stunts like this? No, no way. He can't be there. He needs to be benched until he can stop undermining you."

"Well, here's the thing. He'll go to my supervisor. And trust me when I tell you, everyone in that unit would rather be working with Donovan than with me." Luis made a face. "It's the tan. It's at least mostly the tan. So which one of us do you think gets the boot?"

She covered her mouth again. "Luis, there has to be something you can do."

He rolled his shoulders. "Kevin's been solid so far. I'm relying on him. We haven't always been very tight, but he's watched Donovan over the course of this investigation and he agrees with me. This is pretty bad stuff. So right now, I'm just going to work as hard as I can, defer as much as I can to Kevin, and see what happens from there. After that, I'll try to have him blocked from getting assigned to cases with me."

"Yikes." She shook her head and sighed. "I wish it didn't have to be like this. You guys were so good together. At least I thought you were."

"I did too."

Luis stayed with Alicia and Nick until dinnertime, when he headed back to his own place. He didn't want to be obvious about not being able to choke down any more food. He couldn't make any more progress with the Freetown case right now, and the fact that he'd been wrong about a strict Saturday schedule rubbed him raw, but he could do some work on the other missing persons cases he'd been assigned.

Was there anything he could do about the way Donovan's father manipulated him? He didn't think there was, not even after reflecting on it for a few hours while sifting through documents and fingerprints. He'd done everything reasonable. At the end of the day, Donovan hadn't wanted to believe Luis was faithful. Luis could have worn a GPS bracelet, and Donovan still wouldn't have believed he was faithful.

It didn't matter that his father had been encouraging him. It was bad—evil—of Fred, and maybe some other time Luis could sit down and wonder what would drive a father to behave that way toward his own child. But right now, he could only think about how it had affected him. Donovan hadn't *had* to let Fred manipulate him that way. If Donovan had really trusted Luis, Fred's lies and insinuations wouldn't have been able to gain a foothold.

He found a picture of one of the missing persons on his list at Boston's South Station, only yesterday. She'd gone missing three months ago, but cameras had picked her up at South Station yesterday so that took her off their killer's list. He made a note of it with relief and moved on to the next one.

Her name was Jennifer Bayless. It was hard to tell from a photo, especially since the Jennifer he knew didn't have eyes. This one had striking blue eyes and looked out from a Tinder profile picture while drinking what looked like a daiquiri. It could have been a smoothie.

He touched the photo. She'd been a teacher, last seen on a Tinder date just like his Jennifer. He needed to head back out to Freetown to see if this was her.

It was almost certainly a good idea to wait though. It was late, and he was tired. He'd see if Kevin would go with him tomorrow.

Donovan squirmed in his seat. He couldn't *really* smell Luis from over here. Luis wasn't a cologne or aftershave kind of guy, and even if he had been, he wouldn't wear enough for Donovan to smell him across the room. He just thought he could smell Luis because everything about Luis was everywhere these days.

Where had Luis been yesterday? Donovan had driven past his house again. He didn't know what he'd have done if Luis had been home. He might have tried to talk again. He might have lost his temper and gotten knocked on his ass again. The two weren't mutually exclusive outcomes.

He chewed on the end of his pen and stole a glance at Luis from the corner of his eye. He still looked tired. Had he been out all night, sleeping around, back on Mixr? Donovan had sneaked a look at his profile last night, but it still read as inactive. Donovan couldn't believe it though. Maybe he'd set up a second one at some point, just to hide it from Donovan?

But why bother hiding it now? It sure wasn't to spare Donovan's feelings.

Kevin cleared his throat, jolting Donovan out of his obsessive musings. "So we have a little bit of an issue. The divers won't be able to start looking for additional bodies until Thursday."

Luis made a face. "I'm sure there's a valid reason for it and everything, but it still pisses me off. It's not like water doesn't destroy evidence or anything."

Kevin grimaced, and then he shrugged. "True. But it's also not like a lot of those bodies, assuming he's been killing at the same rate, haven't been down there for a damn long time, you know? It's not like they're going to get any deader."

Donovan nodded. "I'm not sure where the divers are, but it's not like they're just sitting around. We're anxious about our case, but so are folks all over the state. It ain't all about us."

Luis' jaw tightened, but he didn't say anything in response. Donovan wished he would. He wished Luis would give the excuse for another argument or at least speak to him. He knew Luis had to be bothered by the breakup, even if the breakup had been his idea. There was no way he could be so sanguine about it now.

The last time they'd broken up, Luis hadn't shown any weakness in front of him. He wouldn't this time either. That just wasn't who Luis was. He might be burning up inside, but he wasn't about to let an enemy know he was hurting—certainly not the one who'd done the hurting in the first place. This was the guy who'd hidden an injury from not only Donovan but his colleagues and the entire ER staff at Emerson Hospital, even while getting dressed down for letting Donovan get hurt.

Kevin looked over at Donovan and then back at Luis. "Do your . . . other informants have anything to offer?"

Luis looked up at the ceiling. "You can just say the dead, Kevin. They're dead. There's only one that I've spoken to so far, and she's pretty traumatized by the whole thing. She already told us what she remembers about being catfished, and she knows where her body is. The rest of it, she doesn't know."

"You also haven't pressed." Donovan kicked himself for engaging like this. He held up his hands. "I'm not looking for a fight here. I'm just saying, you haven't tried to force the issue or push her out of her comfort zone. Or at least you hadn't the last time we spoke about it."

If looks could kill, Donovan would have been in pieces on the floor.

"That's correct, Donovan," Luis told him in an icy voice. "That's because I'm a civilized human being who knows how to behave around trauma victims. You don't retraumatize them if you can avoid it. That's not the best way to get them to remember, it's the best way to make sure they're screwed up for life. And since Jennifer's dead, she doesn't get to heal. Her injuries stay with her forever."

"You don't know that. Maybe contributing to her killer's capture and bringing him to justice is the only way she can move on." Donovan leaned toward Luis.

"You watch too much late-night television." Luis' lip curled. "There isn't some higher power blocking their access to the afterlife. It's only them, and no one knows why they're here. No one knows why. Lightfoot's still around for whatever reason, but Bundy's not."

"He's not?" Kevin jumped, just a little. "Really?"

"Nope. I did an interview down there for my book, while I was on medical leave. Plenty of ghosts in the death chamber, but not him." Luis scratched at his arm.

Donovan remembered that trip. Luis hadn't spoken much about it, but he'd needed a lot of human contact afterward. Seeing the ghosts of multiple executed killers would do it, he guessed.

Who would give Luis that kind of comfort now? Who would take care of him when the dead overwhelmed him? He liked to think of himself as completely independent, but Donovan knew the truth. Luis needed people. He needed someone to help keep his equilibrium, and without it, he'd spiral again.

"Jesus." Kevin let out a low whistle. "Well, maybe you can interview her about the other girls. Women. Sorry. Old habits die hard, I guess. You don't have to push her about things you think she can't or shouldn't handle. You're the closest thing we have to an expert in the psychology of the deceased, so I'll defer to you on that."

"Thanks." Luis made a face as though he'd just bitten into a lemon. "If we're lucky, I'll be able to avoid our ranger friend."

Donovan crumpled his paper in his hand. He hadn't meant to, but the merest mention of Ruben was enough to set him off. "I'd figure you'd be eager to see him." He tried to keep his voice neutral, but he couldn't keep a little growl from underneath it. "I'm sure it's easier now, without having to hide anything."

Kevin pinched the bridge of his nose. "This is why I drink," he muttered.

"Even if I were interested in sleeping with Ruben," Luis told Donovan slowly, in a voice that could have rivaled outer space for freezing temperatures, "you know I wouldn't have made him aware of the whole ghost thing. I wouldn't have told *you* about the ghost thing if you hadn't found the bandage Lightfoot gave me in my bathroom. And as romantic as I'm sure sex in the woods sounds, I'm not enthusiastic about poison ivy on my bits, thank you very much. You're obsessed with Ruben, Donovan. Not with me, but with Ruben. That's an issue for you. Get help." He got up from his seat and walked away, shaking his head.

Donovan watched him go.

Kevin just looked at Donovan and sighed. "He's right, you know."

"He's the one who cheated." Donovan scowled. Why was everyone acting like Donovan was the bad guy here? Even part of Donovan thought he'd been the bad guy. The guy who cheated was the bad guy, every time. Those were the rules.

"He really didn't. Sure, Ruben's been flirtatious, but we've done a pretty thorough background check on him. The guy's never been interested in men. But here you are obsessing over him, even though you and Luis have been apart for a while. Kind of makes you wonder, doesn't it?" He held Donovan's gaze just long enough to make sure Donovan didn't mistake his meaning, and then he turned back to his work.

Fortunately for Donovan, he wasn't left to contemplate Kevin's words for too long. That would have left him with a feeling far too close to guilt for comfort. He had plans for dinner with his father. At least Fred understood and wouldn't try to make him feel bad about confronting Luis.

He met Fred downtown, at a trendy bar. The place was kind of young and hip for Fred, not the kind of place Donovan would have ever associated with his father, and for a moment, he wondered if he was in the right place. Then he found his dad in a booth, a pretty blonde woman of about twenty-three by his side.

And a girl about the same age, with long, glossy black hair across from the blonde, in the same booth.

Donovan's heart sank. What was Fred thinking? He couldn't mean what Donovan thought he meant, could he? Fred had to be thinking of Donovan as his wingman, which was gross enough. He couldn't expect Donovan to actually show an interest in this woman.

He walked over to the booth, unable to move much faster than a slow shuffle. Fred grinned with delight, and both young women glowed when they turned to see Donovan. They *glowed*. Donovan hadn't seen that before, except maybe in science fiction movies.

"Donnie!" Fred gestured toward Donovan. "Katrina, Lucy, this is my son Donovan. He's a big shot detective with the state police. He works on huge crimes. Right now, he's working on his second serial killer investigation in a row!"

Katrina and Lucy both rounded their eyes and gasped.

"Serial killers!" gasped Lucy, who turned out to be the girl with the raven hair. Donovan couldn't think of her as anything but a girl. She looked like she was barely out of college. "How awful!"

"It can get a little grim." Donovan plastered a polite smile on his face, after a vicious glare at his father, and sat down in his place. A waiter showed up as if summoned, and Donovan ordered a beer and something random from the menu, then continued to address the women. "Someone's got to do it, and at least it's never boring. What do you ladies do?"

Lucy, as it turned out, worked in early

childhood education. Katrina, or Kate as she insisted, was an admin at a bank. Kate had met Fred through Tinder, and they'd really hit it off. Donovan thought he might be sick at the idea of his father having a Tinder account, although he guessed any other man his age had every right.

He observed his father closely during dinner. This was his third date with Kate, or so he said. Their body language was deeply sexual, to a point where Donovan had to look away. Even Lucy had to look away a few times. Donovan frowned to himself. Fred had been trying to get back together with Patricia for months, but he was sleeping with Kate. And he'd mentioned dating another woman, Donna, too. What in the hell was going on here?

And how could Fred possibly criticize Luis when he was philandering like this?

After everyone had finished their meals and Fred and Kate finished another two drinks between them, Katrina and Lucy got up to use the ladies' room.

Donovan had his chance now. He leaned in to his father. "Dad, what the hell are you thinking? You're seventy!"

"So? Katrina doesn't seem to mind." Fred gave a low, dirty laugh. "Age is just a number, especially with the right pharmaceuticals."

Donovan clutched at his stomach. "And I

thought you were trying to get back together with Mom."

"I am. She has to take me back. I'm her damn husband." Fred blinked at Donovan. "She doesn't have a choice here, Donnie. You know that."

Donovan took a deep breath. "She has a lot of choice, Dad. And don't you have another girlfriend? What was her name, Donna?"

"Donna's busy tonight." Fred shrugged and pulled out a wad of cash. "Look. I'm going to take Katrina back to my place. Why don't you go show Lucy what the Carey men can do, huh?"

Donovan pinched the bridge of his nose. He wished he hadn't driven in to work today. "One, I just dealt with a breakup. Two, she's got all the wrong equipment."

Fred narrowed his eyes and pointed a finger at Donovan. "No. That was a momentary lapse in judgment. There ain't no queers in the Carey family. Now you take Lucy home, show her a good time, and stop talking like you were ever in some kind of 'relationship' with that baboon." Fred looked up, and suddenly, he was all smiles again. "Hey, babe. What do you say we get out of here, huh?"

Katrina agreed, and the pair departed. Donovan just stared at the pile of cash his father had left.

Lucy leaned her head against Donovan's shoulder. "I wouldn't mind getting out of here too. It's been a long day."

Donovan sighed and signaled to the waiter. "I've only had one drink. I'll drive you home."

Lucy sat up straighter. "I'm sorry—your dad said . . ." She trailed off, blushing furiously.

"I'm sorry, Lucy. You seem lovely, and you're a beautiful woman. My dad hasn't accepted certain realities. I'm gayer than a whole Pride parade in San Francisco. He didn't warn me he was trying to set me up, and it's pretty clear he didn't warn you. I'll happily get you another drink, and I'll drive you home safely, but as for anything more intimate, I'm completely useless to you. I'm sorry."

Lucy bowed her head. Her hair concealed her face. "I'm sorry. This is so embarrassing."

"It's embarrassing to both of us," he told her, thinking about all of his father's insinuations about Luis' infidelity.

CHAPTER TWELVE

Luis looked over at Kevin. "Is it bad that I'm getting used to this place in the dark?"

Kevin shuddered. "Yes. It's very bad." He pulled his jacket closer to himself. "How many ghosts are there around here, anyway?" He jumped as a handful of leaves brushed his neck. "What was that?"

"Nature, Kevin. It was nature." Luis grinned, just a little, and glanced around. "There are six ghosts around us right now. They're all residual hauntings—they're just memories, really. They're not intelligent and we can't interact with them, but they'll amp up those goosebumps you feel on your skin."

Kevin side-eyed him. "Are they people though? I mean the ghosts you talk to, they're people. They're dead, but they still see things, feel things, do things. These 'residual' ghosts . . ."

Luis thought about it. "I don't know. I don't think so. The alternative is too awful to contemplate, don't you think?"

"What do you mean you don't know?" Kevin turned to face him.

"It's not like there's an official FBI manual on the afterlife and the people stuck in between, Kev. I'm figuring things out as I go along. I'm sure I could go looking for a real psychic, a professional, but the last thing I need is for it to get out that the Boston field office is dealing with psychics now. The stain from John Connolly is going to last for a very long time."

Kevin grunted, but he couldn't deny it. Instead, he stuffed his hands in his pockets. "So there's six ghosts around us right now."

"Yeah. Two gang victims reliving their murders over there." Luis pointed to the left, where the outline of two men having their throats cut played itself out in the brush in an endless transparent loop. "One suicide, up there." He pointed to the Ledge. "A legitimate suicide, this time. And three people from the days when people wore dresses down to their ankles—there, there, and there. Looks like one wandered themselves to death out here and the other two were killed."

"Jesus. And you just see this stuff everywhere you go." Kevin drew back. He hit the leaves again, and again he jumped.

Luis chuckled. "Only if whatever happened

left such a strong impression that it stained the land, and nothing ever overrode it. From what I've read, that doesn't happen all the time. It's hard to find information I'd call reliable, you know?" Luis had gone through a lot of books and even more websites. He could count the ones who'd used anything like scientific methods on one hand. "This place is more active than most, probably because there's been a lot of death here over a really long time." He rubbed at his jaw. "I'm sorry to have to involve you. I know it bugs you."

Kevin stepped away from the branch that kept scaring him. "Yeah, well, it might bug me, but it is what it is. I'm not leaving you alone to run around the woods with a serial killer loose here, you know?" He scanned the dark tree line. "Not that he's the only thing in these woods, but you know. Any sign of your friend yet?"

"No. Let me see if I can reach out to her." Luis closed his eyes and extended his thoughts. Jennifer wasn't always active, but if she was out and about, she should be able to hear him. He always felt weird about this kind of thing. If they wanted to talk to him, they'd come to him. People didn't often become ghosts through peaceful means. They'd suffered enough. If they wanted to talk, they could do so on their terms, not his.

He was a cop though, and as a cop, he had a

murder to solve. One of them was Jennifer's. He had a suspect, but he couldn't rush to judgment. He needed proof. Jennifer was, at this point, his only witness. He couldn't put her on the stand, but she could aim him in the right direction.

Jennifer appeared before him. "Agent." She smiled, and Kevin turned green. He couldn't see her. He wasn't looking right at her but at a point a little over her right shoulder. If the face he was making was any indication, he could smell her, and that wasn't fun. "Agent Luis. It's good to see you. I'm surprised you brought a friend."

"It turns out no one's comfortable with me running around in the woods while a serial killer's on the loose," he told her with a smile. "Especially not when he's got views about people who have enjoyed casual sex. Up until a few months ago, I was very much Mr. Right Now, and not Mr. Right. And who knows, maybe I will be again when I get through this latest breakup." He shrugged and looked away.

"I'm sorry." She put a freezing hand on his shoulder. "It was that pretty detective, wasn't it?"

Luis nodded. "Yeah. Yeah, it was. Turns out he has views about people who've enjoyed casual sex too. But we're not here to deal with that—he's my problem, not yours. You've dealt with enough of that, I think." He managed to give her a little smile.

The wind picked up, just a tiny bit, around them. "If he tries to hurt you because of it, I'll drop him into the quarry and he can find my body himself."

Luis blinked. She'd never threatened violence before. No one had ever threatened violence on his behalf before. "Thanks. I don't think he's likely to try anything though." The wind died down.

Kevin paled.

Luis took a deep breath. "Jennifer, we came out here tonight to ask you a few questions. And they're going to be hard questions to answer—hard in a kind of painful way. You went through something terrible, and it hurts to try to remember through that pain. We want to be able to narrow down a suspect, but we need more information. We don't have any living witnesses."

"Only a dead one." She bowed her head. "I'll try. I don't know if I can do anything, but I'll try. I can't remember his face. All I see is a big black void—like on television, when they edit out someone's face to protect their identity."

"That's good to know, actually." Luis repeated her words for Kevin. "Thank you for that. You mentioned you were upset about the lying—the catfishing—but you went on the date."

She nodded. Her edges flickered. Her appearance was as solid as any living person, but the distress caused a little bit of the simulation to unravel for a moment. "Yes. I didn't care that he was Hispanic. I only cared that he'd lied, and I guess that I bought his reasons. Because I was an idiot."

"Hey." Luis met her eyes. "I'd have bought the reasons he gave too, okay? There's a lot of racism out there, and people evolve different strategies to deal with it. His was sleazy, I just openly excluded white guys, but you're not an idiot for believing him. You are not at fault for what happened to you. He is. Did you have dinner together?"

"We did. We didn't drink. He paid, and he paid in cash." She clenched her hands into a fist. "No credit card, to see his name."

Luis repeated her words for Kevin, and then he managed half a grin. "No paper trail either. Do you remember which restaurant you met up at?"

Jennifer went out of focus for a second. "No. But I remember it served Korean food. I remember him complaining about kimchi and the smell." She came back into focus, and the smell of rotting meat got stronger. "I remember thinking that if I'd been looking for a boyfriend, I'd have ended the date because he would not stop bitching about it. But since it was just going to be a one-night thing, I kind of tuned him out and focused on his body."

"What can you tell me about his body?" Luis asked, after repeating for Kevin. "I know you can't remember his face. Can you remember anything about his body? His skin, his hair, any tattoos or scars?"

She went out of focus again, and this time it lasted for several seconds. "He had amazing abs," she said after a second. "And a tattoo of a lobster on his bicep. It was weird. It wasn't a scorpion, and he said he wasn't from here. He was from California or someplace like that. The tattoo looked fresh too. Not, like, still-scabbed-over fresh, but the ink was still bright and everything."

Luis repeated her words and then nodded. "So, within the past year. That's good, Jennifer. That's excellent. Did you take his car, when you left?"

She hung her head. "It was stupid of me. We should have taken separate cars."

"It would have felt weird, I'm sure. We haven't found your car yet, or else we would have known where you went for dinner. So taking separate cars wouldn't have helped," he emphasized, "and you are not at fault. Okay? This is not your fault. It's all on him. What do you remember about his car?"

She disappeared this time but came back within a few seconds. "He drove a truck. It was a pickup truck." She looked downright transparent now, and the stink of rotten meat was overpowering. "It had a logo on the side." She curled in on herself. "We had sex in the back."

Luis would probably not choose to have sex in the back of a pickup truck. He'd done it once or twice, in a pinch, but it wasn't the most comfortable place for the top or bottom. "Hey. It's okay, Jennifer. You're doing great. You've given us some awesome clues, a lot to work with. The divers should be here tomorrow, and with any luck, they'll find your remains. I'm going to show you a picture of something right now. It's not the suspect. It's not even the truck. Okay?"

Jennifer hesitated, and then she nodded. "Okay."

Luis flipped through pictures on his phone until he got to the Freetown State Forest logo, painted onto the hood of one of the ATVs they'd used. He showed it to Jennifer, stomach twisting. "Is this the logo?"

"Yes," she told him, in a voice no louder than a whisper.

"Thank you, Jennifer. The divers should be here tomorrow, like I told you. I'm going to be there until they pull the last set of remains from the bottom of that pool—I'll be right there with you. I promise."

She took his hand, again searing him with that odd burning-freezing feeling, and disappeared. This time, she took the smell of rotting meat with her. She was gone for now, but she'd left a mark on his hand.

Kevin peered at it under the light of his flashlight. "Yikes. How long do those usually last?"

"A few days. It's like a bad sunburn." Luis took a deep breath. "Let's head back."

They moved back down the trail toward the black SUV, going as quickly as they could in the dark.

Kevin didn't turn on the car's lights until they got onto the road, at which point he slumped in his seat. "I could so use a stiff drink right now."

"You and me both." Luis rested his head on the cool glass. Jennifer's last moments must have been awful.

"I thought you didn't drink?" Kevin glanced over at him.

"I don't. And I'm not going to. That doesn't mean I couldn't use a good stiff drink." He wished he could just go over to Donovan's place and crawl into his bed or find Donovan waiting at his house. He always craved some kind of human connection after contact with the dead, whether sex or just physical contact.

He had the right to go out and just fuck someone, to pick up some guy and screw his brains out, but he didn't want that. The thought made him nauseous. He wanted Donovan, but Donovan was long since out of reach.

Kevin went quiet for a moment. "Can I say something without overstepping?"

"Maybe." Luis closed his eyes. Maybe he could just sleep, for a little while. It felt wrong, when people were dying, but everything inside of him hurt.

Kevin chuckled. "I'm worried about you. You haven't been sleeping as much as you should. And you've lost weight, since things went south with Donovan." Luis opened his mouth to object, and Kevin held up a hand. "I'm not blaming you for what happened. Donovan was being a dick. And he was being weird about . . . everything, really. But you have got to take care of yourself. You don't win by running yourself into the ground."

Luis pouted, just a little. "I'm not trying to 'win.' I'm trying to solve the case, so I don't have to keep seeing and working with him." He slumped down in his seat. Kevin was trying to help. Maybe he should let him. "I miss him. It hurts to see him. And the accusation, after he promised he didn't care that I'd been sleeping around before, that hurts too. It's like, no matter what I do, I'll never stop being that kid who no one wanted. Who couldn't ever do anything well enough to be somebody's." He closed his eyes again. "It's fine, I'll get over it, but I just want to put this case in the rearview mirror and move on, you know? Both because this guy's got a massive body count I'd like to stop from growing and because I just want to start getting over all this, and having Donovan lose his shit is killing me."

Kevin made a soft little noise deep in his throat. "I get it. I'm here for you. For what it's worth, I'm real sorry about Donovan. I thought he was better than this."

"Me too." Luis straightened up. "At least we're wrong together. Okay, let's focus on the restaurant. Korean places in East Providence, right?"

Kevin gave him a tiny smile, and they changed topics. Luis almost felt like he could breathe again.

They found 110 bodies in the quarry pool.

They couldn't all be related to their current case. That would defy logic. The killer, whoever he might be, showed no sign of killing at such an epic pace. The quarry pool had been a popular dump site for people who had become inconvenient for a long time, and plenty of folks who'd been overcome by despair or who'd lost their battle with depression had disappeared beneath the ripples there.

Still, 110 seemed like an obscene number. As Donovan stood by the side of the pool and watched the divers pull body after body from the depths, his gorge rose. How had they missed these people? At what point had Donovan's own agency decided that, no, it just wasn't worth dredging the pond to find them? If someone had just taken the time to look when these victims had disappeared years ago—in some cases, decades—the cases could have been closed.

Budget considerations, said a voice in his mind. *Or likelihood of discovery.*

Donovan called bullshit on that particular voice in his head. He didn't believe it for a second. Waiting until the Feds got involved, and waiting until a secretly psychic FBI profiler made a huge stink about it, meant that instead of paying a little bit of overtime back in the 1980s they were shelling out for overtime for the dive team, overtime for the ME's office staff, paying overtime for DNA analysis, and losing out on time the lab could be spending on more recent cases that had a statute of limitations.

It was all such a waste, and it made him sad and angry at the same time. He looked up at the top of the Ledge and vowed not to go up to the top of it. He remembered the feeling he'd had up there, the urge to jump. It could only exacerbate what he felt right now.

He looked over to Luis. Luis was walking over to one corpse in particular, only just loaded onto a gurney by divers. She'd been in the water for a while, and even at this distance, Donovan had to struggle to contain his disgust. Corpses weren't pretty. Corpses that had been in water—"floaters," even if they weren't floating—were downright ghastly. Parts of the woman's skin had floated away. Her eyes were long gone, and her feet had skeletonized. What skin remained was mottled, but Luis saw something he recognized. He peered closer, somehow without gagging, and checked his tablet.

"Jennifer Bayless," he rasped, and showed Wong whatever was on his tablet.

Wong, being Wong, couldn't leave it alone, but even he had some sensitivity to the scene at hand. "We'll have to get DNA from the family to confirm, of course. The tattoo does give us a starting point, and we'll call them from the office." He wrote the tentative identification down on the victim's paperwork and attached it to her body bag, which his assistants zipped. "Did you know her?"

"Yeah." So this was the ghost Luis had been speaking to, or what was left of her. "Not well. I haven't been in New England that long. But we'd met a few times. She was a good woman. Smart. Brave." He lifted his head. "I'm glad we've got closure for her family, at least. Justice will take a little while longer."

Ruben spoke up. He was there, because he was always there, but he wore civilian clothes. He worked the night shift, so that only made sense. He wouldn't be in uniform in the middle of the day. "She can't have been that smart," he said, and stuffed his hands into his pockets. "I mean she wound up here, didn't she?"

Donovan would have expected Luis to absolutely light into Ruben, but he didn't. He just lifted his chin and met his eyes. There was real grief there. "That's entirely on her killer, Ruben," he said in a quiet, cool voice. "I'm pretty sure she didn't choose this."

Donovan frowned. Something was going on here. Luis wouldn't have hesitated to smack Ruben down if they were sleeping together. Why the reticence—maybe *reticence* was the wrong word. Why would Luis use that kind of phrasing? Why would Luis keep his cool like that?

Ruben was completely oblivious. Even if they were sleeping together, he still didn't know Luis the way Donovan did. "I saw on the news that this killer has been picking his dates from Tinder, right? If she wasn't the kind of skank that just goes off with random guys from Tinder, she wouldn't have wound up where she is now. She made that choice, not anyone else."

"Hm." Luis just shrugged, and that was so out of character Donovan wanted to scream. He opened his mouth to do precisely that, but Kevin stepped on his foot—hard.

"That's an interesting point of view." Luis continued, eyes on the next body being pulled out of the water. "I'm sure plenty of people share it. Me, I'm not religious. I've always been a big believer in personal freedom. If someone wants to enjoy their body and everyone involved is consenting, I don't see why it should be cause for alarm, and not a capital offense." He jerked his head toward the quarry pool once. "But plenty of people think different, and that sex should only happen inside a committed relationship. Or that it's fine for men to have sex when they want, but women should be more chaste about it. I'm not in a position to judge."

Ruben smiled and put a hand on Luis' shoulder. Donovan bit down on his lip, and almost through it, to keep from exploding. "Sure you are.

You must see a lot of this kind of stuff—girls putting themselves in harm's way, it's like a guy can't help himself."

Donovan shoved his hands into his pockets, so no one would see him balling them into fists. He found himself hyperaware of the media presence, just beyond the line of yellow tape. Everything was being filmed—everything. Donovan couldn't afford to look like the odd man out.

And whatever Kevin and Luis had up their sleeves with regard to Ruben, he couldn't afford to blow that up either. He was pissed about it, but he'd have their backs.

"I've heard that from a lot of guys. You know, I'm kind of immune." Luis let out a little laugh. It sounded so real, even Donovan had trouble recognizing it as false. "Wrong equipment for me, I'm afraid. I'm sure you understand."

"Absolutely." Ruben looked up and met Donovan's eyes. He gave a little smirk before standing just the tiniest bit closer to Luis. The little bastard was doing it on purpose.

When the divers finished, the team left the forest. Luis headed to the ME's office with Wong, which seemed like punishment enough for cheating, to be honest. Donovan had planned to head back to Framingham, but Kevin dropped a heavy hand on his shoulder. "I'd like for you to meet me at the Braintree Ninety-Nine. You can follow me there if you like."

Donovan scowled and fussed with the keys in his hand. He didn't feel like meeting with Kevin. He'd just watched 110 bodies get hoisted out of a quarry. The last thing he wanted was meat. "Can it wait?"

Kevin's expression was pleasant enough, but his eyes were hard. "Actually, no. It can't. Braintree is just as inconvenient for both of us."

Donovan sighed. He had the right to say no, but he didn't want Kevin telling his boss he'd been uncooperative. Plus, he wanted to know what that game Kevin and Luis had been playing with Ruben was all about. "Fine." He hopped into his car with ill grace and headed toward Braintree.

Kevin beat him there. Donovan heroically refrained from commenting about how much gas he must have burned in that behemoth SUV of his and slipped into the booth across from him. "So what's on your mind?"

Kevin gave him a thin smile and glanced at the menu. "Let's grab drinks for this. We're officially off the clock, right?"

"Sure." Donovan checked the menu and ordered a crappy draft beer. He wasn't in the mood to get lit, and they both still had to drive a little farther tonight. If Kevin was warning him in this subtle way that this was going to get hairy, he'd listen. They ordered meals as well, and then Donovan looked over at the man he considered to be a friend. "Seriously, Kevin, I've got to know what's on your mind. This whole thing is kind of weird."

"Yeah. Yeah, I know." Kevin sighed and held his head in his hands for a second. "I took Luis to Freetown last night. I wasn't comfortable letting him do his thing with a serial killer running around." He wiggled his fingers when he said "do his thing," indicating he meant talking to ghosts. "Someone had to keep an eye on him, you know?"

Donovan folded over, just a bit. It felt like he'd been punched. "That's not my job anymore," he said quietly. "He dumped me, remember?"

"He did. Of course, he dumped you because you kept accusing him of cheating. Which . . . I mean you're not that stupid." Kevin sat back and toyed with his napkin.

"Excuse me?" Donovan did a double take.

"Stupid. As in, your brain obviously has been taking leave of your body, on multiple occasions, and you've just been letting it happen for reasons of your own. Luis was drowning, getting back together with you was like a lifeline for him. Why in the hell would he start cheating?"

"That's not your business." Donovan licked

his lips. His heart thumped against his chest.

"Actually, it's a hundred percent my business. I seem to recall at some point, over the spring, some state trooper came along and pointed out that part of my job, as Luis' partner, was to have his back. He also pointed out that I'd been doing a shitty job of it at the time—and that was God's own truth.

"I'm Luis' partner. I know how much it takes out of him to do those ghost things. And I know I ain't the one he wants when he finishes. And you know damn well, he hasn't even looked at another guy since he got together with you. You *said* you didn't care about the way he ran his sex life before. You lied. Why?"

Donovan slammed his hand on the table. "I didn't lie, damn it." Other patrons turned to stare, but he pressed on. "He's the one who's out there whoring around right now—"

"With who, Wong? Give me a break. You know what he does when he's upset. He focuses on work to the exclusion of everything else. He's forgetting to eat and he's refusing to sleep. All he wants is to get this case over with so he doesn't have to see you anymore, Donovan. Because it *hurts him.*" Kevin curled his lip in apparent disgust. "You say you didn't lie. But you also said you didn't care about what he did or didn't do before you got together, when you clearly did. Which is it?"

Donovan took a deep breath. "I'm going to pretend you didn't call me a liar."

"Don't. Understand that I did call you a liar." Kevin's eyes burned into Donovan, through skin and bone and right into his soul. "That's because you lied, Donovan. Worse, you lied to a man you knew was vulnerable. You fed him a line of bullshit and you made him believe it, so it hurt even worse when you pulled the rug out from under him *yet again*. We both know you have no reason to accuse him of cheating. You were looking for an excuse."

"He's got no reason to be faithful either." Donovan snarled the words out. "And who the hell are you to come in here and start accusing *me* of things? You never gave a good goddamn about Luis until I got in your face about the way you treated him, and now you're his best friend? Screw you, buddy." He stood up and threw some cash onto the table. "I'm so out of here."

He fled the restaurant, walking until he got out the door and out of Kevin's line of sight. Then he broke into a run. He peeled out of the parking lot in a squealing of tires that would have had the traffic patrol officer hot on his heels, had he not been a state trooper himself.

He didn't stop until he was locked in his

own place in Framingham, shaking in his empty bed that still smelled vaguely of Luis.

CHAPTER THIRTEEN

Luis stared at the whiteboard. Some helpful soul, when designing the new and "improved" office space, had decided to make the "whiteboard" clear glass. Not only had the redesign rendered the words written on it illegible, it also made it a hazard when frustrated detectives smacked their hands, fists, or heads into it in frustration.

According to Kevin, they'd lost three in the months Luis had been out.

He cursed in Portuguese and grabbed a roll of craft paper. Kevin walked in just as he was taping it over the glass and let out an appreciative whistle. "Now there you go, showing us up with that southern ingenuity of yours." He slid into a chair and grinned. "Where did you find a roll of paper like that? I've been looking everywhere for something like that to put on the kids' easel at home."

Luis snorted. "You want the truth? Try the kiddie section of Michaels."

Kevin did a double take. "Are you for real? *You* went into a craft store, and into the kiddie section? Did someone pull a gun on you or something?"

"No, no one pulled a gun on me. I almost pulled a gun on this one absolute pig of a man who was just dawdling in the middle of the aisle, hemming and hawing and scratching at his belly like he had all the time in the freaking world, but I didn't." Luis blushed. "Mostly because Nick stopped me."

"You brought Donovan's nephew to the craft store?" Kevin frowned. "I'm confused. As of yesterday night, I thought you two had split."

And just like that, Luis' good mood evaporated. "Yeah," he said, straightening up. "We did."

"But you're still taking his cousin's kid out to the store?" Kevin leaned forward. "Does his family . . . know? Do they know you broke up, I mean? Or are you playing it cool for their sake?"

Luis tugged at his collar. "No, they're aware. Alicia already read Donovan the riot act once. I'm still coaching Nick's spring soccer team, which means I have to get used to calling it soccer. And that's just one more thing for him to hate me for, you know?"

Kevin glared at the door, like Donovan

might walk in at any moment. "He's not rational right now. I have no idea why, but he's not rational." He snapped his fingers. "Hey, do you think he could be under some kind of . . ." He waggled his fingers, the apparently universal sign for the supernatural.

Luis opened his mouth to object, but he closed it again. The image of purple haze sprang back to his mind, suffusing everything back up on that cliff. He was new to all of this spiritual crap. Who was he to say there wasn't an occult angle to it? He took a deep breath and glanced at the glass walls to their conference room, just in case they could be overheard. Then he leaned forward. "I don't think so, but don't take my word for it. I'm not an expert, not in the psychic junk anyway. This time around, Donovan has shown more than a few signs of jealousy he didn't have the first time, and I guess that kind of makes sense given our circumstances."

"No. It doesn't." Kevin raised an eyebrow and gave Luis a tired look. "Listen, if someone treated my daughter the way he's treating you—or my sons, for that matter—I'd leave them in the swamp, and no one would ever see them again. He's completely lost hold of all reason and logic. This doesn't make sense. I was talking to him about it all last night, and trust me, there was no sense to be found. Other people in the Ninety-Nine got more irrational just from their proximity to him."

Luis started to reply, and then he stopped himself. "Wait a minute, you confronted Donovan about our relationship?"

Kevin blushed. "Well, turnabout is fair play, isn't it? He came for me when I was treating you like crap."

Luis drew back. "I'm not sure what to say. I'm pretty sure I'm grateful. There's a big part of me that's creeped out by the idea of my work partner stepping into my breakups, but it's nice to know you care." Did Kevin care though? Or was he just getting involved because of the case?

His father's voice, banished for months, came back to him. *I told you none of it was real. Kevin just wants to get the job done, which is the right thing to do. He doesn't give a shit about you, and neither does anyone else.*

Luis imagined a nice thick metal door clanging shut on his father's cell. He could still hear the muffled sounds of negativity, but no specifics. It was all figurative, of course. His father couldn't reach out from his dump of a prison in Raiford to harass Luis in Boston. It was just how he saw all of his negative thoughts, his depression, and his self-loathing. Father Geoffrey had helped him to shut it out by visualizing the prison cell, and so far it had worked.

"Yeah, well. I haven't always been a great partner, but I can be taught." Kevin cleared his throat. "Do you think it could be something like possession? Or is he just an asshole?"

Luis tapped a pen on the glass. "My instinct is to say he's just being an asshole, letting that side of himself out. I was willing to cut him a lot of slack because he's not used to being able to date. A lot of things are going to be new and different for him, and we're going to have to get used to them. But there's a line, and he crossed it." He looked over at the stack of cases. He should be focusing on them, not on things with Donovan.

"Also," he continued, "I'm a psychologist by training. And a cop. We don't do occult. We do what we can see and smell and touch and punch and shoot."

"But you can see, and smell, and I'd guess touch and punch a ghost." Kevin drummed his fingertips on the glass tabletop. There was too much glass in this place. Someone was going to get hurt one of these days.

"I can. And that's the thing. All of these issues, they existed for Donovan. They weren't new, and his father started showing up right around the same time as we got this case. His father emphatically did not go to charm school, hates me like we're neighbors in Jerusalem, and has been dumping poison in his ear ever since he and I got together." Luis sat down and fussed with his coffee cup. "That's enough to say, 'It's not a ghost thing, it's an asshole factor carried on the Y chromosome, and there's nothing that can be done.' "

Kevin hissed and waved his hand. "Brutal, man."

"You've seen how Ruben behaves, haven't you? Do you really think I'm cheating with him?"

"Are you nuts?" Kevin held up a hand. "Don't answer that. Really. You're not his type. And while you weren't necessarily discriminating when you were single, you generally tried to stay away from psychopaths you met on the job."

"Right?" Luis sighed, and he tapped the stack of cases. "But there was one incident that sticks out. We went up onto the Ledge."

Kevin frowned and leaned forward. "Did he pull you back? Did something try to push you toward the edge?"

Luis sucked in his cheeks. "You know about the Ledge?"

Kevin moistened his lips. "Everyone likes a good ghost story." He looked down and away, ashamed. "I mean no one wants to live it, and having them peep in on you in the bathroom—"

"Lightfoot has boundary issues, man," Luis

muttered, slouching in his seat.

"He's a serial killer, Luis. He's dead, but he's still a serial killer. He's just mostly over those homicidal impulses. You can't expect him to play by the same rules as the rest of society, especially now that locked doors don't keep him out. Anyone with a passing interest in that kind of thing knows about the Ledge. What did you see up there?"

Luis bit his lip as he tried to think of a way to describe it. "It wasn't human. I know that much. Human spirits I can see, identify, and interact with. Sometimes I'd rather not, but I can. This was just . . . purple."

"It was just purpling around?" Kevin grimaced into his coffee. "What, like a giant plum?"

"No, more like . . . lines, maybe? Or a haze." He sighed. "It wasn't nice. I can tell you that, but I couldn't even wrap my head around it. I'm not an expert at this stuff. Human ghosts I just kind of go with the flow and assume psychology works the same on the dead as it does on the living. This has never been human."

Kevin scratched at his chin. "So, there's an old Native legend about a creature that lives in those woods. I think it's a Wampanoag story, but I could be mistaken. The creature is a pukwudgie, and it's not usually more than three feet tall. It's immensely powerful though, and it *hates* humans.

It doesn't like to interact with us directly. It likes to trick people, and one thing it likes to do is trick people into going off the trail." He swallowed. "Like off the cliff, off the trail."

Luis' heart froze in his chest. "I saw the purple, and I felt the bad . . . stuff. I knew enough to stay back. Donovan, though, he just kept going until I dragged him back. And, uh, we were getting a little snappish with each other before that." He fought against the panic that was rising in his throat. "Do you think that maybe the purple haze influenced him somehow? Is the purple thing the pukwudgie, or is it something else?"

"Next time you see him, see if you can see any indications of the purple whatever around him." Kevin shrugged. "I'm not sure what we can do about it if it's there, but it's a starting place. You're not going to give up on him that easily, are you?"

Luis hesitated. "I don't know. I mean, I love him, but I'm not sure I can trust him. I guess we'd have to see what happened. We don't know if he was influenced, anyway, and if he was, by how much. We can only go by his behavior. Which . . ."

"Yeah." Kevin tapped a pen against the side of his jaw. "Do you think Ruben might have been under the influence of the pukwudgie?"

"I don't know. We don't even know if what's

up there is really a pukwudgie." Luis rolled his shoulders. His suit jacket suddenly felt too tight. They didn't have pukwudgies in Brazil, and even if they did, Luis was pretty far removed from his indigenous heritage. He wasn't qualified to evaluate what Kevin had gotten right and wrong in his retelling of someone else's legend. Everything about this felt uncomfortable to him.

But he had seen the purple . . . stuff. Whatever it was. He couldn't discount the possibility that something was up there, influencing people. "And if Donovan and Ruben were both influenced by the purple thing, know what that means?"

"Um, we'd have a hell of a time proving Ruben innocent in court?" Kevin tilted his head to the side.

"I love that about you," Luis said, with a little smile. "You went straight to proving this guy innocent. But see, Donovan didn't get zapped by the purple whatever and become a ranting homicidal misogynist. He just became a jealous jerk, and if the purple whatever is partly responsible, it happened almost right away." He snapped his fingers. "It means Ruben isn't innocent—he can't be. Just like Donovan had those jealous tendencies, but the purple thing blew them up, the misogyny and the violence were in Ruben the entire time."

Kevin's shoulders slumped. "Which means Donovan is just being himself."

Luis chugged the rest of his coffee. "He's got a lot of insecurities apparently. And that's okay. Whether or not it's the purple crap, or whatever nonsense his father's been feeding him, or whether he just couldn't handle who I am and where I've been anymore, it's all just . . . it doesn't matter. What matters is that I don't need to sit there and patiently let him take it out on me and hope it blows over.

"I loved my mother. She was a great woman. And every time my dad used to lose his temper, she'd tell me afterwards, 'Oh, he's just going through a rough time right now. When we get settled in here, when we're secure, when he's more stable in his job and feels like a man again, he'll get better.' Then he killed her and stuffed her body into a barrel." Luis shrugged, eyes on the table. "Now, Donovan's never raised a hand to me. I have no reason to think he ever would. But I learned real young not to sit around and make excuses for guys. When they start treating you like dirt, the reasons why don't matter. If you take it, they'll know just how much you feel you're worth. And they'll treat you exactly like that, every time. Without fail." He held his head up.

"I am not going to sit there and *pray* for Donovan to get over whatever's going on in his head right now. I've done what I can to try to set his mind at ease. I love him, but he wants to be on his own and that's what he has to do."

Kevin put a hand over Luis'. "I'm sorry. I wish it could be different. With your mom, with Donovan—with everything."

Luis managed half a smile. "Me too. But it can't." He picked up the stack of cases. "How much do you want to bet we'll find a stack of cases just like this back in California?"

Donovan stayed away from the FBI offices again the day after his meeting with Kevin. He just didn't feel up to dealing with the interfering little bastard. Truth be told, he didn't feel up to dealing with Luis either. He didn't want to be around those eyes, so cold and standoffish. He didn't want to be around that voice, which should be full of laughter but was just flat or, worse, angry.

He didn't want to be around that body, that scent, those clothes, the endless cups of coffee, or the little bursts of affection to which Luis was sometimes prone. And he sure as hell didn't want to be anywhere near the overwhelming guilt that threatened to down him whenever he even thought the name Luis.

He did get a cold clinical email from Luis, cc'ing Kevin and SSA Holcombe, informing him that there had been a rash of similar crimes in California that ended two months before their series of crimes seemed to have started. The crimes lacked the degree of overkill seen in some of the Freetown murders, but this was not uncommon in killers who had time to let their urges escalate.

That was all.

He still believed Luis had been cheating, with Ruben at least, if not with other people. Why else would Ruben rub it in the way he had? Fred had been pretty sure Luis was stepping out on him, and if anyone knew about people stepping out on other people, it was Fred. But there was still that little piece of doubt, sawing away at Donovan's mind with all the patience of a saint.

Luis wasn't the kind of guy to hide things. He'd come right out and show Donovan—especially now that they were broken up. It wasn't like he'd have anything to lose, but he still kept resolutely insisting he'd been monogamous and treating this like a serious breakup. But if that was the case, why hadn't he tried harder to earn Donovan's trust?

He headed home, not entirely sure why he was getting status update emails about freaking

Ruben. Ruben wasn't a real suspect. He was just a guy who didn't know how to leave other people's boyfriends alone. Not that Luis didn't make his own choices, even if they were bad ones.

He set about boxing up some of Luis' things. They weren't getting back together, and Donovan needed to streamline some of the clutter in his house. Not that Luis had left much in the way of clutter, but it made him feel better if he pretended he was moving on.

He'd been at it for about an hour when Patricia let herself in.

Donovan cursed under his breath. He should have rethought giving her a key. "Hey, Mom." He turned and smiled at her, but Patricia wasn't in a smiling or affectionate mood.

She sniffed at the boxes. "Well, you don't let the grass grow under your feet, do you?"

Donovan sighed and rubbed at his face. Someday, he would miss his mother. He had to remind himself of that right now. "Mom, this is a personal matter. I'd appreciate it if you let me get through it in my own way."

"Only it isn't quite personal, is it?" Patricia sat down on the couch and looked up at him, eyes tight. "Luis made quite the place for himself in our family. And then you flew off the handle and kicked him to the curb."

Donovan punched the wall. "I think you've got a lot of nerve giving me grief for 'flying off the handle' about Luis' infidelity, when you kicked your husband out of the house for his. All I did was ask Luis to admit to what he'd done."

Patricia's face froze over. "Wow," she said after a moment. "I knew you'd been spending a lot of time with your father, and I thought he'd honor our agreement not to disparage the other parent with the children. The main difference here, Donovan, is that Luis was faithful to you, while your father is a lying, cheating sack of wind, who ran around so much he passed an STI not only to the department admin, who in turn passed it to almost everyone in his unit, but he passed it to his *wife and the mother of his children*. That would be me, the woman you're so cavalierly mouthing off to."

"Luis is no angel." Donovan ground his teeth together and tried to ignore the little part of him that wanted to agree with his mother.

"He's never made a secret of the life he led before he was with you. And neither did you. It wasn't a problem for you until you started spending more time with your father." She stood up. "I raised you to treat your partners well, Donovan. I did that in large part because your father was such a jackass. Instead, you're channeling Fred. What's he doing? Is he paying you to lash out at me? Is he drugging you?"

Donovan took a deep breath. His mother was a good woman and didn't deserve his fury. "He's not paying me and he's not drugging me. If anyone knows about philandering, it's him. He's doing me a kindness, and he's warning me."

"Oh, you think so? So he didn't sit there and try to fix you up with some kindergarten teacher?" Patricia marched into Donovan's kitchen and grabbed herself a beer. She didn't get one for Donovan.

"How do you even know about that?" Donovan scowled and reached for the fridge.

Patricia didn't move. "Beer is for grown-ups, Donovan, and you're acting like a juvenile. I found out about poor Lucy because she teaches kindergarten at little Nicky's school. She knows Alicia, and Alicia told me." She shook her head.

Donovan held up a hand. "Not that I was informed that it was a setup ahead of time," he told her slowly, "because I wasn't. And I wouldn't do that to someone, which I told her at the time. But even if I did have an actual date, with a man, I have the right to date. Luis broke up with me."

Patricia snorted. "Because you wouldn't stop accusing him of sleeping around."

"It's not like I could trust him." Donovan threw his hands into the air. "He didn't even try to make me trust him."

"Come off it, Donovan. Is there anything he could have done?" Patricia leaned against the refrigerator.

"He could have admitted to what he'd done. We could have tried again, with actual honesty this time."

Patricia laughed bitterly. "Now that's cute. You want 'honesty.' You're full of crap, Donnie. What you really want is for him to tell you what you want to hear, so he'll justify your shit."

Donovan brought himself up short. "Excuse me?" He could leave his forced dinner with Kevin, but he couldn't walk away from his own mother. For one thing, in a fight between Kevin and Patricia, he'd bet on Patricia every time. For another, they were in Donovan's house.

"You heard me." She pointed at him. "I know you, Donnie. You're afraid all this will go hideously, horribly wrong. And instead of just waiting for that to happen and dealing with it if and when it comes, you're making it happen on your terms, when you can control it. Your brain is telling you Luis can have any other guy in Boston, and he likely has, so what the hell is he doing with you, huh? So bam. He must be cheating. You're somehow just unable to see the way he doesn't want to step away from you, even for a second. You can't see the way he's always looking for you or looking to touch something of yours if you're not around."

"Oh, for crying out loud, Mom, he's not a teenage girl." Donovan turned away. They weren't talking about the same man. "You're talking about a guy who managed to shoot a suspect in the leg despite having been shot in the chest."

"Teenage girls have done more for the world than you'll ever understand, kiddo." Patricia snapped her fingers at him. "Can we not insult the strength of teenage girls or the masculinity of men who are perfectly okay with showing their feelings? He can communicate and kick ass, Donovan. And in telling you you'd gone too far, he did exactly that."

Donovan deflated. "Mom, you don't understand. There's just no way he could possibly not be cheating. I've tried to look at every other option, and it just doesn't work. You haven't seen the way that ranger guy acts around him."

"And how does he act around the ranger?"

"Normal," Donovan admitted. "But—"

"But nothing, Donovan. Your father's been leading you down the garden path. He has his reasons and maybe he does know what it's like to cheat. I know what it's like to be cheated on. You're not being cheated on. You're acting like every jealous buffoon we see when we get called in on a domestic."

Donovan stood up straighter. They didn't get called in when things were just a misunderstanding. "Mom . . ."

Patricia took a swig from her beer. "Donovan, your father has never liked Luis. And that's before he knew you were sleeping with him."

"Neither did you." Donovan had to point that out.

"You're not wrong, at least not for your college years. Since he came back—well, since that case ended, I'm very pleased to call him my friend. And in this case, he's right. I'd tell any friend of mine whose partner was acting like this to get out.

"Your father has an agenda, honey." Patricia's stance softened. "I know you love your dad. You don't always like your dad, but you do love him. And I know you want to do right by him. I'm not going to sit here and try to convince you to stay away from your father. But, Donovan, you're a detective now. Use those critical thinking skills you're supposed to have so many of, would you? He never liked Luis, he's a world-class homophobe, and he's got all the scruples of a hungry tomcat. If he can convince you Luis is a cheater, he's halfway to convincing you to go back to women."

Donovan groaned. "It doesn't work like that,

Mom."

"I know that. You know that. Your dad, though—well, some minds are downright congealed, they're so set in their ways, and you'll never fix them. He's probably already made some comments to that effect, am I right?"

Donovan looked away. "He might have said something," he muttered.

"Don't take my word for it. I won't be offended. You've already thrown away one of the best things in your life. But you keep your eyes open because, Donovan—he does not mean well. And you know this."

Patricia swallowed the rest of her beer down, and then she left Donovan's condo without another word. He'd had some difficult exchanges with her in his life, but never quite so bad. Seeing Patricia go to bat in such a way, and for Luis, made him want to choke. Hadn't she tried to get him suspended not so long ago?

People could change. Luis had convinced Donovan to come out to his family. While Donovan didn't trust Luis, he knew Luis wasn't the kind of guy to do that and then leave. Maybe his infidelity hadn't been planned. Maybe it had just been a momentary passion?

Maybe he hadn't been unfaithful at all. Maybe Patricia was right. Maybe Fred was trying—

in some kind of weird, underhanded way—to make Donovan straight. Maybe Donovan should have engaged his critical thinking skills before letting his father get into his head.

Should he really suspect his father of manipulating him that badly? Fred wasn't a head games guy. Fred was an action guy. Fred had been put on the bomb squad because he liked to take action a little too directly, and the bomb squad kept him away from the average citizen. That wasn't the kind of cop who played head games.

Then again, the way he'd behaved toward Patricia throughout their marriage proved he was more than capable of head games, when he needed to be. Luis, too, could pull a mean mindfuck when the situation called for it. He had a freaking master's degree in that stuff and had honed his craft at Quantico.

Donovan had no idea who he could trust at this point—if he could trust anyone at all.

CHAPTER FOURTEEN

SSA Holcombe quietly assigned the task of identifying the remains found underneath Assonet Ledge to the state police. She didn't give a reason, and she didn't have to. Donovan didn't fight it. Luis figured Donovan didn't want to be around him any more than Luis wanted him to be around. Holcombe didn't ask about it, and that was fine. He'd already had to spill way too much to Kevin. If he had to share his troubles with anyone else, he might as well write another book.

The work Donovan got stuck with was the shit work. It wasn't just boring. It was depressing. He was going to have to go to countless families and tell them a body had been found, one which "fit the description." There was no better way to phrase it, no gentle way to put it. Donovan was going to have to spend the next few weeks going door-to-door breaking hearts. At least he got to do something he was good at.

Furthermore, before he got the questionable

pleasure of giving people the worst day of their lives, he was going to have to work closer with Dr. Wong. Luis didn't envy him that one little bit. He didn't feel sorry for him either. If he did, he'd call Wong's brother and ask him to intervene. Instead, when Sgt. Wong called him from Boston and asked about Donovan's "harsh" attitude when dealing with his brother, Luis just laughed.

"I don't know, man. We split up. You could call him and ask him, but I somehow doubt his mood will get any better."

"I'm sorry to hear that. I heard he was hanging around that prick of a father of his. I'll make sure Neil knows it's okay to leave the gloves off."

Luis almost told the cop not to, but he held his tongue. The good sergeant had some issues with Fred, and right now, Luis couldn't say he didn't share them. If Donovan wanted to throw his lot in with his father, he was welcome to do so, but it wasn't Luis' responsibility to shield him from the consequences anymore. "Thanks, man. I appreciate it."

"Hey, listen. A bunch of us are having a barbecue in a couple of weeks, kind of a last blast for good weather before we have to dig in for snow and crap. Why don't you come join us? It's all cops, mostly Vice guys."

Luis' instincts were to decline, but he smiled. "I'd love to." Everyone kept telling him to get out and talk to people. Maybe he should try to actually do it. "Let me know where, when, and what I can bring."

"Awesome. See you then."

Kevin grinned at him from across the conference room. He didn't make a big deal of it, which was good since Luis was still feeling kind of unsteady about the whole thing. But as he sat down and got back to work, he found he really was looking forward to the barbecue. Of course, with his luck, he'd be in the middle of chasing Ruben down at that point, but whatever. It was nice to be included.

As far as Luis was concerned, Ruben was their guy. A series of similar murders had taken place around the park he'd worked at in California, just before he'd gotten the job in Massachusetts. He'd displayed the same misogynistic attitudes in front of Luis and in front of Kevin. He'd used the same ruse as the killer, while on Tinder, and he'd been way too conspicuous at the scenes when the bodies were fished out.

Luis was a psychologist. He didn't have a law background. Kevin did, and he insisted they'd need more to get a warrant. While this fact only increased Luis' irritation with this whole case, he appreciated the whole idea of cops needing to be more than "mostly sure" before they went and disrupted a guy's life—especially given law enforcement's track record with brown-skinned people. So he kept his mouth shut and only sought a warrant for Ruben's cell phone records instead.

"After all," he told Kevin and the judge, "those records could exonerate this guy, and there's no reason to bother him if we can just rule him out by virtue of his cell phone records." Luis managed to get all that out with a straight face. He was fairly proud of himself.

Kevin didn't call him on it until they were out the door, with the warrant in their hands. "Really? It's all about Ruben's convenience? You're so full of shit," he said, laughing all the way back to the car.

"I am. But you'll notice I didn't actually lie." Luis slid into the passenger seat and grinned as he buckled his belt. It felt good to relax a little and even to joke around. He didn't miss Donovan any less, but he had to move forward.

The phone provider was more than happy to give them Ruben's phone records. They were a lot more cooperative than they had been with any other suspect Luis had ever chased. Luis grumbled a little bit about that one, but he pretended they were just looking to help out because of the sheer number of dead women they had on their hands. It could be true, after all.

When Kevin chased him home at seven, he brought a sheaf of records with him. It wasn't like he had anything better to do tonight. He guessed he could always reactivate his Mixr account and go distract himself with someone else, but he didn't want to do that. He didn't feel the need to do that anymore, not like he used to. He had people who cared for him, even if Luis didn't understand why. He didn't need to go seek connection through fleeting hookups anymore.

That might change, but for now, he was doing okay.

When he pulled into his driveway, though, he found Patricia Carey sitting on the front porch.

He ran up the ancient wooden steps to meet her. "Are you okay?" he asked, putting a hand on her arm. "Is something wrong? Do you need help?"

Patricia just laughed and gave him a hug. "I'm fine, Luis. You're such a sweetheart. Do you mind if I come in?"

Luis hesitated. He still didn't have a lot of stuff in his condo. It wasn't a place he liked to show off. Still, if Patricia had fought traffic to come all this way, it must be important. "Of course." He opened the door and ushered her in. "Can I get you anything? I have water. And, um. I've got coffee."

"Coffee is fine, thanks." She smiled, and Luis bustled off into the kitchen to start up his Keurig. He couldn't think of a reason for Donovan's mother to be here, but he'd come to like Patricia. Whatever she needed, he'd do. Funny how times changed.

He brought out coffee for both of them, in his old mismatched mugs, and sat down on the couch. "So how've you been?" He turned to fully face her. "I know you were having some pest control issues the last time I saw you."

Patricia made a face, but she chuckled. "That's a good way of putting it. *Pest control.* You know, when I got married, you said your vows and that was it. Divorce was rare, although I don't think it was as rare as we thought it was. People just didn't talk about it. We took our vows seriously back then, at least I thought we did." She looked down and sighed. "Luis, I know you didn't cheat on Donovan."

"I wouldn't. I couldn't." Luis shook his head. "I loved him. I still do. And I get there's something going on there." He rubbed at the back of his neck. "I know there's nothing I could have done to make him trust me or believe me. I get that. I just—well. I just don't think it matters anymore."

"No." Patricia looked away. "I went over to talk to Donovan last night. This is all stemming from him hanging around with that father of his."

Luis sighed and bowed his head. "I think Fred has a lot to do with it. He's always had an issue with me, even before Donovan came out. And while I might not agree with his position, he has the right to his opinion. If all he does is complain and whatever, I don't have a lot of grounds to object, do I?"

Patricia's mouth hung open for a second. "But he's a naked racist!"

"He's not the first. He's not the last. Remind me to tell you about the neighbor who took potshots at me through the windows. That was fun. I'd laugh it off and chalk it up to Florida, but this was in Northern Virginia and the guy was a government contractor with security clearance. He claimed he thought I was 'breaking in.' All six times."

She turned her head away. "I didn't think that happened anymore."

"Well, it does." He shrugged and turned his coffee cup around in his hands. "Not much I can do about what's in people's heads or hearts, you know?"

"I suppose not. Although you and Donovan certainly changed mine." She sipped from her drink. "Luis, I think Donovan's father has some kind of plan. I think he's trying to convince Donovan he's straight."

"Good luck to him." Luis snorted. "I know it's . . . well, I know it's hard for Donovan." He put down his hands and held his hands up. "I'm not trying to judge. I'm just saying, it's not easy for him, being out in the first place. It's uncomfortable for him, like new shoes he's still breaking in. He'll get there, and he knows it's where he belongs. But Fred trying to push him at a woman is going to blow up in his face."

"It doesn't bother you?" Patricia put her cup down on Luis' makeshift coffee table.

"Nope." Luis chuckled. "If he was trying to fix him up with a guy from the bomb squad, I'd be a little put out, but Donovan's never had the slightest interest in women. He'd all but panic, back in college, every time he had to go back to Boston and pretend to 'strike out' all summer long."

"My poor baby." She covered her mouth.

"Hey." Luis put a hand on her shoulder and met her eyes. "You're trying, okay? You know better, you're doing better. That's the important thing. We can't change the past. None of us can."

Patricia took a deep breath. "You're right. I'm sorry. I'm not here to obsess about my own shortcomings. I'm concerned, I guess is the word. It's been enough for Fred to just kind of leave things alone. Now, I'm not a profiler. I'm not a detective. I do know Fred, and I know Donovan. Fred knows just what buttons to press, with Donnie, but what I can't understand is why. Why now? He's been pestering me to get back together, but he's been trying to drive a wedge between Donovan and you by alleging the exact same behavior he says he should be forgiven for."

Luis took a gulp from his coffee, more to hide his confusion than for any other reason. "I don't know Fred well," he said after a moment. "I'd say he's a garden-variety manipulator, but I think you're right. I think there's something going on here. And I don't know what." He rubbed at his face. "And I don't know how to find out. Donovan and I aren't speaking, Patricia. We're not on good terms, and he's been pretty hostile."

Patricia gave him a meaningful look, but her lips curved into a smile. "Is it all one-sided?"

"More or less." He cast his gaze up at the ceiling. "Okay. I might be letting myself react once in a while. I'm trying not to, but I'm just a man. I'm not a saint. And I feel like I'm allowed to get mad about some of this, you know?"

"Of course you are, honey." She stroked his curly hair. "I tried to talk some sense into him. I don't feel like I got through, but who knows? Maybe something penetrated that thick skull of his after I left. Don't give up on him, Luis. The two of you fought too hard to come together."

Luis looked down. "When a guy treats you like that, ma'am, and you allow it—well, he's just going to keep on doing it. Again and again."

Patricia straightened her back. "I think there's a lot to be said for that." She bit down on the inside of her cheek, and then she smiled at him. "I've been sitting here telling myself I can't actually divorce him, but let's be real. He's not trying to get me back, is he? He's telling me I don't have a choice."

Luis recoiled. "I'm not here to tell you how to live your life, but that's repugnant. You don't have to do anything."

She stood up. "Am I correct in assuming your refrigerator is bare?"

Luis blushed. "Look, I'm in the middle of a fairly high-profile murder case—"

Patricia laughed at him. "Men, I swear. Come on. Let me buy you dinner, as a thank-you for hearing me out—and for your good advice."

Luis hesitated. He didn't want Donovan to feel like Luis was alienating his mother from him. "Let me grab my coat," he said, and stood up. Anything between Donovan and his family was Donovan's issue now.

Donovan didn't enjoy making family notifications, but if he was going to avoid going into the FBI office, dealing with identification and notification seemed like the fairest option for him. Much to Donovan's good fortune, the hard part hadn't started yet. Wong hadn't gotten far enough along to send him off to deal with sobbing mothers and angry fathers.

Or worse—the people who had no one at all. They were dead, and technically, they were beyond caring, but Donovan always felt guilty when he couldn't track down some kind of family member to notify. Plus, his time with Luis had taught him plenty of the dead cared very much about what happened to their remains, thank you. Donovan might not be able to see or interact with them, but he could just imagine them sullenly judging his job performance.

At least this part of the game was just legwork, digging through years of missing persons reports and trying to match them to descriptions. They'd already dug out reports on women who'd gone on Tinder dates and never returned during the time frame in question, but not all the women had been reported missing and not all the bodies belonged to women.

Wong informed Donovan, bluntly, that he was going to be tied up with the bodies for a long time. "I can't tell you much yet, not that you'd listen. What I can tell you is that you can see an escalation in the level of violence your killer displays. I'll let you know when I have anything you can use to make an identification."

Donovan had a lot to think about, especially after his confrontation with Patricia yesterday. He'd have liked to talk things over with her, just because he didn't like having bad blood with her, but today wasn't going to be the day. Fred called at five asking for help with a problem, and Donovan couldn't just say no. It wasn't like any of Donovan's siblings were talking to their dad.

He headed into Boston a little later that night, and because he had time and apparent masochistic tendencies, he drove past Luis' place on his way. Luis' condo wasn't convenient, and Donovan knew he was only driving by to justify his own fears, but he still went. In a way, he couldn't not go.

He expected to find a car in the driveway that didn't belong there. It would be Ruben's, or maybe one of Luis' other partners'. Luis hadn't ever brought men home before, but maybe that had changed now that he'd been with Donovan. At least Donovan could say he'd had some impact on the guy.

When he slowed down and passed by Luis'

place, he didn't see an unfamiliar car in the driveway. He did see an unexpected car. His mother's white Ford sat just beside the old duplex, gleaming in the streetlight. Donovan pulled over and stared, letting other cars pass him by. Why would Patricia be at Luis' place? Was she conspiring with Luis?

He smacked his own cheek. What in God's name was wrong with him? This was his mother. Patricia loved him. Patricia had come to love Luis too, but she was Donovan's mother and she'd always done right by him. When Donovan came out to her, she swallowed down her own prejudices and biases to support him. When Donovan had been hurt, she'd pulled out every trick in her book to get back at the person she blamed for his injury.

Patricia wasn't *conspiring* against him, for crying out loud. The thought might as well have come from Fred's lips, and Donovan was ashamed of himself for thinking it.

He pulled back out onto the road. Maybe he should give more credence to her thoughts about Luis too.

He got to the place where his father had wanted to meet. Fred had chosen a neighborhood bar in Southie, one of those places that had been open since Prohibition ended and likely before that too. It was more Fred's style, even if Donovan privately thought it might not fit the neighborhood anymore. Gentrification was inevitable, and dives like this weren't part of the image modern South Boston wanted to present.

Fred was already here, of course. He sat in a half-sized booth, absentmindedly gnawing on a french fry. The seat across from him already had food and a beer in front of it, and Donovan hesitated. Had he gotten the date wrong? Was he supposed to be meeting someone in addition to Fred?

Maybe he'd get very lucky and not have to meet with Fred for long at all.

When Fred caught sight of Donovan from across the room though, he brightened and waved Donovan over. "Hey, Donnie, thanks for coming out. I ordered you a French dip sandwich and a beer. I remember how much you loved those when you were a kid, right?"

Donovan forced a smile. His mother's words from last night echoed in his brain. Fred hadn't cared about his food preferences when Donovan had been a kid, not French dips and not anything else. He didn't care about Donovan's preferences now either. Fred was absolutely up to something.

"It smells good," he lied. "How's it going?"

"It's been a day, Donnie. It's been a day." Fred took a giant swig from his beer. "I really appreciate you helping me out. It's not an easy thing to do, you know? To reach out and ask your son for a hand. I mean, I'm the father. I'm supposed to be the one giving help, not getting it. Right?"

Donovan managed a thin smile and took a bite of his sandwich. "Well, I haven't agreed to anything. I'm willing to hear you out, don't get me wrong, but I try not to agree to anything before I know what it is."

"Probably smart." Fred's laugh sounded a little forced, but Donovan decided not to think too much about that. "So I've gotten myself into a little bit of a jam. Um, do you remember that girl you met a few weeks ago? Kate?"

Donovan thought back. "The one with the friend? The one who's younger than I am?" He put his sandwich down, no longer quite so interested in food.

"That's her!" Fred chuckled and ate another fry. "Boy, she's something else. Legs for miles, tits for days, and let me tell you, she can do things with her mouth that are illegal in six states."

Donovan closed his eyes and pinched the bridge of his nose. "TMI, Dad. Way too much information. And totally wasted on me. I do remember her. She did seem nice. What about her? Did she get a speeding ticket? You already know I can't fix those." He took a swig of his beer.

"I wouldn't even ask. No, she didn't get a speeding ticket." Fred tugged at his collar. "She, ah. She got pregnant."

Donovan's beer shot out of his nose as he choked. "She got what?"

"Pregnant, Donnie. Pregnant. See, sometimes when a man touches a woman in a certain way, they make a baby together."

Donovan held up a hand. "Stop. Just stop. You're a thousand and six years old, Dad. And she's twelve!"

"She's twenty-three." Fred glowered, chewing on another fry. "I get that she's young, but she's not a child. I'm not that bad."

"When you're on the wrong side of seventy, yeah. You are that bad, Dad." Donovan's stomach threatened to revolt. "By the time this kid is her age, you'll be in your early nineties. They'll be bringing their partner to meet you in the old folks' home. Is that what you want? You want to miss out on meeting your grandkids because you died from being old as dirt before they were born? Is that it?"

Fred rolled his eyes. "Oh, come on, Donovan. You should have been an actor, with dramatics like that. Give me a break, would you? Besides, I've got a plan for that." He grinned up at Donovan, although his head was still bowed. "I'm going to know this kid. But he'll be my grandkid."

Donovan blinked. "I don't think you understand how this works, Dad."

"No, no. See, I can't even marry Kate, on account of me being already married myself." Donovan started laughing, but Fred ignored him and pressed on. "But see, I've got a son. And my son's not with anyone right now. And that son, well, he's free to marry her. He's old enough to be starting a family. Too old to be running around making bad decisions, experimenting with guys, whatever." Fred stared into Donovan's eyes.

Donovan stopped laughing. None of this was funny at all. "When did you find out Kate was pregnant?"

"About two months ago. She'd be almost three months along by now." Fred's shoulders lost that hunched look. "See, it's perfect. You get to be the fine upstanding Carey I always knew you were, the baby stays in the family, and everything goes on just the way it should."

Donovan searched for words, but he couldn't find them. "Weren't you seeing someone else though? What was her name, Donna?"

"You're good, son. Great memory for names. You'll go far." Fred bit into his sandwich and smiled. "Yeah, she doesn't know about Kate, but I can't think why she'd care, you know? It's not like you and Kate getting married affects her life at all."

Donovan's head spun. What kind of man just . . . came out with this kind of crap? "Dad, you get that I'm gay. Right?"

Fred sat up straight. All traces of joviality disappeared. Every inch of Fred was a cop now, and he was the cop who'd been transferred from crowd control because of his temper. "No. You are not 'gay.' There are no gays in this family. You're going to marry Kate, you're going to be a dad, and you're going to give my son plenty of little brothers and sisters to play with. Are we clear?"

That tone of voice had terrified Donovan as a child. He was a grown man now. "And Kate's just going along with this. She doesn't want to be with you, she wants to be with her boyfriend's gay son."

Fred's face turned bright red when Donovan referred to himself as gay, but he addressed Donovan's question. "She's more concerned with making sure she and the baby are taken care of than with who does the caretaking. Look, this is the perfect solution. It's the only solution."

Donovan huffed out a bitter little laugh. Fred clearly thought he was some kind of chess master here, moving pieces around the board to try to get control of his family again. Luis had been right, Kevin had been right, Patricia had been right, and Donovan had ignored them all.

"And what about Mom? You truly think

she's going to be okay with you just waltzing back on in, having made a baby with a woman young enough to be her granddaughter if she'd started young?"

Fred scoffed. "Would you stop worrying about that bitch? She's sure as hell not worried about you, okay? You're way too old to be such a mama's boy. She'll take me back because she has to. She's my wife, I pretty much own her. Keep that in mind when you and Kate tie the knot. You have to know who's boss with women, Donovan, otherwise they'll walk all over you."

Donovan rubbed at his face. When he pulled his hands away, he was still in the grungy bar with his father. All of this was still happening. "Look, Dad. Do you feel . . . any remorse at all for having basically engineered a breakup between me and Luis just so I'd be available to marry your mistress?"

Fred laughed. "No. Not even a little bit. Are you nuts?" He pointed a fry at Donovan. "You needed the intervention, Donnie. The way you two were carrying on, you'd think you were going to get married. Some of the guys were saying stuff, laughing behind my back because my son was a queer. I can't have that. I won't have that. No, this is the best thing for everyone. It's best for me, best for Kate, and best for you."

Donovan considered his options. He pulled out his wallet and threw a twenty down onto the table. Then he got up and walked away. Fred called after him, but Donovan ignored him.

How could Donovan have been fooled? His father hadn't been subtle about trying to split them up. Luis picked up on it right away, but Donovan had fallen for it all and asked for more. What the hell was wrong with him? Had he secretly wanted Luis to be cheating?

Was it because deep down, he didn't think he had much to offer Luis?

He drove back out to Framingham. Once again, he passed Luis' place, but both his and his mom's cars were gone again. Whatever it was they were doing, it must have been exciting. Something in Donovan's chest ached. He wished he could be with them, but he'd thrown Luis away and hadn't patched things up with his mother yet.

He pulled over and grabbed his phone. He was, in general, a proud man. He knew it. He could admit when he'd been wrong though, and he'd never been more wrong than he had been about Luis. He pulled up his messages and sent a simple text to Luis. *I'm sorry.*

Then he drove back to Framingham.

CHAPTER FIFTEEN

Luis sneaked out to Sudbury after his dinner with Patricia. It was late, but he wouldn't have gotten much sleep anyway. He wanted to put the time to productive use, instead of fussing and fretting about ways he could have saved his relationship.

He knew the way out to Lightfoot's inn without having to think about it by now. He supposed he should worry about that. Sudbury wasn't his stomping grounds. He shouldn't know how to get around this godforsaken old woodland in the dark, but he did. And when he got there, he found his friend waiting for him, a smirk on his face.

Lightfoot hadn't changed much since they'd met. Sometimes, he looked a little more solid than others, but the rope with which he'd been hanged still hung around his neck like a macabre cravat. "I didn't expect ye to come here tonight," Lightfoot greeted, saluting Luis with his bottle of high-end gin. It never seemed to run out, even though he drank from it all the time. "You're working a case, aren't ye?"

"I am." Luis grinned and sat next to the ghost. Cold radiated from Lightfoot's being, and the sickly glow that followed just about ruined Luis' night vision. He didn't care. "How've you been?"

"Oh, you know. I threw a good scare into a handful of kids here to have a bonfire party. They'll think twice before coming here with their red plastic cups." He sniffed. "Hooligans and rapscallions, the lot of them. If they have so much free time, they should be put out to work. They could be out on the farm, or in a mill. I can remember one of my wee brothers going off to the mines when he was ten, never mind these men of sixteen."

Luis grimaced. "Now probably isn't the time to mention child labor laws."

"Bah. Sets them up for nonsense and tomfoolery, it does. Just you watch, half of them will end up like me, dancing to the hangman's tune." Lightfoot laughed, a creaky and terrible sound. "But you didn't come out here to hear the trouble with the youth today. Something's troubling ye."

Luis bowed his head. "I know travel was an issue in your day. Have you ever been to

Freetown?"

Lightfoot raised his eyebrows. "That place? Bah. Nothing good ever comes out of anything in that part of the commonwealth. The Indians, they put a curse on it or something. Maybe not them, but there's all manner of evil, and it's not just ghosties like me either. You should stay clear of it."

Luis rubbed the back of his neck. "Wish I could. There's been some murder—"

"There's always some murder." Lightfoot rolled his eyes. "Always. Especially down there. At least I killed for money. Down there, they don't even know why."

"Good to know." Luis had to take a second to process Lightfoot's words. Had the place been that bad even two hundred years ago? "Um, listen. Something down there got kind of . . . it seems to be influencing people. I'm not sure how to describe it. I'm not sure it's ever been human."

Lightfoot nodded thoughtfully. "I think I've heard of something like that. I haven't been down there, but I do remember talking with a wise woman who had. She said it was old, older than anything she'd dealt with." He looked off into the distance for a moment. "It would find tendencies in people. So if they had any tendencies toward sadness, they would suddenly feel the whole and entire world had turned its back on them and the only thing left for them was death."

Luis sucked in his cheeks. "That explains the sudden, impulsive suicides."

"Aye. That's what I said. Have ye potatoes in your ears?" Lightfoot shook his head and took a swig from his bottle. "And if a person had tendencies toward jealousy, he would see his rivals under every shrub and bale of hay."

"And a man who already thought certain kinds of women should die . . ."

"Oh, he'd become a complete savage. He'd tear them limb from limb, I'd guess." Lightfoot screwed up his face with distaste and washed it away with more gin. "Say what you want about me, at least I had a decent motive. And I only killed men."

Luis tilted his head. "Is that true?"

"Ah, in my day it was a rare woman indeed who had money of her own. This thing—it's scary, sure. But the wise woman beat it. Other people can too. Usually what happens is the thing tries to get them to go against something more important to them than their jealousy, or their misogyny, or whatever. So the suicidal man we spoke about won't jump off the Ledge onto his sister if he loves his family and so forth."

Luis nodded, scratching at his chin. "That's good to know."

"You've already fought it off. I can see you." Lightfoot brushed a freezing hand over Luis' forehead. "I'd love to stay and chat, but you've a murderer to catch. And he will not stop until you stop him."

Luis took the hint and headed back to his car. He had some research to do. He didn't know where to start, but that had never stopped him before.

Luis got to work the next morning, still numb with shock and exhaustion. Kevin saw the look on his face and must have figured out something was wrong because he immediately pushed everything else aside. "What happened now?" He sat down and leaned in. "Did that jackass give you a hard time again? Because I'll go over and kick his ass myself."

Luis snorted and pulled out his phone. He showed Kevin his ex-boyfriend's two-word text and booted up his computer. He didn't say anything else about it, and he didn't feel he needed to. What else could there be to say? The words were right there in black and gray, on his screen.

"Is he fucking with you?" Kevin scratched his head. "I don't get it. I don't want to think he's the kind of guy who would just go around messing with someone for fun, but that makes more sense than sending a two-word message and leaving it at that." He passed Luis' phone back over to him. "I don't know. Did he want you to do something with it? Did he call? Carrier pigeons?"

Luis recoiled. "That's just unsanitary. No, that was it. I was with Patricia when the text came, and it didn't make any sense to her." He rubbed at his face, trying to wake himself up. "You know, it was so much easier last time. I mean, it sucked, don't get me wrong, but it was a clean break. Uncomplicated. Now it's weird."

Kevin slid back over to his computer. "Define *weird*. Oh, look, here's a message from Wong. We have IDs on four vics from outside of Massachusetts who've been confirmed as having dates with the fake profile."

"The fun never stops." Luis sighed and opened the message. "They're all pretty young too. God, that's disappointing. I was hoping at least some of them escaped, you know? Anyway, the last time we went our separate ways, and we didn't have contact. We didn't have any connections in common because we were graduating and everyone was going their separate ways. This time, I'm still friends with Donovan's mom. I'm still friends with his cousin. I'm still on deck to coach soccer, for crying out loud, and that's just weird. I shouldn't be that guy. I should be the one who just kind of disappears."

"Well, no." Kevin grabbed his keys. "Feel like a trip to Connecticut?"

"Anything to get out of Chelsea for a day, I guess." Luis grabbed his jacket and followed Kevin.

"And it's not that you 'should' be that guy but aren't. It's that you're used to being that guy, and it's hard to get used to a different narrative. You'll get there, believe me. In this case, his family knows he screwed up. They might not know why, but they came to love you as much as they love him. There's nothing wrong with that."

They headed out toward the parking lot as they spoke, and Luis sent a text to Agent Holcombe as they walked. "That's not okay though," he insisted. "It's good to get along with them, don't get me wrong. But I shouldn't alienate him from his family. I shouldn't come between them. That's just gross, you know?"

"If you say so. I think the way he's been behaving is pretty gross, if you ask me. Look, it's okay for them to love you. And if he's been acting in a way they can't support, then that's on him. It shouldn't interfere with the way they feel about you. You're off the hook, buddy. Just like he could be an absolute saint, and it shouldn't interfere with the way they felt about you if you were some scumbag. Right?"

"I guess." Luis managed a little smile. "It's a

weird way for me to look at it, but I can't exactly argue. So I'm just going to go ahead and accept it."

"Good man. You'll go far in life."

"Not if I start dropping my *Rs*." Luis smirked at Kevin and slid into the passenger seat of the giant black SUV.

"One of these days, you'll talk like a civilized man, Luis. We'll get there one of these days." Kevin chuckled.

Two Connecticut state troopers met them in Groton, the town where the first family on their list lived. Both were women, Junia Henriksson and Murphy Russell.

Russell was the younger and more outgoing of the pair. "I can't believe they were killed by a serial killer," she said, bowing her head. "Four girls all from around here, all from the same guy! Of course, you must see this all the time in your line of work."

Luis bit his lip. "Most of my work has been with serial killers, but I'll be the first to tell you this guy's the most prolific I've seen. He's bad news, and we have got to take him down fast."

"How did he fly under the radar so easily?" Henriksson wrapped her hands around her coffee cup. "I mean, from what you were telling me on the phone, it sounds like he's grabbed a woman every week. How does that just go unnoticed?"

"That's a damn fine question, ma'am." Kevin met her eyes. "He knew what he was doing. He knew exactly how to game the system. That does give us some clues as to who he is, now that we know he's out there, but it also means it took a while for folks to figure out he was out there to begin with. The FBI doesn't get involved unless certain criteria are met, and he made very sure no one knew he met them."

"The fake Tinder profile made it easy for him." Luis bit the inside of his cheek. He didn't want to give away too much. What if they were wrong? What if one of the Connecticut cops was in league with Ruben or, worse, was just his friend and shared information with him out of ignorance? "He could meet with people all over the place and convince them to cross state lines on their own, and no one would ever blink an eye. I think it's going to be a good idea to educate some folks sometime soon about the less stellar parts of online dating and the things to look out for." Luis' face got hot. "I've got a little experience in that area myself, so I guess I can help develop that plan if people want. But that's for a later date. Right now, what we're worrying about is talking to the families."

Murphy sighed and stood up. "Well, let's get this over with."

The family of Malena Peña lived not too far

from the coffee shop where Luis and Kevin met the two state police officers. They headed over to the house and formally notified her parents. The Peñas' grasp of English was incomplete to say the least, so it fell to Luis to do the bulk of the speaking and that made it even less fun than it had been before. He got through it though, and even got some good information from it. According to the Peñas, Malena wasn't often promiscuous but she did like to get a little wild when her life got to be too stressful to handle. And she had been under a lot of stress just before she disappeared.

The Peñas had suspected Malena was dead. While they grieved her loss now, they also took some comfort in the fact that they could stop wondering.

The second family, the father and stepmother of Osana Petrescu, lived in New London. Osana was the youngest of the killer's victims so far, clocking in at eighteen years and six months old, but she'd given her parents plenty to worry about in her few short years.

"Her Tinder profile told people she was twenty-four," her stepmother told them, wiping a tear away from her eye. "I don't know why, but I know she acted out a lot after her mother died. I tried to help her, but there was only so much I could do. Only so much anyone could do, I suppose, and this is what comes of it." She buried her face in her hands for a moment.

Luis cleared his throat and put a hand on her shoulder. "Ma'am," he told her, in as sympathetic a voice as he could, "the only person at fault for Osana's death is the man who killed her. No one else. She certainly did have her issues, but I don't know anyone who doesn't. That doesn't mean we deserve to be murdered for them. The person who's doing this likes to sit around and pass judgment on women, but he doesn't have that right. And we're going to do everything we can to stop him."

Luis tried not to judge the grieving parents for their choice of language. They didn't mean to act as if their daughter deserved her fate, or to justify her killer for that matter. Grieving people didn't often express themselves well. Maybe he was just taking the case too personally. He certainly had a right to—if he'd been a woman, instead of a man, his own past behavior would put him square in the killer's sights instead of just having his friends call him a "player."

The third family, the parents of Joanne Hughes, were too upset to have anything to offer. Apparently, they'd become estranged from their daughter after a fight over her "sinful lifestyle" and hadn't realized she was missing.

Family number four, the mother and aunts

of Ella Arrington, were angry. More than that, they were absolutely furious.

"How does it happen that a young woman gets reported missing and seven months go by before the FBI gets involved?" shouted the mother, red in the face. "Hell, this is even the first time we've heard from the Connecticut State Police. How in the hell are we supposed to take you seriously when you didn't give half a crap when she was just some missing girl?"

Russell cleared her throat. "Ma'am, I can't speak to how the original case was handled. I can tell you that if there were no initial signs of foul play and the lady in question was over eighteen, then it would be highly unusual for local PD to consult our agency or the FBI. Adults have a legal right to come and go as they please, ma'am."

"No, they certainly do not. I know my daughter better than anyone. She lived right here at home, with me, and I knew where she was every minute of every day. They knew how close we were, and they knew there was no way she'd just walk right out of here. She'd do it over my dead body!" The mother continued to rant, pointing a stubby finger at Russell as spittle flew from her mouth.

Luis caught a figure out of the corner of his eye, just before the familiar scent of rotting meat caught up with him. He glanced over in the direction from which it came, over near the stairs. A young woman stood there, waterlogged and battered. She beckoned to him and glanced at Ms. Arrington with wide, frightened eyes.

Luis glanced over at the mother, who paused to take a deep breath. "Ma'am," he interrupted smoothly. "I can see you're deeply grieved by what happened to your daughter. If you'd like, I can take a look through her room and see if I can find any clues as to how she fell into the path of this predator." He was laying it on thick, and he knew it, but he needed to get to see the ghost alone. "I'm a profiler by training, ma'am, and one of the things we do is see if the victims have anything in common that can lead us to their killer."

The mother stepped back, almost shocked. "Well, yes. Yes, of course."

Luis had to force himself to walk up the stairs with solemnity. Kevin headed up with him, and Luis didn't know if he was grateful or not.

Once they were in Ella's room, a pink-and-white confection of a space more suited for a six-year-old than anything else, Luis closed the door. He didn't want to have to breathe the dead air, but he didn't need Ms. Arrington listening in either. "Hi, Ella."

Her face brightened when he called her by name. It almost seemed to lose some of its battered look. "You know my name! I didn't think anyone did anymore." She looked down and toward the door. "Even they don't use it now. I'm just *she* to them."

"I'm so sorry for what happened to you, Ella." Luis reached out and took her hand, even though his stomach revolted at the stink. "No one should have to go through that."

"No." She looked down for a second. "But I'm not the only one. I fought him—I did. I fought as hard as I could, but he was a big guy and I never was. He hit me in the head, and I was stunned for a while." She sniffed. "I didn't want it, and I didn't want to go with him. I didn't want to go off the cliff. He threw me. He did. I didn't jump, I wasn't pushed, he picked me up and threw me."

"I believe you." Luis kept his voice soft and even. "You're right. You're not the only one. There were plenty of other people. I can prove that. What I need to be able to prove was who it was. I can't put you on the witness stand, Ella." He gave her hand a little squeeze and pretended Kevin wasn't covering his mouth and nose.

She stuck her lower lip out for a second. It dripped blood, which never hit the floor. "I know," she said in a small voice. Then she brightened up again. "He lost his necklace in the fight. It had a silver cross and a blue stone in the middle. You might find it on the trail—another spirit came along and kicked some dirt over it."

Luis frowned. "Why would they do that?"

"I don't know. The spirit—I don't know, I think it was because I wasn't dead for very long. It looked kind of purple, if that makes sense. But I could hear it laughing before it went away."

"We'll go check for it." Luis smiled. He knew—now—that the length of time she'd been dead had nothing to do with the purple haze's behavior. Ella had no way to know that though. "Thank you, Ella. You've been a huge help."

Ella's shape ebbed into an indistinct white light, and Luis couldn't feel her hand any longer. Instead, he felt only a pleasantly cool sense of peace and cleanliness, and then they were alone in the room. The stink of death disappeared.

Kevin stared. "Did she just move on?"

Luis paused for a moment. "Lord, I hope so. Come on, she gave us a good clue. Let's see if we can go find it."

Donovan didn't hear back from Luis after sending that text, but he didn't expect to. He'd burned his bridges, and it was best he didn't get his hopes up.

He did hear from his father five times before noon the next day though, and once from poor Kate.

He met up with Kate for lunch. He'd heard his father's side of the story. Taking Fred's word for Kate's side of the equation would be doing a huge disservice to her, not to mention to himself.

Kate was looking down at the table when he walked into the little restaurant downtown. And now that Donovan had a better idea of what was going on, he could see more than one sign of stress in her. She was pale, and not in a way that looked natural for her. Her nails were bitten down, but right now, it was her hair that she was chewing on.

She gave him a little smile that didn't reach her eyes. "So Fred says you'll make an honest woman of me?"

Donovan couldn't help it. He laughed. It wasn't the most appropriate response given the situation, but there wasn't anything else to be done right now. "Kate, something I really need for you to understand about Fred is that he's a liar. It's what he does. When he wants something, he does anything in his power to get it, and he doesn't give a rat's ass who he hurts in the process. I told him yesterday I would absolutely not be part of his little scheme, Kate, and I told him that because it wouldn't be fair to anyone involved. I'm so gay I crap glitter, okay?"

He'd come a long way in just a few months, from deep in the closet to announcing his sexuality to people he'd met once with terrible metaphors. He guessed he had Fred to thank for that. He'd have to send him a thank-you card.

Kate's eyes widened. "But Fred said—"

"Fred has a lot of issues with having a gay son. In fact, last night Fred confessed to deliberately engineering a split between me and my boyfriend so I'd be available to marry you, just because he didn't want a 'queer' in the family. Also, he didn't like my boyfriend, who was Brazilian, but that's a whole different ball of wax. Tying yourself to a man who's not going to be able to give you what you need is a punishment you definitely don't deserve, and it's not a dynamic your child should be seeing." Donovan sighed. "I'm sorry, Kate. I'm sorry you had to find out this way. I'm sorry you had to find out at all, because you seemed to be pretty happy with my dad."

Kate snorted and turned her head to the side. "Yeah, well, let's just say he was starting to send up a red flag or two. When he didn't make moves to divorce his wife faster after I told him I was pregnant, I started to get suspicious."

Donovan licked his lips. It wasn't his place to get involved with his father's personal life. It wasn't his place to drag his father's sins out into the light, especially not the ones that involved his mother. At the same time, there was a baby involved here, and Kate needed to know.

The satisfaction from sticking it to the man who'd manipulated him into giving up the love of his life was icing on the cake.

The server came over to take their orders. When they were gone, Donovan ran his hand through his hair. "Look, we're both on the clock. I like you, Kate, or at least what I know about you. I'd like to stay in touch and to be on at least friendly terms, but I don't think either one of us has time to be anything but blunt here. My mom isn't going to appreciate what I'm about to tell you, and it's really her story to tell, but it is what it is. A few years ago, my dad brought home an STI. To my mom. I think she was in denial about a lot of things, but she couldn't pretend anymore. They're both devout—in their own ways—but divorce was out of the question. There was fighting—oh, there was fighting. Long story short, Dad moved out until Mom could 'see things the right way.' Mom changed the locks. He's been trying to get me to convince her to take him back."

Her jaw fell. "He told me, right up until a couple of weeks ago, that we were going to be together."

Donovan managed a weak little smile.

"Well, it's like I told you. Fred's a liar. It's what he does. He doesn't want to have to deal with the division of assets, and he doesn't want to be seen as anything less than in control of his family. It's bad enough that Mom outranked him when he retired. I'm sorry, but he's never going to marry you. He's already been seeing someone else, a woman named Donna, on the side. She doesn't know about you. I'd guess my mom doesn't know about you yet."

Kate bowed her head. "I want to meet her."

Donovan's chest hurt. "Wait, what?"

Kate huffed out a little laugh. "Well, for one thing I have an apology to make. I knew he was married. I mean, he told me it was a bad marriage and he was trying to avoid confrontation because she was mentally unstable, but he really wanted to end it, and blah blah blah . . ."

Donovan pinched the bridge of his nose. "Yeah, sounds like Fred. But why would you want to meet my mom? It's going to be hard for her, hard for you . . . I mean, who benefits from that?"

"Well, we both do. Fred thinks he can get away with lying to us. All four of us—me, your mom, this Donna lady, and you. I mean, you broke up with your guy because of him." She shook her head. "I'm not judging. I obviously know how persuasive he can be."

Donovan's cheeks burned, but he laughed

anyway. "Right?"

"We all benefit because if we can sit down together and compare notes, I'm positive we'll figure out some other areas where he's screwed us over. Or other people he's hurt, that we can help." She gnawed on her hair again. "But to be honest, I also want to get her advice about the baby. I don't know her. All I know about her that's true is she sounds like a strong, smart lady. My own mom isn't much of a role model these days. I need to talk to someone with their head on straight."

Donovan bit his lip. "It's a lot to ask, you know?" He was being diplomatic. Expecting his mother to play nice and advise the woman carrying her philandering husband's baby was beyond unreasonable, especially when her own ability to have more children had been so cruelly robbed from her. But if anyone could give Kate some good advice, it would be Patricia.

"I can ask her," he said finally. "The worst she can do is say no." Their server approached, just as his phone went off.

He pulled it out to look at it. "Sorry, work calls." The message was from Kevin, of course, not Luis. He knew before the server arrived that he'd have to cut it short. "Listen, I'm going to have to ask you to wrap this up for me to go. I just got a call from work, and this is something that can't wait."

He scanned the text while the server set their burden down and went to retrieve a box. *Donovan - got clue about evidence at crime scene. Need all hands to find needle in haystack, asap.*

"You just turned white as a sheet. Is everything okay?" Kate tilted her head to the side.

Donovan debated keeping his silence but decided on speaking. "I'm working on a murder investigation, and I just got a call from the lead FBI investigator on the case. I need to go help with something, but it means seeing my ex again." He tried to take a deep breath, but his chest wouldn't expand enough. "I really hurt him. I was so unfair to him. Fred found all my insecurities and played them like a fiddle."

She smirked bitterly. "Isn't that what family's for?" Then she reached across the table and put her hand on his. "Listen, maybe it's another chance. Not necessarily to get back with him, but to get right with him. It's worth doing, you know?"

"I don't know if it's possible at this point. It's worth trying, at least." He managed a smile and paid for both meals when the server returned. "Look, if you don't hear from me in, say, three days, give me a call. This case is big and important and a little scary, but you're important too. I don't want you to feel like you're being shut out just because my dad is a prick, you know?"

Her smile was genuine this time. "Thanks, Donovan. I appreciate that. I really do."

Donovan took his lunch out to his Ford and ate while he drove. He dictated a text to Patricia, apologizing for his attitude and warning he was planning to call her. He'd behaved worst toward Luis, but he had amends to make with his mom too. There was no point in dawdling when he was making them, not if he hoped Patricia would help Kate.

He met up with Kevin and Luis in the parking lot where he and Luis had hidden out while Luis chatted with his little ghost friend. Alicia stood with them, and just after Donovan pulled in, Patricia pulled in from another direction. Donovan fought down a panicked, choking sensation in his throat. This wouldn't be an intervention. They would never try something like that on him, and they'd all written him off.

Alicia's cold, dismissive sniff and turn of her back proved it. So did the way Patricia immediately stepped between Donovan and Luis.

Luis just looked away. Donovan didn't get to look at his eyes for long, but he thought he saw a hint of real vulnerability there. Did that mean there was still a chance? No, it couldn't. There was no way.

Kevin cleared his throat. "So Luis got a tip

today, about an item belonging to a suspect in the murders." Kevin did make eye contact with Donovan, and he knew it had come from a ghost. "This person said the item had been taken from the suspect in a fight with a victim, and it may be hidden around here somewhere. This would have happened about seven months ago or thereabouts, so watch out for anything that might have had soil washed over it or debris kicked over it. Alicia, Patricia, thanks for agreeing to help."

Donovan almost objected to their having brought family into it, but the light bulb clicked on for him before he could embarrass himself. Alicia and Patricia were veteran cops. They knew how to gather evidence, how to document a find. They might not know Luis' source was dead, but they knew how to deal with the living-world side of things just fine.

They got to work. The struggle wouldn't have taken place very far off the trail because the suspect wouldn't have wanted to go anywhere with a poison ivy rash. The five of them spread out, using sticks to move brush and mud.

It wasn't a five-person job, not with such a limited space, and Donovan found himself moving ahead quickly. He would normally be much more attentive, but he felt like he was going to crawl out of his own skin. Had Luis missed his text? Would he be willing to talk? What would they say to each other? Was he still angry, or could he maybe forgive someday?

Donovan emerged from the trail well ahead of the others, but he soon realized he wasn't alone. A man, young from the looks of him and wearing a threadbare red hoodie, sat up near the top of the Ledge. He was folded in on himself, his face was snow white, and every once in a while, he pawed at his eyes.

The little hairs on the back of Donovan's neck stood up. "Call for backup!" he barked behind him, and raced for the trail to the top of the Ledge. Weird, otherworldly laughter surrounded him.

The young man on the Ledge stood up. His legs trembled underneath him. His knees buckled. "I don't want to do this," he said, in a voice that shook with fear.

"Then don't." Donovan could see the boy had limited control. His knees had buckled, but he still stood upright. His shirt had bunched around his armpits, like someone was holding him up, but no one stood near him.

"I don't have a choice!" the man screamed, but Donovan could barely hear him over the laughter in his own ears.

"There's always a choice." Donovan had no idea if the guy could hear him. The man struggled against an unseen force as he was dragged toward the Ledge.

That ledge terrified Donovan. He still remembered what it had been like to come to his senses after Luis tackled him, breaking him from the spirit's hold. Luis wouldn't do the same for him now. Even if he would, he couldn't. Luis was still on the ground, staring with his mouth round in horror.

The guy on the Ledge had no Luis. It was just him and whatever spirit was here. Donovan pushed himself forward and stretched, reaching for the young man.

It had to be Donovan's imagination. Real or not, he saw hands form in the fabric on the old red hoodie.

No. Donovan refused to let it end like this. He lunged and caught the stranger by the armpits. It couldn't have been a comfortable catch, and Donovan had a moment of vertigo as he landed belly-first on the ground.

Alicia and Luis made it up to the top of the Ledge about a minute later. Alicia, bless her, had some rope. Between them, they got it tied around Hoodie Guy and pulled him up, relieving the pressure on Donovan's aching hands.

Luis examined his hands, while Alicia bustled the man down the Ledge. "Looks like they hurt," he said, running his fingertips lightly over Donovan's swollen knuckles.

Donovan almost pretended it hadn't. "It was worth it," he said instead.

Luis gave him a small little smile. Then he gave him a hug. "I thought I was going to have a heart attack when you lunged for that guy." He turned to the empty space behind Donovan, eyes narrow. "Hands off."

Luis kept a hand on Donovan's back the whole rest of the way down the trail. Donovan had never felt safer.

CHAPTER SIXTEEN

Luis could see the spirt—he didn't think it was a pukwudgie, but he was hardly an expert in North American lore—following him and Donovan back down to the foot of the trail. A small part of him, a little tiny part at the back of his brain, wondered whose side the purple malignancy was on. It could have only had one motivation in hiding the stupid jewelry, and that was to make it possible for someone to tie the murder back to Ruben.

But Luis had seen the spirit grabbing that crying man in the hoodie. And he'd seen it going after Donovan too. He knew what it could do. He just didn't understand what it was, or why it was doing what it chose to do.

He didn't know if he cared either. He was a federal agent, not some kind of witch or shaman or new age guru. He wasn't even one of those ghosty jerks on TV, the guys he always hoped fell down the stairs after scaring the crap out of themselves in the dark. He wouldn't know how to begin clearing something like that out of a place like this, and he wasn't positive it was his job to figure it out.

Once upon a time, he'd have tried. He'd have almost certainly botched it too. He was learning to ask for help. He wasn't quite there yet. He hated doing it, and he was still convinced it would lead to misery and woe somewhere down the line, but he could learn to be part of a team. He'd gotten help from Patricia and Alicia only today, even though it meant the possibility they'd learn his deepest secret yet.

When they got to the bottom of the trail, Luis no longer felt the presence of the purple spirit. He took his hand away from Donovan, even though he wanted to leave it there forever. Even if they were still together, it would be unprofessional, and well, they weren't still together. Damn, it hurt to think about it.

Patricia held up the evidence bag when she saw them. "Got it, just like you said, Luis. I'm dying to know about the CI you heard from, but I'm sure you'll let us know when the time is right."

Luis smiled and ducked his head. He didn't want Donovan to feel bad or to get jealous about the praise his mom was aiming toward him.

But Donovan, surprisingly at this point in their relationship, just grinned. "Awesome job, Luis. Is it enough to nail someone?"

Oh, that was right. Donovan still didn't know Ruben was the main suspect. Oops. "I hope so," Luis told him, blushing under the praise. "The fact that we found a unique earring worn by Ella Arrington in the same location in the same layer should be at the very least enough to get us a very thorough search warrant, wouldn't you say?"

Alicia's eyes gleamed with malice, which Luis couldn't criticize. She'd only barely missed out on becoming one of Ruben's victims herself. "Yes, indeed. I'd like to see you nail him."

Kevin clapped his hands. "Me too. Let's get this warrant and make this happen."

They headed back to the parking lot. The guy in the hoodie was loaded into an ambulance, to be taken for psychiatric evaluation. He would benefit from some help, even if he wasn't suffering from what they thought he was. Luis made a mental note to peek in and see how the guy was doing, later on.

If nothing else, it would do the guy a world of good to know he hadn't hallucinated his experiences up there.

Alicia hopped into her car to head back to whatever she and SWAT had going on right now.

Patricia hugged Donovan and ruffled his dark, curly hair. "I was proud of you today. You saved a man's life, and that's not small."

Donovan blushed. "It is kind of my job, Ma," he demurred, scuffing the ground. "Protect and serve and all that."

Patricia snorted. "That's California, sweetheart. I'll give you a call later, sweetie. I've got my own police work I've got to get back to." She waved and hopped into her car, driving north.

Kevin stuffed his hands into his pockets and looked over at Luis and Donovan. "All right. Let's get this crap back up to Chelsea and enter it into evidence. If we can serve that warrant tonight, I'll be a happy man." He looked over at Donovan so casually Luis almost believed it was casual. "You coming with us or what?"

Luis held his breath. He didn't know what to wish for. Donovan was being normal right now—the good, kind, sweet man he'd fallen in love with. Luis didn't want to put anyone through another flipped switch of jealous rage.

"I think that's a good idea." Donovan set his stance. "I'll meet you up there, okay?"

"Sounds good." Luis slipped into Kevin's vehicle before he could slip into Donovan's, just out of pathetic need or old habits.

"So," Kevin said after a long moment. "How are you doing?"

Luis leaned his head against the cool window. "I'm doing. Dealing with spirits always takes a lot out of me, and that one is more draining than most."

"Maybe it feeds on angst, and it's gorging itself on you."

Luis flipped Kevin off, and they shared a chuckle. "It could be, for all I know. If I'm going to do this kind of stuff on the regular, I need to take better care of myself. But then when I talk like that, I feel like an old man, and then I get stubborn and do things like drink a whole pot of coffee and pull an all-nighter just to prove I can."

"Toxic masculinity in action. Can't show weakness, so I'll hurt myself to prove my strength—even though only dead people can see." Kevin snickered. "Ah, to be in my thirties again."

"Yeah, yeah. At least they don't have to subtitle me when we talk to the media." Luis grinned and slouched a little lower in his seat.

It took them all of two hours to get the warrant. This was a high-profile case, and the judge was more than understanding of the need to move quickly. He didn't just green-light anything they wanted, of course. Luis appreciated the fact that the judge wasn't just going to take their word for it. "So you're just going to go ahead and pin it on the Mexican guy?" he sniffed. "Seems a little too cut-and-dried if you ask me."

Luis smiled. "Thank you for that, sir. All

things considered, thank you for that. Let me walk you through our reasons for wanting to search Mr. Noguera's home." He outlined the unusual interest Ruben had taken in the crime scenes and the way Ruben had tried to insert himself into each scene. He described Ruben's behavior on a Tinder date with Alicia, described as a "Waltham policewoman," and how his alias on their Tinder date had matched the name used by the person who had dates with several victims. His face matched images of the man seen with several additional victims, his phone stopped pinging towers for an hour on either side of each murder for which time of death could be established, and there was a string of murders in California near his place of employment that was consistent with his MO.

"But really, sir, all of that is tied together by a piece of physical evidence. Today, I heard from a confidential informant. This guy isn't the most reliable, and he's moved on out of the area by now. He told me he'd seen a struggle between Mr. Noguera and one of the victims along the trail going to the Ledge. During the struggle, he said he saw Ms. Arrington remove a piece of jewelry worn by Mr. Noguera. We went out this afternoon and found the item where the CI said it would be—along with an earring, with hair visually consistent with Ms. Arrington's still attached."

The judge considered. Donovan presented him with printed photos of the necklace in question, on Ruben's body in a photo of him in California and on the ground in Freetown. "I'm a little skeptical that her hair would have lasted all this time, but with fifty-some-odd victims, it could be anyone's." He signed the warrant with a sigh. "Good luck, gentlemen."

They took Maxwell and his evidence team out to Fall River. Half of the team searched the ranger station in Freetown and half, including Luis, Kevin, and Donovan, searched Ruben's home.

Ruben was at home, of course. He was scheduled to be at Freetown, but for whatever reason, he'd called in sick. Sick was certainly an accurate way to describe Ruben, assuming everything Luis suspected about him was true.

"What the hell is this?" Ruben spluttered, throwing his hands in the air. "I thought we were buddies, man! I thought you had my back!"

"It's a search warrant, Ruben. And I'm pretty sure you know what it's for." Luis met his eyes coldly. It was such a relief to not have to play along or be nice anymore.

Ruben tilted his head. "Oh, come on, baby." He stepped forward. "Don't tell me mean old Donovan put thoughts in your head about me. He's always had a bias against me." He reached out to try to stroke Luis' face.

Donovan and Kevin both stepped forward to block him, but only Donovan spoke. "Actually, I had no idea until today that you were the prime suspect, buddy." He curled his lip. "But good job on trying to divide us. It even worked for a little while. Here's the thing. *Nothing* distracts Luis from a case. Not love. Not money. And sure as hell not some straight pretty boy flirting with him."

Luis got to enjoy the moment for a few seconds, his heart swelling. Then Ruben smirked, wound up, and punched Donovan square in the jaw. Donovan went down, hand pressed to his face, for just a second. It was long enough for Ruben to take off running.

Luis' instincts kicked in before his brain did. Someone was running, so Luis chased him. He hadn't done a good hard run since his injury during the spring. Sure, he'd passed all of his physical requirements, and he'd been working out as soon as he could do so without killing himself. This was different.

This time, there was energy, adrenaline. There was more than that. This suspect, this *prey*, had dared to hurt Donovan. And maybe they weren't together anymore, but Luis had decided a long time ago that the status of their relationship had little to do with the way he felt about Donovan.

Donovan was the man he loved, regardless of who either one of them was with. No one got to hurt the man he loved and get away with it.

Ruben, though, he knew the area. He was in fantastic shape and wasn't recovering from a life-threatening injury. Luis' only advantage here was going to be his rage, so he channeled every ounce of it into his feet.

It worked. Ruben barely got to the house next door before Luis got ahead of him, blocking his path. Ruben had two options—surrender or fight. He brought his fist back and swung for Luis' eye socket.

Luis dodged easily, blocking and deflecting to force Ruben into the ground. He didn't give Ruben the chance to get up. He wanted to. Oh, he wanted to. He wanted Ruben to get up and fight so he'd have the excuse to smash his face into oblivion, just as Ruben had done to Chloe Leifsson, who'd had to be ID'd by an old arm fracture. Her facial structure had been pulped, right to the very bone.

But Luis, much as he wanted the excuse, wouldn't have taken it. He wasn't Ruben. He dug his knee into the small of Ruben's back, yanked his hands behind him, and slapped his handcuffs on him tight enough that Ruben knew who was in charge. It wasn't likely to be a position Ruben was comfortable with, and Luis would have to be satisfied with that. "You have the right to remain silent. Anything you say can and will be used against you in a court of law."

Kevin jogged up beside him, Donovan hot on his heels. His jaw was already darkening into a bruise where Ruben had slugged him, but the blood had stopped.

"I'll take over from here, big guy," Kevin told him. He patted Luis on the back. "Let the techs take over from here. You go on home."

Donovan drove Luis home. Kevin had filled him in on Luis' day. Not only had Luis had to deal with the monster at the top of Assonet Ledge, he'd interacted with a ghost while doing parental notifications in Connecticut, and now, he'd gone and chased down Ruben Noguera. All Donovan had done was stand there and get hit.

Oh, and hold a guy over a fatal drop-off with nothing but his hands, which still hurt.

Luis glanced at Donovan's hands when they got into the car. "You should ice them."

Donovan jumped. He and Luis hadn't said much on the way back to the car. Donovan hadn't wanted to push him. He knew Luis could get tired when he had to deal with ghosts. "Huh?"

"Your hands. They're still swollen. You

want me to drive, so you don't have to hold the steering wheel?" Luis glanced over at him with those luscious dark eyes of his.

"Kevin would shoot me." Donovan shook his head. "I'll ice them later. I'll be fine. A couple of aches and pains will do me some good, you know? It'll remind me not to be an ass."

Luis snorted and looked out the window. "Dude, you literally saved a guy's life today. I think you're entitled to be a little bit assy." He held his thumb and forefinger up. "A tiny bit. Don't go overboard though."

Donovan grinned. God, he missed this, the easy banter. "Yeah, well, you took down a serial killer without ever pulling your gun. How's that for badass? I think you win, man."

Luis shook his head. "You're forgetting, Donovan. I could see what you were saving him from." He shuddered. "Trust me. You're the badass here."

Donovan licked his lips. He wanted to know, of course he did. The supernatural stuff was just one more area in which Donovan fell short though. Was it a great idea to open that can of worms when they were just getting a fragile peace back? "How bad was it? Like, demonic?" He swallowed. "I could hear laughter, but it was weird. It's hard to describe."

Luis closed his eyes. "Um, *weird* is a pretty good word for it. There isn't a word in any language I've heard. When I see spirits, they have a shape. This one is just . . . purple. And it's not good. It's not evil. It's so far outside any frame of reference we have, I don't know how to classify it. It's malevolent. It doesn't like us—but then it hid that evidence just so we'd be able to nail Ruben."

Donovan pondered that for a second, while his aching hands gripped the steering wheel. He wanted to reach out and hold Luis' hand, but he didn't dare. The scent of Luis was driving him insane. "Do you think it's something like why Lightfoot got involved with that killer in Sudbury?"

"What, tarnishing its legacy?" Luis opened his eyes and glanced at him.

"Er, maybe. Not exactly." He squirmed. "Like, okay. Hear me out. You ever get called to a domestic and the father's super controlling of everything his kids do, including the sons, but then wants the kids to 'stand up and be a man'?"

Luis wrinkled his nose. "Dude, I *lived* that domestic until my dad went to jail."

"Right? So, I think it's something like that. The thing—the malevolence—it doesn't like people. It wants them gone, but it wants them gone *its* way and not in whatever wackadoodle way

Ruben has going on."

"But it's not evil. It doesn't like humans, but let's be honest, as a species we kind of suck." He tapped his jaw, lost in thought. "But let's think about this for a second. We know it's a trickster-like figure, right? Hiding the jewelry, and then revealing it at just the right time. Tricking people into walking out over the Ledge, thinking they're on the trail."

"Right. But it also . . . I mean, that first time I went up there, I was *pissed*. I'd been a bit annoyed, but I was absolutely livid when I came down. You weren't affected though." Donovan couldn't stand to look at Luis now. "You were calm and cool."

Luis snorted. "Like hell."

"You weren't?" Donovan mopped a little piece of sweat from his temple. "What do you mean?"

"I mean, all my issues—my depression, my anxiety, all of it—it all kicked into overdrive up there. The main difference is that I could see the influence of the spirit." He gave a bitter little chuckle. "I never thought having depression or anxiety would be good things, but in essence, I'm already trained to block out those voices and those thoughts. I'm used to it. It doesn't always work, but when you can actually *see* the thoughts coming at you, it does give you an advantage in fighting them." He snickered. "That's why I knew to tackle you."

"Jesus." Donovan whistled. "Can I get something off my chest?" He refrained from adding *besides my shirt*. It would be inappropriate, and he didn't want to ruin the moment.

"I'm kind of a captive audience." Luis hunched his shoulders, just a little bit. He likely didn't even realize he was doing it. "Go for it."

Donovan hated that he was causing such a reaction in the man he adored. He didn't want Luis to have to resign himself to talking to him. "I know I sent you that text. I didn't know when we'd have the chance to speak in person, and I wanted to make sure I said it." He swallowed. "You know, just in case."

Luis bowed his head. After his injury, neither one of them took tomorrow for granted. "Yeah. Okay."

"I, um. I'm an idiot, in essence. My dad got someone pregnant, and he wanted me to marry the girl. So he figured he'd kill two birds with one stone—he'd magically get me to stop being gay by marrying me off to his girlfriend, and he'd deal with the little problem of having a newborn at seventy or whatever he is."

Luis widened his eyes so much Donovan could see the whites. "Jesus Christ. Is that normal for family stuff, or no?"

Donovan laughed. "No, Luis. It's not normal family stuff."

"I don't know these things, you know. I've got work and your family to go by, and that's the kind of shit that gets you put into a case file." Luis covered his mouth with one hand. "I'm sorry. I shouldn't be trashing your father to you. Whatever he did, he's still your father."

"For all I know at this point, he's half of South Boston's father. Trash away. The guy took every insecurity I have and played me like a harp. And I fell for it. He wasn't even subtle." Donovan swallowed hard. Luis wasn't moving, and Donovan didn't know if that was good or bad.

He pressed on. "The reason you couldn't convince me you were faithful was because I couldn't think of a single reason you should be. I mean, you're gorgeous, you're brilliant, and you're a complete badass. Add your psychic . . . whatever . . . to it, and it's like, the dude's not going to go from being with whoever, whenever, wherever, to being with just me. I mean what the hell was I bringing to the table, you know?

"And Dad took that clay and he made a damn solid pitcher out of it. I'm ashamed of how easy it was for him. I'm so sorry."

Luis stayed silent for a long few moments.

Donovan hardly dared to breathe. If he were Luis, he wouldn't forgive. Donovan had not only impugned his word, he'd done it at work, in such a way that it impinged on a case. He'd done it in such a way that the suspect picked up on it and used it against them.

"Donovan, I need you to understand something. What you brought to the table was you. Your love and your trust. It was the way you made me feel—safe, in a way I hadn't remembered I could feel until we were back together. I could be myself around you. I could relax around you. I could feel free to just *be*.

"When I was alone, yeah, I had a lot of one-night stands. I was convinced I couldn't have a loving monogamous relationship. Between my job and just me, the way I am, I was convinced it wasn't worth it. Those hookups were just there—for me—to fill a void and to give me the illusion of a sense of connection for a few hours."

Luis blinked a few times and toyed with his seat belt strap. "I didn't need to be with anyone else when we were together. I'm not saying everyone who has multiple partners does it for the same reasons I did, and it's so not my place to judge people who do that. I'm only speaking *for me*. And when we had what we did, one person was enough for me, and I never even briefly thought about anyone else. Not even for a threesome."

Luis cleared his throat. "But . . . I mean . . . now, I'm sitting here and wondering how much of that was a lie, you know? I didn't have your trust. And I appreciate you telling me what was really on your mind and what was really behind that jealousy stuff, but at the end of the day, you still didn't trust me. You didn't trust me enough to be faithful, and you didn't trust me enough to come to me and say, 'Look, Luis, here's what's on my mind. I'm feeling a little inadequate here, can we maybe talk through this?' "

Donovan squeezed the steering wheel. It was agony on his hands, but it cut through the shame and the need to cry. "Yeah. I hadn't thought about it quite like that, but you're right."

"I know this is going to give you hives or something, but give some thought to talking to Father Geoffrey. He's amazingly good at what he does, and I've never felt like a doofus sitting there and talking to him. And he's discreet. He won't go blabbing to your mom or your supervisor." Luis twisted in his seat so he could look directly at Donovan. "Even though we're not together, I still love you, Donovan. I want you to thrive. I want you to be happy. And if you're going to thrive and be happy, I think you need to work through some of these issues. With a counselor," he emphasized.

Donovan pouted. "Can't I just come and talk to you? You've got a master's degree in this stuff, right?"

Luis laughed. The way his face lit up would never fail to be beautiful to Donovan. "The guys I work with are locked up for a good long time and usually shackled to the floor for added security. But hey, if that's what you want, we can do that." He rubbed his hands together.

"Hm. Kinky." Donovan waggled his eyebrows, making Luis laugh even harder. It relieved some of the tension in the air, not all of it but enough.

Donovan didn't invite himself in when he dropped Luis off. Instead, he headed back to Framingham, where he called Patricia and told her everything. He told her everything Fred had told him, everything he'd talked about with Kate, and everything he and Luis had just discussed.

Patricia was silent for a few seconds after that. "For a second there, I was actually livid that you'd told that woman about what your father did to me." She took a deep breath. "But you know what? I have no cause to feel any shame about that. *He* did that to *me*. I was the victim, he made every choice.

"I'm glad you told her, Donovan. Under the circumstances, the poor dear deserves to know exactly who she's hitching her cart to. And oh, Donovan, I'm glad you've finally come to your senses—but I wish it didn't have to be so painful for you."

Donovan managed to laugh a little. "Well, you know, I am half a Carey. We don't learn unless you hammer things right into our heads there, you know?"

Her laugh was light and airy. "Well, you said it, not me. And since we're having all of our big confessions, I have a big announcement for you. I filed for divorce today."

Donovan gaped at the phone. "Congratulations, Mom. He'll flip out, but I'm proud of you. With all the stunts he's pulled, I think it's ridiculous that you should have to stay knitted to that man."

"And so do I." She sounded firmer, more sure of herself. "I'm proud of you for talking to Luis. He's a good man."

"He's the best. I know I ruined everything, but he really was the best thing to ever happen to me." Donovan wiped away tears. "And Dad might have shown me the way, but I took it."

"You did. But, Donovan, last time you both thought was forever too. And this time, you know. You know what's in your heads and in your hearts. You know where the other one is. And you know what you can do about it."

Donovan squared his shoulders. "It's a lot of rebuilding. I think I have to start with friendship first, Ma."

"More people should."

CHAPTER SEVENTEEN

By the time Luis got to work the next morning, Maxwell's team had done their thing. They'd collected an astounding six thousand pieces of evidence, some of which tied back to crimes in California. Some of the evidence would take time to analyze, like women's undergarments that needed to be tested for DNA and a pair of boots with human hair still stuck to the soles.

Other evidence more or less spoke for itself. The underwear that needed to go for testing could be compared with items known to be missing from victims' belongings—and already, in eighteen cases run while Luis was wasting time on sleep and wringing his hands over Donovan, they'd found a match.

Donovan came to the Chelsea office to help prepare the case. Luis relaxed as soon as he walked into the room. He knew he shouldn't. He knew he should keep his guard up and not get complacent about Donovan, but how was he supposed to do that? As the hours moved toward lunch and the list of trophies got longer, their chairs seemed to migrate toward one another almost of their own accord.

Luis stopped fighting it by nine.

They ordered pizza for lunch because they didn't want to waste time. The volume of evidence, like the sheer number of victims, was too great. Luis didn't mind not splitting up for the meal. He knew he had a tendency to lose himself in the work, and this way, he knew he'd eat.

Donovan frowned as they looked over the reports. "What I don't get," he said around a mouthful of pizza, "is why this guy keeps evidence lying around like this. I mean, would you look at all of this stuff? He kept dead women's underwear lying around in his house. His actual house. Who does that? We don't need the DNA to nail him for Masha Bertolini's death." He used his free hand to wave a folder. "Her underwear was found in his house—stashed, I should add, under his pillow and crusty with, er, 'deposits.' " He made a face at his pizza. "Why do we talk about this stuff while we're eating? That's just nasty."

Kevin snickered. "Perks of the job, I guess. I had six brothers. They still try to take all the food. I've got to be sneaky if I want to get my share. You do have a point though. These guys always want to hoard the evidence, and then we use it to nail them, and they're all 'Oh, wait, you can't touch that, it's my stuff!' Every time."

"Well, I mean the Fourth Amendment is a thing." Luis took a bite of his own pizza. The gross stuff didn't bother him anymore. He was more than used to it. "Think about it though. When's the last time either of you took down a criminal who believed anyone was going to bring him down?"

Kevin glanced at Donovan, who huffed out a little laugh. "You've got a point."

Luis nodded. "It's kind of chilling, if you think about it, because somewhere out there is a guy who's not keeping trophies." He paused and corrected himself. "A woman, actually, because women serial killers tend not to be motivated by sex and it's generally the sexual killers who keep trophies. It helps them to prolong the pleasure. When women kill, it's for a purpose. Aileen Wuornos, for example, at least believed she was killing in self-defense."

Kevin and Donovan stared at him. "Keep a cheery thought there, professor," Kevin said, and took a drink. "So they're getting off on the trophies." He pushed the files away from him and wiped his hands on his pants. "Well, that's just gross. I want to go steam clean my hands."

"Oh, come on, Kevin, you've seen this all

before. They don't all do it, just the ones who are killing for sexual gratification." Luis smirked into his pizza. He couldn't deny he got a kick out of their discomfort. He liked watching them squirm. He couldn't deny it, and he didn't want to.

"Dude. Gross." Kevin gave a full-body shudder. "They know it's going to be their downfall, but they keep doing it. Is that part of what gets them off?"

"Sometimes." Luis had to give that one some careful thought. "It's not much different than people who get off on public sex, for some of them. For most of them, they just don't think anyone's going to find them. They think of their victims as things, not people, so it's not something they even worry about. And of course you've got the few who just truly don't believe they're doing anything wrong, which is a whole different ball of wax."

Donovan swallowed the piece of pizza in his mouth. "You know, I understand that someone has to think about these things. I get that, I do, but really—is this the stuff floating around in your head over coffee?"

Luis laughed. "Sometimes. Sometimes, it's a lot more prosaic than that. Sometimes, I'm just thinking about my own basic needs. Hunger, sleep, sex, putting on pants and leaving the house, that kind of thing. And sometimes, I'm like, that guy at the door looks sketchy. I wonder what he's guilty of."

Both Kevin and Donovan nodded at that. Every cop had those moments. It was only natural, given their jobs.

"I had a guy tried, convicted, and sentenced for trying to bomb a mail truck the other day," Donovan said after a second. "Turns out his cat had escaped and was hiding under it, just to be a little shit."

"That's cats for you," Kevin chuckled. "What did you do?"

"Well, I helped him get the cat, of course. But the letter carrier came out, and *she* was pissed because she thought we were both deranged stalkers putting a tracking device on her car, and until we got the cat out, it was a huge mess." Donovan blushed. "I put her in touch with a detective from our abused persons unit. They should be able to help her with the stalking."

"I hope so." Luis had more to say about stalking, but his phone buzzed and interrupted him. "Hey," he said, glancing at the message. "Looks like they brought Ruben in for a visit. Along with his attorney. Isn't that exciting?" He looked up and glanced at Kevin and Donovan, although he didn't dare look too long at Donovan. He didn't want to risk making a *thing* about Ruben.

"Awesome," Donovan said, and leaned back. "Let them stew. I happen to like pizza." He gave the two federal agents a sheepish look. "I have to admit I don't have a lot of questions for him. I was a little blindsided by him being a suspect. When were you guys going to let me know about that?"

Luis tugged at his collar. "Er, I don't know."

Kevin cleared his throat. "That was my suggestion, not Luis'. You weren't with us when we started to suspect him, and to be honest, you weren't exactly being your most rational self. So I suggested we keep quiet about it until we had more evidence."

Luis' lungs filled with guilt. He hated keeping secrets from Donovan, but he hadn't felt he had much choice. "I'm sorry. It's just—you were so angry about him, and if he wasn't our suspect, he'd stop cooperating if you said anything. And if he was . . ."

"My big mouth would make him destroy evidence and go to ground." Donovan hung his head sheepishly. "I should never have put you in that position. I'm so sorry."

Luis hesitated. It was too soon for forgiveness, too soon for anything like it. His chest hurt to see Donovan so low. "Hey, it's okay. We got him, and I think Ruben was a small part of the problem." He put a hand on Donovan's and gave a squeeze. Maybe it was early for forgiveness, but it wasn't too early for support.

And maybe Luis didn't want to put a timetable on anything, anyway.

Despite their bluster about making Ruben and the lawyer wait, none of the trio had any intention of doing so for long. Pizza would keep, overnight if need be. Whatever Ruben had to say, or whatever cooperation he intended to offer, might not.

Luis led the way into the interrogation room. Ruben was one of very few people who looked good in orange, and even the shackles didn't do much to diminish his appeal. Luis couldn't help but sigh as he took his seat across the table from the park ranger. "I truly didn't want it to be you, Ruben," he said, folding his hands together. "I mean I was rooting for you."

Ruben, whose hands were shackled to a bar under the table, spread them as wide as he could. "Sorry to disappoint, man."

His lawyer, a short pudgy man with balding gray hair, gave Ruben a pissy look. "You're not supposed to say things like that until we've seen what they're willing to concede."

Ruben snorted while Luis exchanged glances with the other investigators. Was Ruben confessing?

"Come on, Hershey. They've got me dead to rights, and I know it. They don't even have to do the DNA on some of my more personal keepsakes." He grinned, toothy and bright and soulless. "I am what I am. And they know it. Right now, all I give a crap about is not getting the chair."

Hershey cleared his throat and tapped a file folder. "Mr. Noguera is prepared to make a full and detailed confession in exchange for not facing the death penalty for those crimes committed in California."

"And Utah." Ruben winked at Luis.

Hershey recoiled and gave his client a look of shock. "For real? Utah? You haven't even been charged with crimes in Utah."

Ruben shrugged, jangling his chains. "I will be, when it all comes out. I don't care where I serve my time. Considering everything, I expect it'll be in Colorado. That's where Supermax is, right? I don't even care if I get shanked in there my first day. I'm not going to lie down and let the damn state do it. Not when I don't feel like I did anything wrong."

Luis looked at his friends. His stomach should have turned at Ruben's last sentence. Kevin's lips were curling, and Donovan looked downright green around the gills, but Luis had heard it a million times before. He just accepted it now, part of the *I'm a creepy killer* package like the trophies and the unsavory personal habits. "We're not prosecutors. But I will reach out to the prosecutors myself and request that the death penalty be taken out of the equation. Assuming that all of your crimes remain in federal jurisdiction, which I think likely, I'll double down on my request that you not face capital punishment."

Hershey moved his chair aside, a little bit away from Ruben. Luis didn't blame him. "I've included language in the confession that declares it to be null and void if the death penalty is included in any way, as well as if he should choose to make any attempt at falsehood. I know we'd like to avoid a lengthy trial, and I suspect you'd prefer to avoid the same."

"We care about justice for the victims," Donovan told Hershey. "I'm not sure a long trial would serve justice." His hands, underneath the table, were balled into fists.

And Ruben began his story. He'd grown up in Northern California, not much different from any other kid until his father died. His mother had done what she could to keep food on the table, but it wasn't enough. So his sister said she'd get a job. She started bringing money home, but she wouldn't tell her family where or how she got it. And she came home bruised or bleeding at least once a week.

They found her in a ditch with her throat cut a few months later. Police said she'd been "hooking." Young Ruben hadn't known what that meant, only that it meant the police weren't going to do anything to try to find her killer. Mama wouldn't even claim her body. "She brought it on herself," she said, as they walked away from the medical examiner's office. "She deserved it."

As Ruben got older, he understood. And he took that early lesson to heart. He didn't hurt good girls—women who were well behaved, who respected their bodies and their families. Women who whored around, though—they deserved everything they got, and no one was going to care.

His first kill came during an internship at Bryce Canyon National Park in Utah. A pretty girl had come up to him and invited him out, but once she got him alone, she told him it would be fifty bucks if he wanted to get off. He broke her neck, right then and there, and took all of her cash before tossing her body into a ravine.

A guy came around to the park a few days later. Ruben thought he was her pimp. He told the guy she'd gotten into a car with some guy and driven east. Then he described some guy who'd used an ethnic slur toward him, even going so far as to give the guy's license plate.

It was so easy, so goddamn easy.

Once he got back to California, and his first real job, he picked up where he'd left off. He got a Tinder profile and started trolling for dates. He didn't kill a lot at first, maybe once a month. As time went on, he got more comfortable with it. Just as he'd learned as a boy, no one cared. He could up his count without fear.

When he found out he was being laid off, he got a little nervous. His job gave him plenty of room to play with his victims, and to dispose of them. Half of them were picked clean by vultures before anyone knew they were missing. When the job in Freetown came through, he almost did a little dance.

Not only was it even more secluded than his California job, it came with a reputation for being haunted already. It was perfect.

"You got sloppy." Luis could view it clinically here, in this bland and boring interrogation room. "I don't want to seem like I'm provoking you or anything, but you got sloppy. You left that one girl floating, and that's what brought you down." It wasn't the whole truth, but Luis couldn't very well point out the ghost who'd helped.

Ruben shrugged again. How much of his apathy was an act, and how much was genuine? "I didn't think anyone would care. Again, these aren't people. They're whores. No one cares about them. No one's going to miss them. I mean, it's basically what they're for, right?"

Donovan ground his teeth. "It's not what they're for, Ruben. They were human beings, with friends and families who loved them. I've spent my week talking with those friends and families. But it's not worth trying to convince you. Enjoy Colorado. I hear it's a survivalist's paradise up there."

Donovan walked out, and Ruben chuckled. "I like him. He's got so much anger in him. It's fun to wind him up. The laughing guy likes him too."

Kevin wrinkled his nose. "The laughing guy?"

Luis sighed and rolled his eyes, but his insides froze. "It's a local legend around Freetown. They say it lives around the Ledge and laughs at people. He's using it to cop an insanity defense." He stood up and shook Hershey's hand. "Thank you very much, Mr. Hershey. I'll run this by the prosecutor, but I can't see why they wouldn't accept it."

He almost ran from the room. Why would Ruben bring up the laughter?

Donovan paced outside the interrogation room until Luis and Kevin left it. "I'm sorry I freaked. I said I wasn't going to do that again, and then I went and did exactly that, didn't I?" He hung his head, unable to look either of them in the eye. "I really shouldn't work cases like this anymore." What he shouldn't be doing anymore was working cases with Luis. That was his real poison, and he knew it. He was so turned around about Ruben he couldn't govern his temper.

"Did you walk out in a jealous fit, or did you walk out because a very bad man said something astonishingly shitty?" Luis put his hand on Donovan's shoulder.

"Well, it was shitty!" Donovan winced at his own volume. "I mean, did you hear him? It was disgusting! He should be ashamed. Everyone should be ashamed, for crying out loud."

"I don't know about everyone." Kevin jerked his head toward the hallway, and all three of them started walking. "I don't think serial killers feel a whole lot of shame, you know? But it's normal to be disgusted by people who see women who enjoy sex as less than human. And I don't have a problem with you saying something. Do you?" he asked Luis, looking over at their resident profiler.

Luis didn't miss a beat. "Not even a little bit."

Kevin grinned. "See, you work a pretty wide variety of crimes, and Massachusetts doesn't get a whole lot of serial killers. This guy, he's new to you. You reacted to him because he's disgusting, and damn it, he had to know he was disgusting. Whereas you've got the other extreme, he's all like *serial killer, yawn* because that's all he does."

Luis snickered as they headed back up to their bull pen. "I wouldn't go quite that far. But, yes, I'm a little more used to them than most people are. It's more like *Oh good, here's the standard serial killer self-justification list, let's move it along now*. And, Kev, you're somewhere in between the two."

"But he did let something slip." Kevin wagged a finger. "Which he wouldn't have done if he hadn't had the chance to 'wind Donovan up.' His words, by the way. He was hearing that laughing thing."

Donovan licked his lips. "Wait a minute. He could hear it too? The purple spirit?"

"It's purple now? Wait a minute, is this monster like appropriating the bi flag or something?" Kevin folded his arms over his chest. "We might want to have words, now." Then he shook his head. "In all seriousness, we talked a bit about the purple thing, but what is it? Could it have caused Ruben to act the way he did?"

Luis shook his head. "Nope. No way. It

seems to amplify emotions, but it doesn't cause them. Someone who was happy and well-adjusted would have no problem at all. Whereas someone who wants to hurt women he perceives as promiscuous . . ."

"Right." Donovan gulped. "So—wait, you think the Purple Menace might have 'enhanced' my responses to Ruben? Or my dad?"

Luis opened the door to the conference room they were using. "Anything's possible, I guess."

"Because the insecurities are mine. I'm not hiding that. I just—I mean, I'm not usually that easily taken in. And both my dad and Ruben pulled it off." Donovan scratched at his arm.

Luis sighed and opened up his computer. "Whatever it is, it's old and not nice. I don't know what it's capable of. I'm not your magical spirit guide, I'm a cop who happens to be able to see a ghost or two. But it's logical to say sure, it could have enhanced what was already there."

Donovan sagged with relief. He didn't care who saw it. "It was bad enough having to realize I was a petty first-class jerk. Knowing I was a petty first-class jerk and knowing I was stupid? I couldn't handle that." He massaged his temples. "So are we really taking the death penalty off the table?"

"Yup." Luis leaned back and put his feet up. "I'm not a huge fan. I'm positive we've got the right guy, don't get me wrong. But the death penalty means a minimum of two long appeals, even with his confession and guilty plea. It means dragging the victims' families through decades of hell rehashing this whole thing, and it's just a mess. I don't think he'll last long in any prison, not in Supermax, not in any state prison, not anywhere."

Donovan gave Luis a long look. "You're awfully sure about that." He knew Luis knew his stuff, but no one could know that. Could they?

Kevin took a deep breath and leaned back, hands laced behind his head. "He's right, actually. Ruben's thing is all about women, controlling women. He tried to manipulate you and Luis, but that was just a way of trying to get away with what he'd done. It had nothing to do with you guys. There aren't going to be any women in prison, except some of the COs. And they're not going to cut him any slack at all. There won't be anyone for him to charm or to push around."

"I give him eight years, tops." Luis shrugged. "It's not my problem, to be honest, and I don't care. I mean human life is important, and you don't want to squander it, but some guys can't be rehabilitated."

Donovan considered Luis' words. Were they meant for him, as a reminder that they wouldn't be getting back together? Or were they exactly what they sounded like—a normal law enforcement professional expressing an opinion about a scumbag? "Do you think his upbringing played a role?" he asked, to see if he could get a better read on the situation. "I mean the trauma with his sister, you know?"

"Absolutely. And it should be brought up at sentencing, if we can corroborate it." Luis reached for his computer. "What happened with his sister, and his mother's response, was absolutely a factor in how his ideas developed. And there were probably some other latent ideas, and blah blah blah. The thing is, plenty of guys grow up in poverty. Plenty of guys grow up and lose a family member to violence. Plenty of guys have relatives say terrible things as a defense mechanism. Statistically speaking, most of them can manage to avoid taking it out on innocent people. It's a factor, but it's not a mitigating factor or an excuse. It's just one part of what went into it."

Donovan pursed his lips. He didn't know if he quite liked that answer or not.

Kevin got up and patted Donovan on the back. "Stop overthinking, man. I'm out. Macha has a soccer game, and I'm not going to miss this one."

Kevin left, and Donovan was alone with Luis. He tugged at his collar. He had so much he wanted to say, but he figured he should quit while he was ahead. There was no reason to rush things, after all. "It's kind of astounding that Ruben just confessed like that."

Luis considered and wrinkled his nose. "Kind of, I guess. I mean, on the one hand, yeah. I was kind of shocked. I didn't expect it, but in hindsight, it makes perfect sense, you know? I mean, we have got so much evidence. So, so much evidence." He grinned. "Ruben's a lot of things, but stupid isn't one of them. I think he just realized, you know? There's a time to put up and a time to shut up. He wasn't going to get bail, and he wasn't going to get out, so he might as well cut his losses and get what he could out of it."

"I guess." Donovan looked down. "Luis, do you think I'm like Ruben?"

"What?" Luis pulled back. "Did he hit you harder than I thought he did? Are you having double vision?"

"Cute. I'm serious, Luis." Donovan chewed on his fingernails. "I mean he was passing judgment on these women, when he had no right to judge anyone. And I did the same thing to you."

Luis sucked in his cheeks for a second. "Donovan, you did judge me, and you judged me pretty harshly. I won't pretend I don't resent the hell out of that. I mean, you told me you didn't hold it against me, and then you turned around and you did exactly that. But I'm not sure . . . it's not the same thing."

Donovan slumped down in his chair. "I don't know. It feels the same. I was willing to throw everything we had away because you'd enjoyed your body as you saw fit. And he was willing to kill over it."

"True. But you know what? You didn't kill anyone. Ruben had some truly sick ideas. There are reasons he had those sick ideas, but they're his sick ideas and he's responsible for them. Your feelings about my past relationships come from insecurities of your own, or at least that's what you told me when we spoke last about them. Right?"

Donovan swallowed hard and nodded. "The thing is, though, those insecurities are always going to be there."

"Maybe, maybe not. I'd like to think they'll start to clear up, at least a little bit, now that we've talked about them." Luis reached out and put his hand on Donovan's arm. "Whatever happens going forward, Donovan, you're a good guy. Someone like Ruben would never acknowledge he'd done something wrong or that he'd listened to bad advice or he'd made a mistake. You did all of those things. And you didn't come at me from a place of hatred in your heart or burning spite toward everyone who'd ever had more than one partner."

Donovan laughed, startled out of his self-flagellation. "Yeah, that would be kind of ridiculous."

"I know, right?" Luis grinned and pulled his hand back. "That's why I know you're going to be just fine. You'll work on shoring up those insecurities."

Donovan took a deep breath. He had to speak. If he didn't, he'd lose his nerve. "I don't want us to be apart, Luis. I get if you don't want to get back together. I won't pressure you. But I felt like I had to say something or forever hold my peace, you know? I had to get the words out, so you know. So we're not going on assumptions and missed opportunities anymore."

Luis didn't wrap his arms around Donovan and claim his mouth with a kiss. Donovan hadn't expected him to, although he'd have taken it if Luis offered.

"I'm not sure what to say," Luis said after a few long blank seconds. "There's the part of me that wants to be all over this. I hated to walk away, you know? I didn't see an option, but it was kind of like digging a bullet wound out of your own thigh. Not something you want to do for yourself, but not something you can get away with letting fester."

"Fester?" Donovan winced.

"Yeah, fester." Luis raised an eyebrow. "I

couldn't let myself be treated like that anymore. It's about trust, at this point. I love you, Donovan. And I want to be with you, but the past few weeks, or whatever it was, were pretty brutal. You were this kind of rock, and I built my whole world on that rock. And then you pulled that rock out from under me and replaced it with Styrofoam or something, I don't know—"

Donovan held up a hand. "I think I understand what you're getting at, even if your metaphors are tortured at best."

"I'm a cop, not an author." Luis ducked his head ruefully. "Look, the point is, I love you and I want to be with you, but I'm afraid to trust you about this now. Can you, I don't know, can you understand that?"

The tightness in Donovan's chest loosened. "I can. I can, and I do. I want to do everything a man can do to earn your trust back, Luis. I'm going to make an appointment with Father Geoffrey tomorrow. I'm going to get myself—us—back to a point where I'm not convinced you've got one foot out the door. I should know better, and part of me does know better. I just—I get scared sometimes."

Luis squeezed Donovan's hand. "We all get scared sometimes. You know I spend plenty of time sitting around and wondering why the hell you'd saddle yourself with a basketful of issues like me, right?"

Donovan snorted. "Aren't we a pair?"

"We are." Luis rested his head on Donovan's shoulder. "We can take things slow and see how they work out."

"Deal," Donovan said, and wrapped his arms around Luis. "First things first though." He pulled out his phone and took a selfie of himself and Luis together. He sent it to his father without comment.

Luis just laughed. "Isn't that a little petty?" His tone lacked disapproval.

"Nope. It's super petty, and I don't care a bit." Donovan held his hand out to Luis. "Let me give you a ride home."

CHAPTER EIGHTEEN

Luis had misgivings about getting back together with Donovan. He had a lot of them. He didn't want to be with someone who was going to fly off the handle and accuse him of sleeping around again. He knew from harsh experience that people who had those tendencies rarely got better. They escalated, and it never ended well.

At the same time, Luis didn't think he was being arrogant when he said the same experience that informed him of the likely outcomes for jealous and angry men told him that wasn't likely to be the case with Donovan. Donovan understood what had gone wrong. He understood why he'd done the things he had, and he understood that it had very little to do with Luis at all.

It was one thing to know Donovan wasn't likely to relapse or escalate, and it was another to *feel* it. Luis wasn't there yet. He wanted to be. He couldn't get there without time and a lot of effort on both of their parts.

And Luis wasn't prone to giving his trust easily.

He did love Donovan though. He was willing to put the effort in. He had to hope Donovan was too.

The case didn't end with the confession. It would have been fantastic if life worked that way, but the sheer number of bodies found meant they would spend a lot of the next few months trying to identify remains and notifying families. Some remains had no one to claim them. Luis didn't fail to notice that for a long time, he'd have been one of them, if Ruben's hatred ran toward promiscuous men as well.

He didn't spend all of his time on the Noguera case, once prosecutors accepted the invitation. A noncustodial parent in Laconia, New Hampshire, absconded with an infant and a two-year-old, and living people always took precedence over the dead. It wasn't like the dead were going to get any deader, after all.

Luis threw everything he had into getting into the head of this unstable father and figured out that the man (Jules Irvin, twenty-five, occupation: none) had connections in Ogdensburg, New York, up by the Canadian border. He wouldn't go directly there though. The one thing people who knew Irvin always said about him was that he might be unstable, but he was smart as hell. That meant he'd have the sense to take a roundabout route to get there.

Luis and Kevin commandeered a helicopter to get them to Ogdensburg. If Luis had thought Boston was cold and miserable, nothing could have prepared him for Ogdensburg. He made Kevin stop their SUV, borrowed from the guys at ICE, and stop to buy a parka. Kevin laughed at him, and their local companions gave him odd looks, but he didn't care. He was going to be comfortable, and that was all there was to it.

The relatives—an uncle who was drunk as a Vegas mogul at ten o'clock in the morning, a pregnant wife whose black eye looked like the result of a fall down stairs their double-wide didn't have, and no less than five kids. Not all of them looked like theirs, but Luis promised himself he wouldn't judge. It wasn't his place, and what did he know about kids?

The uncle slurred that he wasn't cooperating with no Feds at all, at which point he poked one of the local cops in the chest. It was enough for an assault charge if the cop in question was feeling petty, and apparently, Officer Ruggles had just enough pettiness to spare.

Once the old man had been dragged into the patrol car, the other local turned to the wife. "How you doing, Susan? Still not ready?"

She sighed. "What am I supposed to do on my own? Five kids and one on the way, Bill. And it's not like those Irvins will just leave us alone."

"Let my friends hang out here. Let us take a look around. I've known the old man for a while now. It ain't like he's not going to leave something in plain sight." Bill made a face as he glanced around. "Like that gun he ain't supposed to have. It's around kids, Susan. I know you know better."

She flinched.

"Hey." Luis slipped between her and Bill. "I get it. It's not like you could get it away from him, right?" He held his hands up, the universal signal of innocence. "It's going to be okay, Susan. We'll get there. But that gun's got to be enough to get us a warrant, right? Why don't you let Bill here take you and the kids somewhere safe. You don't have to listen to them about getting out if you're not ready. It takes time and planning. I get that. But in the meantime, do you want to put two more kids in his path?"

Susan paled. "Jesus, no. He just said his sister's kid was coming up to get his head straight."

"He kidnapped his kids, and now he's on his way here. We just want to be here to meet him. That's all. We don't want you or yours in any danger." Luis met her eyes and projected as much sincerity as he could.

Donovan was always better at this stuff.

Susan bought it, at least. More local cops came to clear out Susan and the kids, and then Luis found himself alone with Kevin, Ruggles, and Bill. He didn't even know Bill's last name, and it felt awkward to ask him now. God, he wished he was back in Boston.

Boston was becoming home. He wasn't sure how he felt about that either.

Jules Irvin pulled up to his uncle's trailer two hours later. He was driving a car with Vermont plates.

"How much do you want to bet he bought that car fair and square?" Luis murmured to Kevin.

"No bet." Kevin checked his holster. His gun was ready, but he didn't want to draw if he didn't have to. No one wanted to pull his gun with kids in the room.

The car door creaked as it opened, and Luis heard sobbing immediately. He wasn't the kind of guy to get panicked about crying kids, and definitely not when one of them was an infant, but something about these sobs pinged him as different. They were hoarse, for one thing. Most kids didn't scream and cry themselves to the point of pain.

He forced himself to stay still. They had to

get Irvin away from the car.

"I told you to shut up, or I'd give you something to cry about. There ain't diapers. Aunt Susan will have some. At least she'd better."

Luis exchanged glances with the others. The children had been taken more than twenty-four hours ago. Surely, Irvin had planned to take them and brought diapers with him?

The door to the trailer flew open. "Uncle Al? Aunt Susan?"

Luis slid in front of the door. Kevin blocked the path to the back of the trailer, and that was all there was to it. He was trapped. Jules Irvin, with an infant in one arm and a toddler's limp arm held in one hand, was caught. He looked much worse for wear than even the mug shot the FBI had to go on, with lank and greasy hair and three days' growth of beard.

"What the hell is all this then?" Irvin had to shout to be heard over the screaming children. "Where's my family? Where's their kids?"

"Jules Irvin, you're under arrest for kidnapping, violation of three restraining orders, and child abuse." Luis met the man's beady gray eyes and stepped forward. He held his hands out. "Hand over the baby."

"I ain't handing the little shit over. He's my baby, and I can do what I want with him." Irvin sneered and jerked the toddler toward himself. The little boy howled anew.

"There's only one way this is going, Jules, and that's with you in cuffs. You want to tell the DA you cooperated, or do you want to say you put the kids at risk and made us do it the hard way?" Luis tensed. What would Donovan do in this situation?

He met Kevin's eyes. Kevin nodded, just a little bit.

"I'm an American. I got rights. And no screwed-up bitch has the right to take my kids from me, just because I put her in her place for getting mouthy—"

Luis moved fast. He stepped in and took the sobbing, stinking infant from his father's grasp while turning away, preventing the father from hurting the baby. Kevin caught the toddler under the arms at the same time, pulling him away from his father. It had to hurt—Luis suspected a dislocated elbow. It wasn't anything he hadn't seen before, and the little boy would be fine once they got it set.

Once Luis and Kevin got the kids away, the two Ogdensburg troopers swooped in and got the cuffs on Irvin.

"Nice work," Bill told them, as Luis cradled the baby to himself. "Our crime scene techs are on their way to search the house. It should be okay if you grab some diapers for the kids though."

"I think they're going to need a bath, but we can deal with that at the hospital." Kevin wrinkled his nose. "Diapers first."

They got the two kids out to the SUV while the locals dragged Irvin to their patrol car and read him his rights. The adrenaline was starting to fade from Luis' body, and he just wanted to go home. He had other priorities first though. He took the diaper Kevin brought out for him, stripped the infant, and cleaned him up as best he could. Then he bagged his clothes and diaper as evidence.

Kevin was busy with the older child, but he spared a glance for Luis. "I had no idea you knew how to change a diaper."

Luis huffed out a little laugh. "Believe it or not, I do. I've changed hundreds. I've fed babies, rocked them to sleep, helped them take their first steps, you name it. The neighborhoods where I grew up, everyone's parents were busy all the time. Everyone worked hard, you know? So older kids pitched in where they could. It's been a minute or two, but I do know what I'm doing." He cradled the somewhat less foul baby to him. While the baby was almost certainly hungry, its most pressing comfort need had been satisfied. When Luis wrapped him up inside his coat, the baby fell asleep.

The toddler was less easy to satisfy, likely because of the dislocation, but Kevin had a great way about him. He settled down into just a few sniffs and big fat tears rolling down his cheeks when Kevin got him clean. "Why clothes in bag?"

"So we can make sure no one hurts you again, okay?"

"Why?"

Luis hid a grin inside his jacket. He'd been that kid once, always asking *why?* It was kind of a reflex action, and there would be no stopping it until a distraction showed up.

Thankfully the distraction arrived quickly in the form of an ambulance. Luis and Kevin accompanied the children to the hospital, where doctors examined them and treated them for dehydration and, in the case of the older boy, a dislocated elbow and bruising.

Photographs were taken, to press the case for abuse. Luis had a hard time remembering to stay calm. Cradling the baby helped.

A quick meeting with Social Services to establish chain of custody—and to get clothes and other necessities for the kids, for their trip back to Laconia—was all that remained. Federal marshals would bring Irvin himself back to New Hampshire when extradition proceedings ran their course, and Luis would have to do the paperwork.

The toddler was excited about riding in the helicopter back to New Hampshire. Their mother was ecstatic to be reunited with her sons. Luis and Kevin drove back home, exhausted but satisfied.

"I love it when a case has a happy ending like that." Kevin grinned. "I could live without having to drive around with a bag full of dirty diapers, but you know. Details."

"Right?" Luis sighed. "It's weird. It was the first case I had where I had to travel since I started seeing Donovan. You know, back in the spring."

"Huh." Kevin pursed his lips and nodded. "How are you feeling about that?"

"I'm not sure. I mean we're taking things slow and trying not to push anything too far, you know? I don't want to push things. We've both got a lot of stuff to work through around this whole mess, and it's important to get it right if we're going to make it go at all. But . . . I missed him. While we were gone, I missed him."

Kevin looked at the car ahead of him for a moment or two. "I think you should call and tell him that, you know? Or at least text him. He should know your thoughts on the subject. Don't hide things like that from him."

Objections rushed into Luis' mouth like early bird shoppers on Black Friday. He stopped them. Instead, he pulled out his phone. *On my way home from a work trip to Ogdensburg. I missed you.*

Donovan texted him back in seconds. *I missed you too. What's your eta?*

Luis glanced at the GPS, a flush coming over his face. *Um, hour and a half maybe?*

I'll meet you there.

Luis' text went a long way toward eroding the barriers between them. Donovan knew, intellectually, that Luis wouldn't cheat. He had to feel it, and to get there, he had to get little emotional cookies from Luis like that. He hadn't understood that about himself before, and now he did. He tried not to be ashamed of it, and most of the time, he succeeded.

Luis was learning to trust Donovan again too. That part wasn't as easy. Donovan understood that. Rebuilding bridges was hard, harder than building them in the first place, and Luis could be prickly when he was afraid. But Luis wanted to rebuild just as much as Donovan, and he'd made a career out of understanding people's brains.

So they worked on it.

Ruben Noguera's sentencing happened around Halloween. Some of the bodies pulled out of the pond were still being analyzed, and so not all of his victims' families were available to give impact statements. Not all of his victims' families knew they *should* be giving statements. Luis brought Jennifer and Ella's families to the sentencing himself. They might not have known the reason for the personal attention, but Donovan did, and that was enough.

Donovan had been to sentencing hearings before. He'd listened to victim impact statements. Listening to *these,* so many of them all in a line, was a lot like having his heart cut out. Each and every one felt like an indictment of him personally. It wasn't rational. He understood why Ruben had managed to evade capture for so long, but it still burned him up inside that each and every one after the first could have been prevented. If only they'd picked up on the clues a little faster. If only Donovan hadn't flown off the handle. If only his jealousy hadn't gotten so out of hand. If only he hadn't fallen prey to the Purple Menace or whatever.

Luis squeezed his hand. Obviously, Luis would understand what Donovan was thinking. The same stuff would be going on in his head too. He would be grieving just as much as Donovan. He still wanted to reach out and show Donovan support and love. If that wasn't the best kind of man, Donovan didn't know what was.

Ruben wound up sentenced to life without

parole. Luis had a lot to do with that. The judge asked him for his professional opinion, as a profiler and forensic psychologist, as to the likelihood of rehabilitation. Luis explained, in a calm and dispassionate tone Donovan could only dream of in a case like this, that between the trauma that had incited Noguera's misogyny and the absolute conviction on Noguera's part that he'd done nothing wrong, allowing him back out into a mixed-gender public would be reckless in the extreme.

"Mr. Noguera has suffered loss, and that is a contributing factor to his crimes. I don't feel like that should be ignored or discounted in any way. I also don't believe it excuses what he did. Mr. Noguera could have made many other choices, as have other men who either dislike women or who have suffered through the murder of a loved one. The fact is, Mr. Noguera wanted an excuse to hurt women, and he took it.

"He is a likable man. He is an intelligent man. I think his life in prison can still have meaning and purpose, and if he so chooses, he can still offer some benefit to society. But I do assert that to allow him into the company of women would be to endanger those women."

And so Ruben was packed off to Supermax, to live out his days. He wrote Luis letters. Luis even replied to him. Luis made sure to translate both the letters and the replies, just so Donovan understood what was going on. He didn't have to, and Donovan told him so, but Luis did it anyway.

Fred was furious when he found out Patricia filed for divorce. He called and screamed into her voice mail for a while. Then he screamed into Donovan's voice mail, and into Luis' voice mail. Furthermore, Kate decided she didn't want anything to do with Fred either. She was livid over the way he'd tried to "marry her off" like some kind of political pawn, and the next time she saw him, it was in company with Patricia and the elusive Donna.

Fred was now left with no wife, no girlfriend, and no emergency backup girlfriend. He didn't like that much, and he let them know it. It was Patricia, though, who pointed out that leaving threatening messages on a federal agent's voice mail was usually considered a one-way ticket to a very exclusive retirement home, "one with distinctive decor and limited fashion choices."

The phone calls stopped. No one heard from Fred who didn't want to hear from Fred, and the whole family had a little celebration.

There was just one more loose end to tie up, and only Luis could do it. After Ruben had been sentenced, Luis headed down to Freetown on a

Saturday evening. Donovan went with him because he didn't want to leave Luis alone for this kind of thing. They brought a newspaper clipping of the article about Ruben's sentencing.

Luis sat on a boulder near the quarry pond for a few minutes, and then he smiled. "Jennifer. Hi. Thanks for coming. I want you to know, we got him. He's going off to Colorado, the single highest security prison we've got. And he's never getting out." He handed her the clipping.

Donovan couldn't see or hear Jennifer. He could smell the rotting flesh scent that came with ghosts. He'd smelled it off and on all his life. Luis said ghosts were everywhere, so that made sense. Now, he could see the newspaper clipping float over from Luis to a spot in front of him.

Then he saw light, beautiful pure light emanating from the center of that space. He had to look away. When he looked back, the paper was gone.

He took Luis' hand, and they walked back to the car together. He could still feel something watching them, but it didn't feel hostile anymore. Maybe it was curious, but it didn't seem to have any interest in attacking anyone. Whatever lived in Freetown State Forest had been here long before humans walked the earth, and it would be here long after humans breathed their last. Donovan could respect that—as long as they kept their distance from each other.

For now, he and Luis would just go home. He wanted to put Freetown as far behind him as he could.

ALSO BY J. V. SPEYER

Hunter (2018)
Professional Courtesy (2018, MLR Books)
Snowed In: Ross and Ashton (2019, JMS Books)
Paper Hearts (2019, JMS Books)
Whirlwind (JMS Books, 2018)
Carriage House (NineStar Press, 2017)
The Dented Crown (2017)
Rites of Spring (Less Than Three, 2017)
Starlit (MLR Books, 2017)
Midnight (Less Than Three, 2016)

ABOUT THE AUTHOR

J. V. Speyer has lived in upstate New York and rural Catalonia before making the greater Boston, Massachusetts, area her permanent home. She has worked in archaeology, security, accountancy, finance, and nonprofit management. She currently lives just south of Boston in a house old enough to remember when her town was a tavern community with a farming problem.

J. V. finds most of her inspiration from music. Her tastes run the gamut from traditional to industrial and back again. When not writing, she can usually be found enjoying a baseball game or avoiding direct sunlight. She's learning to crochet so she can make blankets to fortify herself against the cold.

J. V. can be found on Twitter or Instagram at @JVSpeyer, or on Facebook at https://www.facebook.com/JVSpeyerAuthor. You can get exclusive updates, cocktail recipes, and other notes here: http://eepurl.com/dtlwBH